SKAGWAY

IN DAYS PRIMEVAL

SKAGWAY

IN DAYS PRIMEVAL

The Writings of
J. Bernard Moore
1886-1904

Cover Art by Peter J. Lucchetti

Lynn Canal Publishing
Skagway, Alaska

ISBN: 0-945284-06-3

Direct inquiries to:
Lynn Canal Publishing
P.O. Box 498, 264 Broadway St.
Skagway, Alaska 99840-0498

skagnews@ptialaska.net

Printed and bound in Canada

Contents

Foreword

Master William Moore of Emden, Germany and wife Hendrika of Holland emigrated to North America the hard way – via Cape Horn – looking for an opportunity to earn a living doing what Moore knew best: the business of boat building and shipping. Moore succeeded at this business, plying the Fraser and Stikine rivers in western Canada and hauling passengers and freight. But the opportunity for his final venture came with the discoveries of gold in northwest British Columbia and the Yukon.

In June 1887, Captain Moore accompanied Canadian surveyor William Ogilvie on an expedition up Southeast Alaska's Inside Passage and over the Coastal Mountains into the Yukon. During this expedition, Capt. Moore was guided by Skookum Jim, a Tlingit Indian, over the White Pass trail through these mountains. Moore was so impressed with this new route through the mountains, that he returned in the fall and laid claim to one hundred sixty acres at the trail's beginning. With the help of his son, James Bernard, Moore built a cabin, constructed a wharf, and waited ten years for the great Klondike Gold Rush. Their homestead became the boom town of Skagway, Alaska.

J. Bernard Moore was one of six children of William and Hendrika Moore and the recorder of these passages. Accompanying his adventurous father, young Ben rubbed shoulders with many sourdoughs. He was a keen observer of people and events, and those observations were recorded in diaries that encapsulated gold rush lore.

In the winter of 1889, Ben attended a Tlingit potlatch near Haines where he romanced Klinget-sai-yet, the daughter of Chief George Shotridge. She became Mrs. Minnie Moore, my grandmother.

Ben saved the diaries and used them to prepare a speech – entitled "Skagway in Days Primeval" – to a group of pioneers in Skagway in 1904. Minnie and Ben died in 1917 and 1919 respectively. After his death, Ben's speech and the diaries collected dust for decades in careful storage by his son, Benny Moore, my uncle. When the diaries came into my possession, I realized that I possessed recorded Alaskan history that needed sharing.

Our family first published these writings in 1968, and we are pleased to see them return to publication in 1997 for the Skagway Centennial and the dedication of the restored Moore family homestead by the National Park Service in Klondike Gold Rush National Historical Park.

The original diaries have been donated to the Archives of the Alaskan Polar Regions Section of the Elmer E. Rasmuson Library at the University of Alaska Fairbanks.

Donald A. Gestner
Seattle, Washington
April, 1996

Don Gestner with sisters June and Mildred on a ship.   *Lu Gestner*

Notes from the Editor of this Edition

I am grateful to Donald A. Gestner, the grandson of J. Bernard Moore, for allowing Lynn Canal Publishing to produce this new edition of "Skagway in Days Primeval" at the height of the Skagway Centennial. Most of the original text has been left undisturbed. However, in some cases, we updated the spellings of locations and names to make them identifiable to the reader on modern maps. The most prominent of these is the Chilkoot Pass on the trail from Dyea to Lake Lindeman. Bernard Moore identified it as the Chilkat Pass in his writings, no doubt because the Chilkats controlled it for many years before white settlers like himself arrived on the scene. By 1897, it was known throughout the world as the Chilkoot Trail. The name Chilkat was given to the pass on the old Dalton Trail above Haines. In early accounts, the upper Yukon River also was known as the Lewes River before meeting up with the Pelly River. The Hootalinqua River is now known as the Teslin. In most first references, we left the name intact and placed the modern name or spelling in parentheses.

If the reader gets confused along the way, refer to Moore's distance guide at the beginning of the book, which is still an excellent reference for travelers on the route to the Klondike today. Moore prepared this guide and updated information from his diaries in the early 1900s, when he prepared these writings. I didn't think he would mind a few more updates for this edition.

A small publishing house relies on the help of many in producing a book. I would like to thank the following: Don Gestner and his wife, Lu, who assisted in all phases of this publication and loaned me their previously unpublished family photos; researchers and archivists Debbie Sanders, Diane Olthuis, Doreen Cooper, Karl Gurcke and Paul Lofgren of Klondike Gold Rush National Historical Park, Judy Munns of the Trail of '98 Museum in Skagway; Kathleen Joy, who typeset the manuscript from the original 1968 publication; and Dorothy O'Daniel, who assisted in proofreading the new manuscript.

William J. "Jeff" Brady
Lynn Canal Publishing
Skagway, Alaska

Partial Notes for Preface

Distances (are) approximated and, of course, in some instances would vary from actual surveys made later.

In turning over the leaves of this diary and logbook, a great yearning comes over me as I read the lines written over twenty-two years ago now that they are before me, clear and distinct as though recently written to live it all over again. . .

Between the leaves in book marked Number One of my first trip into the Yukon in '87, I noticed a large mosquito, dried and flattened out, which had been caught there in shutting up the book.

The strong resolve to hold on to our location at Skagway shaped my future destiny, as will be seen.

It may, I admit, be perhaps tedious for some of my readers to follow me step-by-step on my long, detailed trips down the Yukon River and return, and up and down Lynn Canal and during our first work in detail done at Skagway Bay. But I wish to set forth word-for-word as my diaries were written at that time; and, moreover, to show the long struggle and deprivations I went through in the early days to accomplish what we did up there, and then allow the magnificent and valuable wharf property and town-site interests slip from my grasp.

Many of those to whom I have referred and known and met in the Yukon and on the coast of Alaska at Juneau and Douglas have passed over their last divide, among them both Wheelock and Flannery, also Morris Horton, John J. Healy and others.

J. Bernard Moore
Circa 1908

Distances Recorded by
J. Bernard Moore during his Travels

FROM JUNEAU - MILES:

To Haines Mission, Chilkat 80
Dyea 100
Head of Canoe Navigation (up Taiya River) 106
Summit of Chilkat (Chilkoot) Pass 114 3/4
Head of Lake Lindeman 123 1/2
Foot of Lake Lindeman 128 1/2
Head of Lake Bennett 128 1/2
Caribou Crossing (Carcross) 156 1/2
Foot of Tagish Lake 173 1/4
Head of Marsh Lake 178 1/4
Foot of Marsh Lake 197 1/4
Head of (Miles) Canyon 223
Foot of (Miles) Canyon 223 3/4
Head of White Horse Rapids 225 1/4
Tahkiena (Takhini) River .240
Head of Laberge Lake 256
Foot of Laberge Lake 284
Hootalinqua (Teslin) River 316
Cassiar Bar 342
Big Salmon River 349
Little Salmon River 385 1/2
Five Fingers Rapids 444
Rink Rapids 450
Pelly River 503 1/2
White River 599 1/2
Stewart River 609
Sixty Mile Post 629
Fort Reliance 682 1/2
Forty Mile Post 728
Fort Cudahy 728 3/4
Circle City 898
Mouth of Cook's Inlet 700
Turnagain Arm 800
Six Mile Creek 825

DISTANCES ON THE YUKON - MILES

Fort Reliance was a trading post about eight miles downriver from present-day Dawson City, which sprang up at the confluence of the Yukon and Klondike Rivers in 1896 after the nearby discovery of gold on Rabbit (Bonanza) Creek.

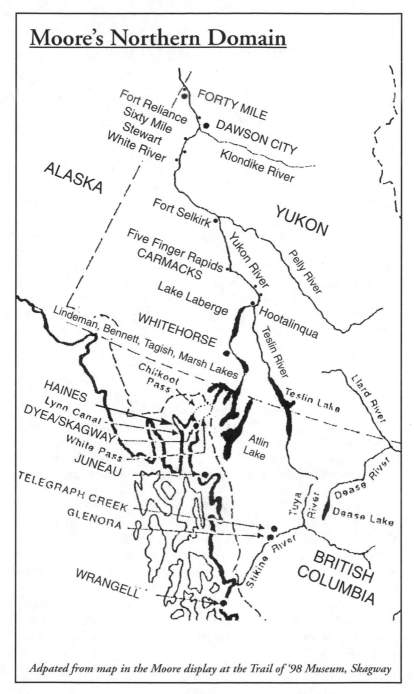

Moore's Northern Domain

Fort Reliance
Sixty Mile
Stewart
White River

FORTY MILE

DAWSON CITY

Klondike River

ALASKA

Fort Selkirk

YUKON

Five Finger Rapids
CARMACKS

Yukon River

Pelly River

Lake Laberge

WHITEHORSE

Hootalinqua

Lindeman, Bennett, Tagish, Marsh Lakes

Teslin River

Llard River

Chilkoot Pass

Teslin Lake

HAINES
Lynn Canal
DYEA/SKAGWAY

White Pass

JUNEAU

Atlin
Lake

TELEGRAPH CREEK

Dease River

Tuya River

Dease River

Dease Lake

GLENORA

WRANGELL

Stikine River

BRITISH
COLUMBIA

Adpated from map in the Moore display at the Trail of '98 Museum, Skagway

Introduction to Diaries

Notes and memorandums taken from my diary and logbooks, and from memory of my life, including early trips and experiences in the Yukon country and southeastern Alaska, also steamboating on the Stikine, Fraser, and Yukon Rivers, and on the coast .

At this writing, January 1, 1908, I am a little over forty-two years of age. I was born at New Westminster, British Columbia, on September 6, 1865. Part of my childhood was spent in Caribou, B.C., with my parents, in the early mining days. Afterward we lived in Victoria, B.C., and in my boyhood I attended the public schools there and the old St. Louis Catholic College somewhat irregularly until I was about fifteen years old.

During those years, when on summer vacations, I made trips to southeastern Alaska and to Fort Wrangell on the steamers *Grappler*, *California* and the *Otter*. The first-mentioned vessel was originally built and used many years before as a British gunboat, and about 1880 my father purchased her and remodeled her into a freight and passenger boat and operated her on the run between Victoria and Fort Wrangell and way ports in opposition to the Pacific Coast Steamship Company.

I made my first trip to Wrangell when about nine years old on the steamer *California*. This vessel was at that time operated by Capt. John Hayse, master, who died some twenty years ago. Mr. Vanderbuilt, her purser on that trip, was afterward occupied in the mercantile business at Sitka. The steamer *Otter* was owned by the Hudson Bay Company.

The steamer *Grappler* was burned to the water's edge in Seymour Narrows several years ago on her way to the canneries of Northern British Columbia, when seventy of her Chinese passengers and many others were burned to death and drowned together with most of the crew; her commander, Capt. Jaeger, was severely injured but saved.

The steamer *California*, some years later, was put on a run on the southern coast of California and her name changed to *Urica*. The old steamer *Otter* was dismantled and, I believe, her hull was used as a barge.

These three vessels were propeller boats and averaged a speed of eight to ten knots per hour, the *California* being about a five-hundred-ton vessel; the other two carried some three hundred and fifty tons.

I have dwelt somewhat on the subject of these steamers for the reason that they carried a great many passengers to and from Fort Wrangell, among whom were miners, prospectors, traders, and storekeepers on their way to the then rich gold diggings in the Cassiar country which was discovered in 1873. To reach these diggings, canoes and light draft steamers would be taken at Fort Wrangell and thence about one hundred fifty miles up the swift Stikine River to Telegraph Creek landing, the head of navigation, thence over a trail of seventy-three miles to Dease Lake and the mines.

I have met quite a few men within the last four or five years, who are sixty to seventy-five years old now, who traveled to that country at the time I write about, some of whom remember quite well having traveled on the same steamers with me. Old Fort Wrangell was then quite a busy place. Many miners used to winter there. – J. B.M.

To The Reader

Chapter lengths vary greatly, because they were organized by Mr. Moore according to their logbook numbers. — *Ed.*

1. STEAMBOATING ON THE STIKINE AND FRASER RIVERS (early 1880s)

I steamboated on the Stikine River during the summer months, off and on, till about 1880-1881, when I was about fifteen. Most of these trips were quite exciting and at times even perilous.

My father, at that time, built expressly for the Stikine River a very powerful light-draft steamer called the *Gertrude* (named after my youngest sister who is now residing in San Francisco, California). This boat was, of course, a stern-wheeler, about one hundred twenty five feet long, with a pair of sixteen-inch cylinders and six-foot stroke. She was built on Laurel Point at Victoria B.C., on the right-hand side entering the inner harbor and just at about the present location of the Pendray Soap Works.

The steamer drew about sixteen inches of water with her boilers filled, and used to make the least time of any of the other three steamers on the river, namely, the *Nellie, Beaver,* and the *Glenora.* These boats would be often stuck on the bars, and at other times with lines out with a dozen men on the capstan heaving them over the bars and engines working full power, while our boat, the *Gertrude,* would walk right by them; and sometimes we would sound the whistle and shake a line over the stern at them as we passed by.

The Stikine is a very swift stream with many snags and shifting bars, the latter necessitating the picking out of new channels every trip - especially toward the fall of the year when the water is falling permanently - it would mean perhaps a total loss of the vessel, for if she could not be backed off the bar she would be frozen in for the winter and then, in the spring break-up, be demolished by the ice.

1

This steamer, *Gertrude*, was certainly my father's pet boat out of the numerous steamers he owned both before and after her time, and I and all our family loved this grand little steamer, to say nothing of endless praises spoken of her by all who traveled on her. Those were our palmy days too; our family were all together, and we were young.

One trip going up the Stikine, the opposition's steamer *Glenora*, then owned and operated by Capt. John Irving, was also on her uptrip. From the deck of the *Gertrude* we saw the *Glenora* take a shear across the current, heel away over, with guards under water, and spill a lot of freight overboard. We thought that surely she would sink right there, but she righted herself and went on.

At this time I wish to say that the mouth of the Stikine is about five miles from Fort Wrangell and up to about forty miles to what afterward was made the boundary line. The river is easy navigation, and at the time of which I now write these river steamers and many large canoes too used to, of course, have to continue right to Wrangell to load freight deposited there by the coast vessels of which I spoke before. But later on my father built a fine, large, staunch stern-wheel steamer, the *Western Slope*, one hundred sixty-five feet in length with a twenty-six-foot beam and a hold eight feet deep, with heavy circular hog frames running right down to kelsons in stern and bow supported by heavy posts and knees.

This steamer he ran direct through from Victoria to the boundary line on the Stikine, making connections there with our other steamer, the *Gertrude*, for the head of navigation, Glenora Landing. This steamer, *Western Slope*, made regular trips right up the coast and had good success for a stern-wheel vessel.

We used to run up alongside the steep rocky shores in Granville Channel on our way to and from Wrangell when the tide was on the rise, and hang up with lanyards a long canvas hose with mouth shaped like a bell two feet in diameter tapering to three inches. We would place this under a waterfall, and fill up the boat's tanks with fresh water for the boilers in a short time. We had no regular surface condenser, but a large galvanized pipe oil condenser ran along in the fan tail at the rear of the wheel; this condensed considerable water, but not enough.

These waterfalls, some of which are quite large, come down the steep hills and mountainsides from thousands of feet above, and there are a great many of them on either side of this beautiful stretch of water. Granville Channel is eighty miles or so in length with an average width of about three miles.

The Stikine River has a canyon pretty well up which is about three miles through and steep wall rock, and in many places there is barely room for a steamer to turn around; and during high water and freshets at times it is impossible for any ordinary steamer to stem the current.

On one occasion, when I was still a boy, I was up the river on a trip in the *Gertrude*. She had been convoyed up to Fort Wrangell by our other coast steamer, the *Grappler*, and during the trip in, going over Queen Charlotte Sound in the long rolling swells, we on the *Grappler* would sometimes see the frail little *Gertrude* almost disappear from sight between the rollers, and the next moment see her riding like a duck on top of another smooth top sea. It is needless to state that with such a light-draft boat as she was, we had to pick our weather to make a spurt to cross Queen Charlotte and Millbank Sounds, and Dixon's entrance.

In taking such frail light-drift steamers as these up and down the coast, they are temporarily braced diagonally from main deck to beams of upper deck; also extra hog chains are put in for the trip.

But to return to a trip up the Stikine:

I was in the pilot house with my father and brother William on our way up through the canyon. The river was fairly high and still on the rise, the *Gertrude* was bowling along under a full head of steam with a stick of cordwood jammed in between the safety-valve lever and the boiler on the upper deck (to keep it from blowing off steam), and in looking over the sides of the boat at the water, one would think she was surely making twenty miles per hour. But in reality she was hardly moving. (Any swift-water man or pilot will know that a man at the wheel in the pilot house has to be clearheaded in going through narrow canyons similar to this one in the Stikine or the one on the Skeena River which is even worse than the former.)

We were just about halfway through the canyon, and just at the time when there were some very large whirlpools directly in front of our bows and abreast, when there appeared all at once a huge, dark-colored and apparently water-soaked log that shot straight up into the air endwise some ten feet and right into the center of one of those big boils.

Well, I just looked with mouth and eyes wide open, then rushed out on the upper deck and my hat blew overboard. The log disappeared again, end on, and our bows to the whirlpool nicely; but the great danger was, as we all had realized from the first, that this log would make another rise before our boat passed over it and probably punch a hole through the steamer's bottom. However, when we glanced back a moment or two afterward, we saw it rise up again beyond our stern.

At times, on most any trip through this canyon, the water piles right over the forecastle and especially when a boat takes a heavy shear or run in a canyon like this one, then she is likely to founder at once. In going downstream around bad curves and bends, drifting is resorted to very often, which means to stop and back and fill either stern or bow first.

I made a trip through this canyon once on one of our steamers, the *Alaskan* (though this is jumping ahead of my story), when we had to turn back and wait for three days for the water to fall a little. The mosquitoes were very thick, and we cut about ten cords of wood while we were tied up just below the canyon. Then we started out in the afternoon to take advantage of the strong upriver wind that invariably springs up every afternoon and which is such a help to the canoes going upstream.

Well, we had a large square sail temporarily rigged up in the mast, and we had on one hundred seventy pounds of steam with the safety valve blocked, and even then we could not make it on the first attempt; but this boat was, of course, no comparison to our *Gertrude* of other days whose machinery, I understand, is still doing good work in some sawmill. Her hull was hauled to the old steamer bone yard.

Oh, those were the good old days; the happiest I ever knew. And how proud I felt when I was entrusted with the wheel in the pilothouse of the *Gertrude* and *Western Slope*, at first for half an hour or so, in a good reach of the river; then later for longer periods until I could handle a stern-wheel boat pretty well. I have wished that I had followed it right up as a business.

After this I put in the time partly working in a machine shop, and also put in six months at the carpenter trade; and later acted as assistant pilot and purser on one of our steamers, a twin

4

propeller called the *Fraser*, plying between Victoria and New Westminster. Also I put considerable time steamboating on the Fraser River and was aboard our large steamer, *Western Slope*, when we took the first load of steel rails from Esquimalt to Fort Yale for the Canadian Pacific Railroad when they began to work.

I witnessed many exciting incidents on the Fraser River such as steamboat racing, mutiny among railroad men while carrying them up river to Fort Yale; and on one occasion, headed by one of their smart ones, they tried to take charge of the steamer and actually forced their way into the pilothouse by kicking in the door. We captured the ringleader and shoved him down into the hold and fastened the hatches down on him till our arrival at Yale, then turned him over to the police.

The steamers *William Irving, Reliance* and *Western Slope* were the principal boats on the Fraser River, all good large vessels and good carriers: the two former had been built and were operated by Capt. John Irving, and the latter, our boat, was the first to inaugurate through trips from Victoria across the Gulf via Westminster, to Fort Yale, the head of navigation.

There was much activity on the Fraser in those days during the construction work of the Canadian Pacific Railroad. Later on Capt. Irving had a very fine large stern-wheeler built, a passenger and freight boat called the *Elizabeth Irving*.

It was about a standoff for speed between her and our boat, the *Western Slope*. We had been racing a little after leaving New Westminster, and Irving's boat made a landing at Chilliwack about sixty miles up river. We landed a few moments later, putting our bows into the mud bank just inside of her fan tail. After a little (time), Irving's boat pulled out and started out upriver. This was only her third trip. She was a brand-new, elegant boat. Capt. Irving himself was on board. They tooted her whistle at us, and someone on board of her shook a hawser (rope) over her stern at us just as we pulled out immediately after them.

Well, it was quite a race all day long, nip and tuck; but the Irving did keep just about a mile or two ahead of us. We could not pass her, and the distance between the two vessels varied but little. At last we neared Fort Hope Bend where there is a sharp turn or elbow in the river with a bluff rocky point on the right, and which at certain stages of the river it is exceedingly difficult -

especially for heavily built boats such as the *Slope* was - to make this turn.

I was aboard our boat in the pilothouse with three men at the big double wheel. We made three attempts to round this curve, and had the steamer turn around and look at us three times and drift downstream a couple of miles, and on the fourth attempt got through. The *Irving*, of course, got out of sight, having made the turn around the point successfully. But we did not know, of course, whether she intended to make a landing at Fort Hope, or continue on through to Yale fifteen miles farther on.

My father and brother William, myself, and, I think, my brother Henry were in the pilothouse too, all four of us at the wheel (we had no steam-steering gear on our boat then), when all at once we noticed through the trees and an opening over the point, a large mass of smoke rising high up in the air which we all, at the first moment, thought was a slab-pile fire at the Fort Hope Sawmill.

At this time we had just gotten to within a short distance of the critical curve or bend referred to, when I spied a smokestack in the middle of the huge mass of smoke.

"Oh! It is the *Elizabeth Irving* on fire!" I cried aloud.

A moment later this magnificent brand-new steamer, which cost her owner some eighty thousand dollars, was a mass of flame from stem to stern and came bearing down on us with her wheel slowly turning, head on downstream just as though still being steered by her pilot.

We were in imminent danger. Immediately reversing our engines, we drifted back downstream out of the way of this floating mass of flames and smoke, but we could already feel the heat of it all. That is as plain to me now as though it had happened yesterday. It was an extraordinary sight to see the way that boat came around the bend, heading downstream with her engines slowly turning over the wheel.

By this time we had gotten well out of danger, and very soon the burning vessel grounded on a bar perhaps five miles below Fort Hope Bend, where she burned up completely and nothing was left but the charred shell of the hull.

Of course it will be seen that during all this time none of us knew whether or not all the *Irving*'s passengers and crew had perished. But on our arrival at Fort Hope we learned that the

Irving had only just landed and got her lines out when the fire alarm was given, and that not more than two minutes later, when the whole vessel was a mass of flames and smoke, the passengers and crew had all jumped ashore, some into the water at the bank. It was reported at the time that one or two persons had been burned to death. The colored steward, quite an elderly man whom I knew well, saved a large dog by jumping to shore with him. Capt. Irving cast off the steamer's lines as soon as he felt sure that everyone was off the boat, to save the town from getting afire.

The steamer's engines working and wheel revolving are easily accounted for and would readily be understood by river men. But for the sake of those who do not know, I will explain that at Fort Hope, at the steeply cut bank there, as at many landings on river banks, the stream runs quite fast, and nearly always on landing at places like this the engines are allowed to turn over slowly ahead to take the strain off the steamer's lines which, of course, was done in this case.

The steamer had a large load of hay aboard too, which helped to make the fire so much worse. The charred hulk of this once-beautiful boat was hardly cold when Capt. Irving commenced arrangements to build another vessel just as good and even better. That steamer is running today, and is called the *R.P. Rithert.*

On one occasion on the Fraser River, one of the steamers belonging to Capt. Irving on her up trip, ran into a long swifter snag striking it on the end and under the steamer's guards. The impact of the boat caused the snag to rise high up and crash right through the guards and into her house work, running through a stateroom where a passenger was asleep in his bunk, but who, by a miracle, was saved from being crushed to death, though for a time he was pinned in tight where he lay till extricated and the snag was cut away at the guards.

On another occasion on a trip down from Fort Yale, I was aboard the *Western Slope.* We used to leave Yale during the summer months at about 3 or 4 a.m. when it began to be fairly good daylight, and used to arrive at Victoria, B.C., by 3:30 or 4 p.m. on the same day.

About fifteen miles below Yale there are two huge rocks towering high up. The river along there runs very swiftly and great care and experience are required in handling a large heavy boat like the *Slope* in making the shootdown through the Sisters. This trip she took a shear on us and struck a sunken rock. I rushed down to the fire room to see if any water was showing up in the hold. When I got there, I saw at once that the boat was already leaking heavily, for chips and bark and small sticks were afloat in the fireroom.

I sent word to the pilothouse and we headed her for the nearest shore, where she lay for a while with her nose on the beach while we built a copper dam around the hole in the vessel's bottom which, fortunately, was in the fireroom and away from the boilers where we could work at it. After a few hours we proceeded on our trip through to Victoria.

Emory's Bar used to be a hard place for the steamers. The water was very shallow here at times, and swift. Often the boats would stand still with a full head of steam on, trying to head upstream, and one could hear the loud coughing of their exhausts through the funnels for miles; and at time cinders as large as your hand would shoot up in the air and mingle with flame and smoke.

On another trip down we had the honor to have as passengers, General (William T.) Sherman and about twenty of his men. They boarded us at Fort Hope, after first sending word to us at Yale to meet them there. They had along fourteen head of horses, having reached Hope overland. We arrived at Victoria about 9 p.m. on that trip. A brass band was at the dock to meet the boat, and the band played "Marching Through Georgia" as the boat landed, while the General walked ashore over the gangplank with his hat in his hand.

There is a great fascination about river steamboating, especially where there are opposition lines and lots of freight and passenger traffic, as was then the case on the Fraser River; the boats of owners vying with each other to make the quickest trips, securing the most passengers and freight, many landings, one boat endeavoring to reach a certain woodpile before the other, one owner trying (and often succeeding) to buy up most of the woodpiles, and so forth.

Our boat, the *Slope*, used to consume on an average of forty cords per trip, for which we paid at the river bank three dollars per cord. Our steamer had a firebox boiler forty feet long and a

8

pair of twenty-inch cylinders and six and one-half-foot stroke.

One season there came a freshet on the Fraser and some of the lighter draft boats could run into some of the farms along near Chilliwack and Sumas.

One fall, the river began to go down somewhat sooner than usual and we experienced considerable difficulty in getting up. At one point, where we had to put out a long line leading well ahead, we enlisted the services of some native woodchoppers from a camp and also bargained to take their whole woodpile which consisted of some ten cords.

The only way we could get the large full coil of new rope fastened to the point above was to put the whole thing in a canoe and then have a couple of our men, with the natives, pole up and make one end fast to a staunch tree, fasten a large wooden buoy to the other end, and then pay out the rope downstream till we could reach it with the help of the canoe and take the end to our capstan. It was quite a job to get this end aboard, but we succeeded and finally started to heave on the capstan.

About this time the head one of the natives with whom we had bargained as to the amount to be paid him for his services, became leery or wrongfully thought we might not stop to take on his wood and pay him for their services, and half a dozen of them were standing up in their canoe alongside our steamer and holding on to the guards of the vessel. A French carpenter whom we had on board, who did not speak or understand English too well and knew nothing of the Chinook (native) language, apparently did not know what they were jabbering about and ran and got a long heavy sounding pole (which is used aboard stern-wheelers at the forecastle head to take the depth when nearing shallows and cry out the number of feet in halves and quarters up to the pilot or captain in the wheelhouse), and was just about to plunge it down through the bottom of the canoe with all his might to sink the canoe - which no doubt at all would have caused all the occupants of the canoe to drown.

But I quickly saw this Frenchman's motive, and before the end of the pole reached its mark, I grabbed hold of it and turned the pole aside; the pole disappeared overboard on the outside of the canoe. These poles usually have, as this one did, a steel pike and an iron ring on the end.

Well, there was something doing then at once. The head

native and one other man made a dash to get up on the steamer, leaving the other four to look after and hold the large canoe head on to the current and alongside the steamer on our river side. All was excitement. Of course we had not started to heave around on the capstan and hawser as yet, but were lying too near the bank. The leader of the natives made a rush up the main stairway near the pilothouse, chased the French carpenter through the cabin and threw a hatchet at him, barely missing his head. But the Frenchman got away and hid.

In the meantime we gradually got the natives quieted and explained to them that this Frog – oops I mean Frenchman – was wrong in the head and so forth, and eventually got the matter patched up all right by paying them quite a little over and above their bill for services in assisting us in running the line and for what their cordwood amounted to. However, none of us could blame these natives for going after the carpenter, and we all thought we got out of it cheaply; the carpenter especially thought so when he began to fully realize what it would have meant to all of us, particularly to himself, had he succeeded in foundering the canoe and drowning its occupants.

We got through that trip all right, and arrived safely back at New Westminster where we put the steamer into her winter quarters. In a few days it became quite cold and froze, and something having happened to the regular boat plying between Victoria and Westminster, and wishing to go to Victoria as soon as possible, we, including the carpenter, launched one of our metallic lifeboats and provisioned her with food, blankets, a tent and so forth. Four of us started for Victoria downriver to its mouth and thence across the Gulf of Georgia and reached our destination, a distance of about one hundred miles, after four days' rowing and camping overnight.

From this time on, for the next three years, I stayed home in Victoria. Part of the time I attended school; and off and on I worked aboard our steamers as purser and assistant pilot.

I still lived at this time with my parents, over the bay in Victoria near the waterfront where we had a shipyard, a set of ways for hauling steamers out on, a warehouse, a small wharf, three dwelling houses, and some half a dozen of large lots. A portion of this property is now owned, I believe, by D. Warren;

and I understand that a coal-and-wood-yard business occupies the portion where we had the shipyard.

In November 1885 I resided in Seattle for about six months. During that time the anti-Chinese agitation was on, and that city was placed under marshal law. Eight hundred soldiers were sent there from the Vancouver barracks in Oregon under General Gibbons, and I witnessed the shooting down of a couple of men on the street during the riot. A large hole, caused by a stray charge of buckshot, was also found in the doorcasing of the old New England Hotel.

I was deputized on the fire patrol, among several other young fellows, for three weeks, and still have my passport from General Gibbons pasted in one of my scrapbooks.

In the early part of May, 1886, I went again to Stikine River, leaving Seattle on a new river steamer called *Alaska*, which had been hurriedly built there by my father and brother-in-law during the last three months of my residence in Seattle. This boat was only eighty feet long.

We proceeded up the coast to Fort Wrangell under our own steam, carefully picking our weather, and ran on the Stikine River between Wrangell and Telegraph Creek one hundred fifty miles under contract for the firm of Calbtaith, Grant & Cooke at a stipulated figure of eighty dollars per ton for their own freight. We were guaranteed by the above firm one hundred tons for the season, and our little steamer could take up on an average about thirty tons per trip.

We completed our contract, and left Wrangell again some time in August bound for Victoria, after experiencing the usual happenings which always attend swift-water navigation. The old points along the river and the landmarks appeared quite natural to me after my absence. At this time our steamer was the only one plying on the Stikine.

11

2. MY FIRST TRIP INTO THE YUKON TO THE BERING SEA AND RETURN (1887)

On March 11, 1887, at the age of twenty-one and a half years, I boarded the steamer *Idahoe* at the outer (or ocean) dock at Victoria, B. C., Buckman purser, and left there just after midnight bound for the interior of the Yukon country. My objective was Forty Mile Creek situated on the left hand side fifty miles farther down from where Dawson is now located.

This, I felt, was really my first homeleaving. Little did I dream what the near approaching years were destined to work out for my future life. Had it all been different, would I have been better off, or happier? Perhaps not. Who can tell? I promised myself when I started to write this modest and unembellished record of my past life, to withhold any of my strong, emotional feelings and regrets for what has or what might have been. Those who have known and do know me as I am will readily read between the lines of this paragraph and be charitable in their judgment of me.

But to return to my story:

Few people at this time, namely in 1887, except some of those who resided in Alaska, and those who were directly connected with the fur business and coastal steamboat companies of Alaska, had much real understanding or knowledge of the great interior and surrounding country of the mighty Yukon River and its many long navigable streams and tributaries.

Therefore, the many thousands who entered that country in the great rush of 1897 from almost all parts of the world thought that that year was the first any white men had arrived. But as a matter of fact, at this time, namely in the spring of 1887, there had been a few men in the interior of the Yukon for twenty years, and, as many know, the Hudson Bay Company was represented there by their trappers and traders even some time prior to this. And later the Alaska Commercial Company took hold of the fur business.

This company also had a couple of small steamers on the river, the largest of which was called the *Yukon*, some eighty feet in length, and one called the *St. Michael's*, which was sunk just prior to my reaching there; and one steamer called the *Explorer* formerly taken up there and owned by Lieut. Stoney.

There was also another little fifty-foot steamer called the *New Racket*, which was taken up to St. Michael's on the deck of some large vessel in 1880 or 1882 by the Sheffland Brothers with the view of exploring, trading and mining. The last mentioned, at the time of my arrival in the Yukon, was owned and run by Messrs. Harper, McQuesten, Hart and Mayo.

These four men, at the time of my arrival in that country, had been in there for fifteen years without once being out farther than St. Michael's. These men were all big-hearted fellows and thought a great deal of by everyone who knew them. They had assisted many a poor miner to get a grubstake and otherwise perform acts of kindness to different people.

No man I have ever met, either in or out of that country, had anything but a good word to say of the firm of Harper, McQuesten and Company.

I wish to explain here that these four men first entered that country overland from Canada by striking the upper part of the Porcupine River, a large tributary of the Yukon, putting in on the right-hand side going down, just above Fort Yukon and very close to the Arctic Circle.

Descending this stream, they engaged in trapping and put in one or two hard winters. They were also at the head of the White River, another stream coming in on the left a few miles above the Stewart. In fact, these men no doubt really saw more, and went over more of the interior of the Yukon country, and roughed it more than any other men who have ever been there.

Later, they traded for furs for the Alaska Commercial Company, and still later, at about the time of or just prior to my arrival there, they traded for themselves; and had first a post at the mouth of the Stewart River and later, one at Forty Mile Creek. These men were held in the high esteem and respect of all

13

who knew them; not alone for their ever fair and proper business dealings with their fellow men, but also for their great loyalty to their native wives, whom three of the men had married in the first early days of their entrance into that country.

Mr. (or, as we all called him) Jack McQuesten has been residing for the past few years in Alameda, California, with his wife and family, where he has a beautiful home. Poor Mr. Harper died several years ago in the Yukon. Fred Hart also died a few years ago, and Al Mayo is, I understand, still somewhere in the Yukon. His children, like Mr. McQuesten's, are grown up and doing fine. One of Mayo's daughters holds a responsible position, in or near Alameda, and resides there with some of her family, or Mr. McQuesten's.

I have not heard of Harper's family lately, but his children were all well-educated and very likely some of them are still living in the Yukon. I met and saw much of the families of all three men quite often in the Yukon, when some of their children were quite young.

Bishop Seighers, formerly of Portland, Oregon, who during the winter of 1886 was murdered near Nulato, on the lower Yukon, and whom I personally knew, was also an early traveler in that country, as were Professor Dell and Lieut. Schwatka, the latter two having gone in there on their first trips in 1879 and just a year prior to the discovery of Harrisburg, or as it is now called, Juneau.

The Treadwell mine was also discovered about that time or a year later, and two brothers, Captains Dan and Alex McLean (several years later they engaged in the sealing business in the Bering sea), worked at a small placer mine on the beach where the present gigantic Treadwell stamp mills are now located.

Joe Juneau and Dick Harris were the discoverers of Gold Creek, which empties into the Gastineau Channel just behind Juneau. The source of this creek heads up into the Silver Bow Basin back in the steep mountains, the discovery of which led to the location and building of Juneau City.

For about two years prior to my going to this country, a few miners and prospectors used to leave Juneau and go into the upper Yukon in the spring over the old native trail by way of Dyea and the Chilkoot Summit, striking the head of Lindeman Lake and then proceeding down the lakes and river to Cassiar Bar and portaging their boats over the canyon and White Horse Rapids. They built boats, as we did ours, by whipsawing the lumber from spruce trees. Then these men returned in the fall to winter at Juneau, with pokes averaging from five hundred to a couple of thousand dollars in gold dust.

About the same time, or rather some months later than this time (1885), pretty rich diggings were found several miles up the Stewart, quite a stream, and navigable for small, light-draft steamers for some seventy-five miles above where Dawson is now located. Probably a couple of hundred men went in, and good pay was found.

Messrs. Harper, McQuesten, and Company took their little steamer, *New Racket*, up there to the placer mines, rigged a set of Chinese buckets and used the steamer's machinery to run them, furnishing water for their sluice boxes, and for a while made as high as two hundred dollars per day.

Quite a few individual miners made some good stakes mining bar diggings on the Stewart, and a few kept on working their claims on Cassiar Bar on the Lewis (upper Yukon) River, of which I spoke before.

3. DEATH OF TOM WILLIAMS ON THE CHILKOOT SUMMIT WHILE BRINGING OUT NEWS OF THE GOLD STRIKE AT FORTY MILE CREEK (1886-1887)

Now, late in the fall of 1886, after the river navigation had closed and all communication to the outside world was shut off for the time being, a party of stragglers discovered what was reported to be very rich diggings up Forty Mile Creek, the mouth of which is some fifty miles below Dawson coming on the left-hand going down.

There was no way of getting this news to the coast just then. It was not until the river was firmly frozen over that any mail could be sent out. So a man by the name of Tommy Williams, who had gone into that country by way of St. Michael's, and who was in the employ of the Alaska Commercial Company, volunteered to take that company's mail and other letters up the river over the ice and Chilkoot Pass to Dyea, a route he had never been over before.

There were no roadhouses or places to replenish provisions or travelers to meet, as there were some years later. (Today, what a change! An excursion trip for tourists from all parts of the world). Some of his friends tried to dissuade him from going, but he was determined to start. So, some crude maps and charts were marked out for him along with other information; and particularly of the Chilkoot Summit, for that was the place where the difficult part of the journey would be encountered at that time of the year.

Williams pulled out from Forty Mile with the mail sack

containing letters from the Alaska Commercial Company to their headquarters in San Francisco, and also other mail which, of course, it was understood, told the news of the rich strike. He had a dog team of four or six dogs (I am not sure of the exact number), and also a young Indian boy named Bob.

Well, it appears they made good time and had fairly good luck till they came to the Chilkoot Summit on the Dyea trail, when a blinding snowstorm overtook them. After making down this side to what used to be called the Stone House (s large mass of rocks and boulders with cave-like placer among them), Williams commenced to fail, and their dogs, which had been getting short rations for some few days, began to peg out.

The young Indian boy fixed some kind of partially sheltered place in among the rocks and snow, and he and Williams crawled into it. But, of course, they could not make a fire. They remained in this snowhouse for three days. In the meantime Williams was frozen pretty bad, and the Indian boy's feet were frostbitten; some of the dogs got lost, and a couple died right near them and were buried in the drifting snow in a few moments. And the mail pouch which, as was learned afterward, contained three thousand dollars in gold dust, and was also lost and buried in the snow.

At the end of the three days there was a moderation in the weather. So Williams, by this time helpless and having contracted pneumonia, and Bob, the Indian boy, started out with Williams on their sleigh. After lightening it all he could by stripping off the networks and sideracks, and by a superhuman effort, this young boy eventually got Williams down to Healy and Wilson's little trading post at Dyea - and this boy had never been out over this route before, either.

The saddest part, though, was that poor Williams survived only a few hours after reaching the post. The Indian boy was obliged to have most of his frostbitten toes cut off at Juneau.

When a snowstorm is raging on this summit one cannot see anything; and the snow being light as powder, the tracks of someone close ahead of you would be filled up before you could see them. Everywhere you look is the same white mantle of snow, in places a hundred feet deep, and there is nothing to guide one.

That winter of 1886 will be remembered by many, for it was an extremely hard and cold one; and I judged it as having been

17

so from the great depth of snow and thickness of ice I noticed on arriving at Juneau and Dyea.

The trip was made by Williams in December, and they arrived at the post at Dyea along about the first of January. Before he expired, considerable information and news was gleaned from Williams regarding the rich new strike at Forty Mile Creek; and, of course, the boy Bob also told all he knew and had heard about it. So the news went flying down to Juneau by the same canoe engaged to take Bob there for medical aid, and where he had his toes amputated. Then from Juneau, the news went to the states together with a few loose letters carried out aside from the regular mail pouch that was lost.

Well, it was the news of this rich gold strike at Forty Mile Creek reaching Victoria that started me as well as some five hundred other people for the Yukon the succeeding spring in the early part of March.

FIRST TRIP INTO THE YUKON CONTINUED

Now to return to my trip in, where I left off. On boarding the steamer *Idahoe* on the night of March 11, 1887, at Victoria, as I stated before, I became acquainted with an old man named Joe Wilson. He was also on his way to the Yukon, and three years later experienced a very hard trip out over the same route that Williams had taken. He had to live on the inner skin of the barks of trees for four days, and also retrace his steps twice from the Chilkoot Summit forty miles to an Indian camp where he lived and was fed by the natives for six weeks until suitable weather afforded an opportunity to cross the divide.

There was among the passengers Richard Nelson, on his way to Juneau where he was soon afterward in the employ of Mr. Reid, a merchant, and for some years held the position of postmaster at Juneau, and who is now one of the foremost business men of that city and the owner of a large stationery store and other valuable property.

Ned and Jay Decker, two brothers, were also among the passengers bound for Juneau; they afterward became very prominent business men of that place.

I took second-class passage, fares then being thirty and fifty dollars first class to Juneau. The trip up lasted seven days, and

18

since it was uneventful of any unusual incident, I will pass over the details of that portion of my diary.

On the evening of March 18th, now just twenty-one years ago, and after passing the Taku Inlet where the fierce north wind careened our boat over to her port gunwales, our vessel steamed up the channel and it was then that I first saw the twinkling and many lights of the great Treadwell mine and buildings on our port breast. And farther in the distance ahead on our starboard bow were the lights of the little town of Juneau, built mostly in a side hill or ridge to the water's edge.

A cannon shot from our bow followed by a short sound of the whistle was the signal of our approach, and shortly afterward, at 8 p.m., the *Idahoe* tied up to the old first dock (long since abandoned) at Juneau.

I met my brother William there, and next day he and I proceeded to repack my outfit of provisions and supplies into fifty-pound packages. The supplies consisted of about a thousand pounds of general provisions I had shipped from the firm of F.H. Page in Portland, Oregon, to Juneau by the Pacific Coast Steamship Company's steamer *Alki*, three or four days prior to my departure from Victoria.

The *Alki*, at that time, was altogether a freight boat. But several years later some cabin work was done on her to accommodate a limited number of passengers. This steamer has been right along ever since on the Alaska route, and is still considered a good staunch vessel. On many occasions I have heard good jokes sprung among the shipping men at Skagway and elsewhere about this old boat, but the old *Alki* always used to reach port O.K. even if behind time once in a while. Whenever I think of her, I always remember that she was the boat that brought my outfit to Juneau; a heavy load we double and triple tripped into the Yukon.

Well, to return to my story:

On the 19th, the next day after arrival at Juneau, and after preparing our flour, bacon, sugar, dried fruit, rice, coffee, tea and some other miscellaneous provisions in fifty-pound packages with oil sacks around them, then purchasing two good oak runner sleighs at ten dollars each, and two pairs of snow shoes, brother and I left Juneau on the little iron steamer *Yukon* with Capt. John Healy as master, for the head of Dyea Inlet - the then only traversed route to speak of - into the head waters of the Yukon, and which lie some hundred miles in a northwesterly direction from Juneau; to reach it, Lynn Channel, or canal as it is sometimes called, had to be run out.

The transferring or reshipment at Juneau from the *Idahoe* to the small steamer *Yukon* would not have been necessary, were it not for the reason that the large vessels in those days scarcely ever extended their trips to Dyea. But two or three times a year they did go up as far as Chilkoot, which is now better known as Haines Mission. Adjoining the little town are now the fine U.S. Barracks called Fort William H. Seward.

On these particular trips the large boats had to have freight enough on board to assure them at least two hundred dollars in order to go up as far as Haines Mission, or to the Canaries at Pyramid Harbor across the Chilkoot Inlet. On this trip the *Idahoe* was to continue to Haines, which is some nineteen miles from Dyea; hence we were obliged to take passage on the little *Yukon* at Juneau.

About fifteen other miners and prospectors were also aboard the *Yukon*. We were obliged to anchor in Berner's Bay during a heavy snowstorm.

On the morning of the 20th at 8:30, we got under way again, though it was still blowing hard and snowing some. We overtook and passed a little steamer called the *Seal*, which also had a load of passengers for the Yukon via Dyea.

Arrived at Haines Mission and dropped anchor there at 1 p.m. We went ashore and made some little purchases at the old Dickinson store. This building still stands not far from the shoreline, about a quarter of a mile to the right of the U.S. Barracks of Fort William H. Seward, completed a couple of years ago.

March 21st: Got under way again at 7a.m.. Arrived at Dyea, the head of Lynn Canal and our salt water destination. A couple of hours later, passing on our right, but not aware of it at that time, the little bay and river of Skagway. I little thought that this place was to play such a part in the future years of my life and become the main gateway into the great interior of the Yukon with large shipping wharves and railroad facilities, with a thriving little city of (at one time) several thousand people nestled in the valley between its high mountains.

We found the channel frozen solid about two and a half miles out from its head, including the Dyea River. The ice was nearly a foot thick. Our little steamer ran up alongside this natural frozen wharf. We chopped notches in the ice, moored the steamer by planting her anchors, and after getting all our outfits ashore we made double trips with our sleighs till we struck the river ice, which we followed up to about half a mile above the little trading post of Healy and Wilson, where we camped in a thick cluster of spruce timber about a hundred yards from the river's bank.

Judging from the great number of sleigh dogs brought in by miners in subsequent years, it has since often made me ask why did none of us who went into the Yukon that spring take dogs; but out of the five hundred men who did go that spring, I saw only one little black puppy among the miners.

March 22nd: Commenced overhauling our outfit preparatory to hauling up river over the ice; weather turned somewhat softer, and it is snowing. Wrote letter to Mother this afternoon.

March 23rd: Broke camp at 8 a.m. and proceeded upriver ice with about six hundred pounds between William and me, to the mouth of the canyon eight miles or so distant and made camp there at noon. Weather turned quite mild, and sun out bright all afternoon. William took about one hundred twenty-five pounds on the sleigh up to some two and one-half miles farther on.

March 24th: Started down to our first camp at 7:30 a.m. for remainder of our six hundred pounds of stuff. Weather clear and frosty. Returned to camp at the canyon at 4 p.m.. with remainder of outfit, and very tired, making the round trip of some sixteen miles or more in eight and one-half hours. This was heavy work, hauling three hundred pounds each upriver, and our appetites were something awful. We learned today at Healy's post that a canoe arrived at the ice at (the) head of the inlet with six miners who had started from Juneau on February 20th. They were unable to get here sooner on account of the severe weather and heavy northerly winds. It is now 6:30 p.m., sunset. The high snowy mountain peaks, with the reflection of the sun on their tops, look grand this evening.

March 25th: Made three trips each up through the canyon to Pleasant Camp some two and one-half miles between 5 a.m. and 2 p.m., taking about two hundred fifty pounds on our sleighs each trip. Very rough and hard traveling through these canyons. Large boulders and holes in the ice to contend with, and quite dangerous. We are often obliged to unload our sleighs and lift them up five to eight feet and then load one sack at a time.

These canyons, or narrow gorges, during the open seasons, of course, are totally impassable; water rushes and tumbles over and around boulders large and small, and pitches over shelves, and forms, in places, little falls. And late in the winter or early in the spring, at which time I write, the vast amount of snow has partially leveled the holes and depressions formed by the large boulders and rocks some eight and ten feet in diameter. And in sleighing up through these canyons one has to wind around these boulders and pick the way as best as one can; and the snow being very soft and light, we would many times sink clean up to our shoulders in it and the sleigh would topple over and over.

We also had to be very careful in getting around the open pools where we could see the water running swiftly under the edges of the ice. Several times we nearly fell into these pools, sleigh load and all, sometimes when coming to a steep pitch, almost perpendicular, of several feet. Then one of us would have to climb up on top with the sleigh rope and pull hard, while the other lifted and pushed up at the back end of the sleigh. In this way we often got the sleigh and load up without unlashing the stuff, which saved considerable extra work and time.

Toward evening William took three hundred pounds up to Sheep Camp, a distance of about two and one-half miles, the same as from Mouth Canyon to Pleasant Camp.

March 26th: Left Pleasant Camp at 8 a.m. with all our stuff, and arrived at Sheep Camp at 10 a.m.. Make a new camp, pitching tent, and so forth, and took a load each up to Stone House. Very steep grade and pitches. William took one hundred seventy pounds, and I one hundred pounds; wind is blowing strong down off the Chilkat (Chilkoot) Summit. Stood still for a moment and looked at the summit: The men on their way up resembled small black spots. In coming down from the summit, after having cached our packs up there in the snow, we would just sit down and slide down at great speed. In this way we had a regular ditch or trough worn in the snow, eighteen inches or two feet deep. Then from Stone House, which is about three miles from the summit, we coasted considerably the first part of the way to Sheep Camp.

March 27th: Sunday. Weather very rough, blowing heavy from the north and drifting snow; therefore we concluded to lay off and make up some packs and straps in readiness for our climbs to the summit. Toward 5 p.m. weather moderated. Got news that the little steamer *Yukon* had arrived at Healy's place with twelve more men for the mines.

March 28th: Sheep Camp. Very strong southeast wind during the night and all day with drifting snow. Took three loads each in our sleighs to Stone House, distance of about two miles; sent down to Healy's store this morning for twenty-five pounds of bacon, fifty pounds rice, two tins syrup, one tin lard, and a dozen cans of yeast powder. Got news today that the U.S. gunboat *Pinta* had arrived at anchorage near Dyea, to remain there for a couple of weeks or more to quell any disturbance that might arise among the natives until the miners got their outfits over the divide. Wind died down at 6 p.m..

March 29th: Strong southeast wind blowing, and snowing heavily. William and I took about seventy-five pounds each on our backs from Stone House to the foot of the Summit. Very steep grade, and heavy traveling; freezing hard. On returning it was almost impossible to face the drifting snow and wind. Distance from Stone House to foot of Summit is about one and one-half miles.

Paid four dollars for some tobacco, yeast powder, and a tin of syrup from Healy's. The bacon and rice did not come up because the natives wanted twelve dollars to bring it to Sheep Camp.

About 6 p.m. a native arrived here with the fifty pounds of rice and twenty-five pounds of bacon. Cost for the rice and bacon nine dollars and fifty cents, and charges for bringing them from Healy's post, seven dollars and fifty cents.

Two men started to cross the Summit late this afternoon, and on arriving on the other side, a large snowslide came down. They dropped their packs to run out of the way just in time, but their packs were buried forever by tons of snow. About 11 p.m. a strong wind set in from the north with considerable snowfall.

March 30th: Morning. Wind hauled around to the southwest; weather clear, but very few men turned out to work. Wind still blowing hard at 7 p.m.. Impossible to go to the

23

foot of Summit today, so we stayed in camp. It was rumored today that the little steamer *Seal*, from Juneau, with twelve men bound for the mines, was lost. The snow in places is twenty and thirty feet deep at Sheep Camp, where it has drifted, and from time to time we are obliged to select new places for our campfire.

March 31st: Fine weather all day, with a sprinkle of snow. Early this morning took five packs from the Stone House to the foot of the Summit. About sixty men were packing their outfits up the Summit today. We stood at the foot and watched them sliding down the mountain in the worn snow gutter for a long distance, going very fast to the foot.

April 1st: Weather clear at 7 a.m. but very windy from the northeast; impossible to pack to foot of Summit. Several men started out but were obliged to return. We took one load on a sleigh to Stone House; wind lulled down at 1 p.m., and so we took two packs each from Stone House to foot of Summit. A great many men were out packing over the Summit. Native women and their young daughters and sons from ten years of age up were also packing from fifty to seventy-five and one hundred pounds on their backs for miners, earning from ten to twenty dollars per day. I noticed that the few small trees and shrubs in vicinity of Stone House were bare of bark on the north side, a condition caused, as some said, by the wind and snow beating against them.

Today, the first party of men crossed the Summit with their camp outfits. These men had left Juneau about six weeks ago. Among them were McCue and Bill Stuart.

April 2nd: Very stormy all forenoon from the northeast and freezing hard; no men leaving camp. Six natives arrived here today from Healy's to pack for miners over the Summit.

Weather moderated about 12:30 p.m. Took two packs each from Stone House to the Summit, and returned to camp about 4:30 p.m. There were about sixty men packing between Sheep Camp and the Summit this afternoon.

Going up the last pitch is similar to going up a stairway. We felt quite warm in our exertion and many times in ascending; when we became winded, we would just turn around and lean back against the snow and rest a while without removing our packs.

My appetite is simply enormous from working in the snow

and stormy weather as, of course, were the appetites of all on the trail. We would fill our tin plated - some used granite pans a couple of inches deep - with boiled beans and bacon, then ate a big plateful of boiled rice and mixed dried stewed prunes and apples; then we had from two to three large tin cups of tea, and several pieces of our homemade camp bread with very little butter, for this luxury had already pegged out, as had also our condensed Eagle Brand milk.

We judge that this summit is approximately forty-one hundred feet above sea level.

April 3rd: Made an early start from our camp here (Sheep Camp), and went up to Stone House. Strong northeaster blowing; freezing hard. Engaged three natives to take nine packs from foot of summit to the top for thirty dollars; pack ranging in weight from seventy-five to one hundred pounds. We worked all our own outfit up from salt water to the foot of summit ourselves, the two of us, except the extra pack bought from the Healy post previously mentioned.

Quite a number of men got over the summit today with their camp packs. I stood on the Summit this morning and could see a fine blue sky as far as the eye could reach. Had very hard work pulling our sleighs up to the Summit from its base with less than forty pounds.

April 4th: Weather fine and no wind. Got all ready. Broke camp here (Sheep Camp) at 5 a.m. and started to cross the divide. But on reaching Medlow's Camp at 7 p.m., a strong northeaster sprang up, and it is freezing hard with drifting snow, so we are obliged to remain till the morning. I was blinded, which is very painful, and had to go to bed. Quite a number of men are also troubled with snow-blindness. It is caused by continually seeing the snow, for when the sun is out it causes the snow to glitter and this is very hard on the eyes.

This ailment can be avoided if one wears blue or green goggles before the complaint comes on. The natives blacken their faces with a mixture of oil and other stuff to avoid it, as they also do to ward off the mosquitoes. I applied warm moist tea leaves, which helped me some. At 1 p.m. the weather moderated, but it was then too late to start to cross the Summit and reach camping timber on the other side. We could see along the mountain tops; the drifting snow resembles fog.

April 5th: Started for Old Man Medlow's Camp, one mile above Sheep Camp, at 6:30 a.m.. Wind still blowing some, and freezing hard. We both had light packs, blankets, and so on. Arrived at the Summit at 10:00 a.m., loaded all our outfit on our two sleighs and took them down the mountain on the other side. About fifty tons of miner's outfits were piled up on the Summit in different piles, most of them in fifty and seventy-five-pound packs. We traveled down to within one mile of Lake Lindeman. About sixty men crossed the Summit today with their camp packs. We reached a place to camp in timber about 8:30 p.m. and dug down nine feet in the snow. Weather balmy and nice on this side of the divide. Felt an agreeable change as soon as we got over. We cached six hundred pounds (about half) of our stuff at the foot of the summit on this side; the loads were too heavy to pull all the way to camping ground.

We have traveled just about fourteen miles today with packs and heavily loaded sleighs; crossed two lakes between our camp and the Summit. A great deal of snow lies on the lakes' ice. We call the largest one the "Two-Mile Lake" (now called Deep Lake). We experienced very hard sleighing in the canyon between Lake Lindeman and the Two Mile Lake because of the many short pitches and large holes and crooked turns.

April 6th: Started out at 12:30 p.m. with our sleighs for the foot of the summit for the remainder of our outfit, but were obliged to return to camp on account of bad soft trail and drift snow.

April 7th: Made an early start again this morning to get our stuff to camp. Reached the cache at 10:00 a.m.. I took two hundred fifty pounds on my sleigh, and William three hundred fifty. Very hard pulling. Reached camp again at 4:00 p.m., making the round of some twenty miles in eight and one half hours. Several men are now suffering with snow-blindness. One man's sleigh ran over a bank into the canyon today and was badly broken.

April 8th: Started from here today at 7:30 a.m. with half our outfit (six hundred pounds) for the head of Lake Bennett, a distance of about nine miles. Crossed the ice on Lake Lindeman. Wind blowing with us, but we had not yet rigged up sails on our sleighs.

The snow on Lake Lindeman covered the ice to an average

depth of two feet through which it was heavy sleighing. Reached the foot of the lake, and proceeded about one mile down Payer Portage at the canyon, or outlet, which connects these two (Lindeman and Bennett) lakes. During the open season this outlet, or creek connection, is very swift-running water and very rocky, and boats are always portaged.

At noon cached our sleigh loads, had lunch, and returned to camp near the head of Lindeman Lake at 3:20 p.m.; distance for the round trip, about eighteen miles. In returning, met several parties with large square sails rigged up on their sleighs. Many times the men pulling their sleighs with rope over shoulder and gee pole in one hand have to run to keep ahead of their sleighs, especially when the trail becomes well traveled and no fresh snow falls.

April 9th: Payer Portage. Arrived here with the balance of our outfit (camping stuff, etc.,) at 2:30 p.m. Weather warm and bright; sun all day. Commenced rigging our sleighs with masts and sails in bobsled fashion, one behind the other, with a bolster on the hind one and a pole on each side leading to the forward sleigh to pile our outfit on, and a gee-pole on hind sleigh.

April 10th: Sunday. Got up at 5:30 a.m. Finished rigging our sleighs, and left here (Payer Portage) at 11:00 a.m. Reached head of Bennett Lake 11:30 a.m. This lake we estimate to be about thirty miles long. We found quite a number of men here busily engaged in rigging up their sleighs for sailing. Our sleighs worked fine, but instead of finding mostly glazed ice on Lake Bennett, as we had expected and hoped, there was about one foot of snow on an average.

Weather fine. Sun shining brightly, and a clear sky. At about 2:00 p.m. we were obliged to camp, for the snow was very soft and the sleigh pulled hard with all (our) outfit stuff on them, about thirteen hundred pounds. This was about four miles down the lake. As soon as the sun goes down behind the hills it commences to freeze. The best time for traveling here is very early in the morning when the snow is more firm.

April 11th: Monday. Made an early start this morning at 2:30 a.m. Intense frost during the night and morning. When we had traveled a short distance we found the sleighs pulled very hard, so we uncoupled them and took half our load on each one. Things then went much better. Good fair weather, no wind, made camp at 12:30 noon, after making ten miles. At 2 p.m. William took a load ahead about three miles, while I remained in camp to make bread and cook.

April 12th: Started at 7 a.m., no wind to fill our sleigh sails. About 11 a.m. were forced to halt again. Made camp for the night at 3:30 p.m., about six miles from the foot of Bennett Lake. The snow appears to be getting thinner here; it is about two feet on shore, and about six inches on the ice.

April 13th: Made a start this morning at 3 a.m. with a good fair wind; made fair time for a couple of hours, then the wind died out again. Some patches of good glare ice here and there, but scarce. In going over it we were obliged to get on the sleighs and ride or run to keep up with the sleighs during the brief time it lasted. Our sail was about ten feet square.

In the afternoon the wind freshened up again and helped us along considerably. Camped for the afternoon and night at 1:30 p.m. just this side of Windy Arm, after having covered about fifteen miles in the ten and one-half hours with our two sleighs coupled together with a load of nearly thirteen hundred pounds. A large number men passed here this afternoon with their sleigh sails set and heavy loads.

The first party that crossed the Chilkoot or Dyea Summit this spring ate lunch about one mile from here today. The sunset here this evening looks beautiful as it sinks down behind the snowy mountains and throws gleams all over the snow and patches of ice here and there.

April 14th: Made a start at 7 a.m. Wind dead against us. Struck in by Windy Arm and camped at 10:30 a.m.

The Stuart party were just a few hundred yards ahead breaking trail through the snow; several men camped here to wait for fair wind. This lake (Taku Arm) is, according to our estimation, some twenty miles long, leads approximately northeast for about seven miles, then takes a turn northward, where Windy Arm comes in, which arm is some fifteen miles in length. There are thirty-two miners' hand sleighs pulled up by this camp this afternoon, all like a little harbor full of small craft. Blowing very hard this afternoon out of Windy Arm as usual; not in our favor, but with what would be called a beam wind.

April 15th: Got under way this morning at 8 a.m. traveling very hard; snow very soft. Went about four miles when it became too much for us, the sleigh runner clogging up and piling the snow up in front, and our shoulders becoming sore and chafed by the straining and pulling on the sleigh ropes. Went into camp for the afternoon and night at 1 p.m.

Found at this point forty-five loaded sleighs pulled up nearby on the ice. Strong wind blowing from the southeast; snow lies from six to eight inches on the ice here. Game seems to be very scarce through this portion, at least in and about the line of travel; saw only a few ptarmigan on the trip thus far. They resemble a white pigeon very much, but are a little larger, have considerable small fluffy feathers on their feet, and are called by some "Arctic Grouse". Last spring, along about April 20th, the ice here was as clear as crystal, no snow lying on it.

April 16th: Started this morning at 7 a.m. as also did most all the other parties. Sleighing good for light loads, which could be drawn over the light crust of snow; but our loads were too heavy for that, so we went into camp again at 10 a.m. for the rest of the day and night after making only four miles.

At 10:30 a.m. a strong southwest wind sprung up which soon caused all the sails of passing sleighs to be unfurled. The majority of these sleighs went into camp about a mile below us on a point. We cut a hole in the lake ice about five feet deep to get some good water instead of melting snow.

April 17th: Sunday. Made a start this morning at 4:30. Light frost during the night; sleighing good. At 9:30 a.m., a southwest wind sprang up which assisted us along considerably. Reached the foot of Taku Lake at Five Mile River where it leads into Marsh Lake, at 11:30 a.m. and camped for the night. Snow becoming too soft and wet. Found quite a portion of the lower end of Taku Lake and the Five Mile River open. Traveling distance today, twelve miles. Saw quite a number of large white swans flying this afternoon, but could not get a good shot at them.

April 18th: Got under way at 4 a.m. Sleighing heavy. We were obliged to double trip for a couple of miles. In some places we could travel over the snowcrust with snowshoes and light loads. Made our way down to within a mile of where this stream empties into Marsh Lake. We were then obliged to camp again, for the snow gets very soft along about 11 a.m. Weather still continues warm and fine. No rain, and no fresh snow. During the nights and early mornings we often see the beautiful

Northern Lights. The whole heavens are streaked and lit up by them.

April 19th: Got started this morning at 3:15 a.m. sleighing hard, double tripping, and when we were obliged to go into camp again we found several other men camped also. No wind all day, and quite warm about noon. This evening weather indicated good frost for coming night, which is what we need for traveling.

Saw a fresh fox trail in the snow. I learned that on or about the middle of last December, when Bob the Indian boy came out from the Yukon, all these lakes had glare ice.

April 21st: Got up this morning at 12:15 (just after midnight) and were under way in our sleigh ropes at 2 a.m. Very good going until about 9 a.m., when hauling became very hard; caught up to the head crowd on their way this morning, the Ashby and Leak's party; went into camp at noon, three miles this side of or above the foot of Marsh Lake. Just opposite here the McClintock River comes in on the right. William took a load on ahead to near the foot of the lake this afternoon, and found the Sixty Mile River*, as some call it, was open but how far down he could not tell, of course. This morning early, the thermometer registered at zero just before sunrise.

April 22nd: Started at 6 a.m. and proceeded down to the foot of the lake or mouth of Sixty Mile River*. There we made a good comfortable camp, built a raft thirty-three feet long and about ten feet wide, taking thirteen dry logs averaging about nine inches in diameter; after trimming them close, we hauled them down with ropes on to the edge of the river on the ice, and arranged them, butt and small ends alternately, to keep the widths uniform as much as possible. We fastened all together with four heavy cross pieces of timber, first boring two-inch holes through each log and fastening same with wooden pins two-inch diameter.

A great number of swans are flying all around the river here.

* Moore is referring to the mouth of the upper Yukon River, the first stretch of which is about sixty miles between Marsh and Laberge lakes. The better-known Sixty Mile River flows into the Yukon sixty miles upriver from Fort Reliance, hence the name.

4. FOLLOWING THE YUKON ICE JAM DOWN BY RAFTS AND BOAT TO FORTY MILE (April-May, 1887)

April 23rd: Got up at 5 a.m. and shortly completed our raft and launched it off the ice into the river with all our goods and sleighs on it, including Bill Best's and Tom Manley's outfits, making in all about twenty-five hundred pounds. The raft floated rather low in the water, so we put six extra logs under it. Our goods were piled up on a deck of poles about a foot above the main raft logs.

I broke through the ice and fell into the river just after launching our raft, but hung on to the edge of the ice and was hauled out by William. Weather cloudy today; had a light shower of rain only lasting about five minutes. Quite a number of men are strung along the river here, all engaged in building rafts.

When we got about five miles down we were stopped by an ice jam which extended right across the river. We chopped our way through it, and camped for the night. At 6:15 p.m, there was quite a breeze blowing from the northwest.

April 24th: Started with the raft this morning at 5 a.m.. Proceeded but a short distance (some two miles) when we came up to another jam; found several rafts stuck there and apparently abandoned. One party was camped nearby. We finally got through and went down about one mile farther, when we found still another jam. Two parties, Kennedy and Hasser, fell into the river with all their stuff and nearly lost their lives. Several others were out on the ice today. Tommy Ashby and Billy Leak came down to here on a cake of ice with their outfit.

The country along here shows many high gravel-and-sand banks, also table lands. Snow is beginning to get thinner. Weather very fine, resembling that which I remember on the

31

Stikine River at Glenora Landing about this time of the year. As it seemed impossible to force our way through this jam, we went into camp at 10 a.m.

April 25th: River still jammed with ice here. William and Tom Manley went down on foot to Cummings Creek, about six miles from here, and found the river had closed there again. Three more rafts arrived from above today, but all were obliged to stop here on account of the jam. Two more men fell into the river, but they got out all right.

April 26th: Jam gone; started again with all our stuff on the raft at 7:30 a.m. Drifted down some two miles when we came up to another ice jam. Two rafts ahead of ours got through, then the ice immediately closed in again and shut our raft out. We then took everything ashore and went to hauling with our sleighs again, abandoning our raft.

Sleighing exceedingly hard. Two more men fell into the river today and damaged their outfits. We came down the river thirteen miles (to eight miles above the canyon), and camped for the night. The river thus far, from where we left our raft, is completely closed; ice in many places along here very bad and dangerous. Saw fresh otter tracks from ice up into the woods.

April 27th: Started out at 5:30 a.m. Sleighing good; not much snow on the ice; fair wind all day. Arrived at the head of the canyon at 10:30 p.m. Had dinner there; then went on through this narrow gorge with high perpendicular walls of rock on either side, hauling our heavily loaded sleighs (four, including Tom Manley's and Billy Best's). This canyon is about three quarters of a mile long and averages about fifty feet in width. We sleighed through this canyon instead of going around on top over the hill.

We found a shelf of ice about ten feet in width frozen onto the canyon walls. We took the right hand side. The middle of the canyon was very swift running water with large whirlpools, running at the rate of about fifteen miles per hour or more. From this it will readily be seen that taking this route through the canyon on this ledge of ice was a great risk, but it saved us much heavy work in avoiding the route over the hill.

As we looked back over this, we realized more fully the danger of it all. For a little piece below the canyon it was open water, then closed again until we got down to the White Horse

Rapids, along which, over the ice near shore, was very rough going. Had a strong fair wind here; proceeded down to about twenty-two miles from the head of Lake Laberge and there camped for the night at 1:30 p.m.

April 28th: Started out at 6 a.m. Found sleighing very good in places, there being occasional spots of glare ice (that is, places where the ice had sunk and the water risen above it froze again). Traveled fast, and made fifteen miles by 1 p.m. Then the ice and snow became too soft, so we camped for the night. Tahkiena (Takhini) River comes in about two miles above here, or about ten miles above the head of Lake Laberge.

April 29th: Started this morning at 5:15. Quite a frost last night, which made sleighing good; also had a good fair wind. Found long stretches of glare ice along near the edges of the river, and also some very bad stretches. The latter were caused, as I understand it, by anchor ice rising up to the surface and forming large blocks which made these places heavy sleighing. Found the head of this lake (Laberge) also like this, with about eight inches of snow, but this condition began to change for the better when we got farther down. Came down the lake some thirteen miles, and camped for the night at 2 p.m., making twenty-one miles today.

April 30th: Got started at 7 a.m. with good sleighing and fair wind, and by 3:30 p.m., at which time we made camp, we had made twenty miles. This camp was about six miles above the foot of Lake Laberge. Today I am suffering considerably with snow blindness.

May 1st: Sunday. Started at 7 a.m. Arrived at the foot of the lake or head of the Lewis River (Lewes/Yukon) at noon. Here we found a number of men camped, some building temporary rafts to drift down to where fit timber could be found for more substantial rafts or for boat building.

The river along here is open, but jams are anticipated farther below. The weather today was very warm at noon. The snow was hard on my eyes, which felt as though they were full of hot sand, for the glittering snow is hard to look at.

May 2nd: Started out from camp this morning at 5:30 to look up suitable timber for another raft. Went another mile downriver and managed to gather fifteen dry logs averaging about ten inches through at the butts. Worked hard, and got the raft all ready this evening for an early start downriver tomorrow morning.

May 3rd: Our raft being all ready, rigged up with good long steering sweeps on each end in the center, and built similar to, but better, than our first raft. We loaded our stuff, including our sleighs as before, for we did not know how soon we might have to take to the sleighs again. But we were in hopes that this time we would be able to travel quite a way without encountering another jam.

Got started at 8 a.m. When about a mile down we met four men, one called Joe Dotey; one was from Stewart River, and two from Salmon River, all on their way out. They reported three white men killed by the Indians down on Stewart River . They also reported that the fifteen men who wintered at Salmon River were nearly starving; some had been living on a sack of flour for three months. These men spoke favorably of the coarse gold diggings on Stewart River. They had been in there since last September.

The weather today was quite a change; blowing, freezing, and snowing while we drifted downstream on our raft. Twice we had to make a landing on account of heavy hailstorms, not being able to see far enough ahead to be sure of steering our raft in safety. The river along here at this stage of the water is very rocky, the bars are mostly of heavy boulders and gravel. The ice on either side in places appears to be five feet thick; large cakes of it are continuously breaking off and coming downstream. Large flocks of geese are beginning to fly about searching for breeding ground.

Camped at 4:30 p.m. about six miles above the mouth of the Hootalinqua (Teslin) River. Saw a lynx walking on the opposite side of the river, but was too far off to get a shot at him. It was reported that a number of Indians from the interior started out to head off the white men who are now going in, to take their provisions away from them.

May 4th: Started out with our raft at 6 a.m.. Weather fine. When down about three miles above the mouth of the Hootalinqua, we found the first parties that had crossed the summit this spring. Their rafts were tied up to the bank there. A large jam had just broken loose before we got there. We all shortly pulled out in the stream again, and drifted down to where the Hootalinqua comes into the Lewes (Yukon) River; there we found the river completely blocked by an ice jam. Some parties intend taking to their sleighs again, and others intend to build boats.

Sleighing along here is now rough, for we have to keep along the shore edges and the ice here is rough, broken and sliding toward the river; and our sleighs keep sliding down and often rolling over. We remained in camp today and got our whipsaw filed and set.

May 5th: Got swung out into the stream this morning at 6 o'clock; went about two miles farther down the river to an island where we understood fair timber could be found for boat building. All the other parties also came down, some to build their boats there. Ahead of us we could see another complete jam of ice on both sides of the island, and tried to work our raft into the left hand shore with two men on each long steering sweep. But being well out in the middle of the stream, and the current here pretty swift, we could not make the landing above the jam. So we struck the ice jam with our raft full force, and the force of the river began to sink the hind end. We had to work fast to throw all our outfit on the ice, then sleigh it to shore on the island and to safety. Then we took ropes and managed to get our raft hauled around to where it would be safe in case the jam broke away.

We put up a whipsaw kit today, and also commenced making mining rockers, buckets and the like.

Very large cakes of ice continued to break off along the shore edges and float down to pile up in front of the jam here. Toward evening the whole jam broke loose, and the whole blockade went shooting downstream.

May 6th: Made two rocker frames today; rolled our first medium-size log up onto the saw pit and sawed out two pieces of lumber.

May 7th: Sawed out seven more spruce planks ten inches wide by twelve feet long.

Two more parties came downriver today on their rafts. Billy Best and I gathered a gold pan full of spruce pitch to be used later to pitch the seams of our boat. We all apprehend a short season to mine before high water, as the nights are still very cold. Last night it froze harder than it has for the last three weeks.

May 8th: Sunday. Got up at 6 a.m. and went to work getting out timber (round young spruce) for boat, and hewed them out one and one-half by two inches. Whipsawed some more lumber, gathered more pitch, and made some boat frames.

Our boat is to be thirty feet long overall; twenty-six inches extreme breadth of beam on the bottom, with a forty-four-inch beam in the widest place at the gunwales, and a depth of twenty-four inches.

Weather cold and cloudy all day. River fell about fourteen inches today on account of ice jams again breaking loose farther below.

May 9th: Large quantities of ice went out of this vicinity today. Got a large log rolled up onto our sawpit today, thirty feet long and twenty inches in diameter at its butt end. We figure it will make nine boards one inch thick by ten inches wide. Faced it up this evening, and lined it out ready for sawing in the morning. Finished one rocker completely this afternoon.

May 10th: Weather fine. Finished another rocker, also made eight wooden buckets and two tubs for packing sand and washing out the rocker blankets. The buckets are fourteen by six inches by twelve inches on top, chamfered down on the open end, with handles made of young spruce bent round.

A little scow came downriver this evening with Alex Fraser, Joe Hasser and another man also bound for the Forty Mile Creek mines. Some parties here are building their boats sixteen and eighteen inches in width on the bottom and thirty feet long, so that it will be easier to pole up the Forty Mile Creek or River, and also to pole out upriver to the lakes on their way out in the fall - provided they wish to come out.

May 11th: Finished sawing the lumber for our boat this forenoon, and got her all in frame this evening. Worked from 6:30 a.m. till 8:30 p.m. Her length overall is twenty-nine feet, length of keel twenty-seven feet, breadth of beam on the bottom twenty-six inches, and beam on top four feet. Twelve sets of timbers one and one-half inches, placed two feet apart. Bottom planks one by ten inches, siding three quarter by ten inches, shear forward two inches, sheer aft one inch; stem and stern pieces five-inch side, tapered down to one and one-half inches in front and three inches on the inside edge. She is very good model with a long draw aft. We set the first frame one-third distance from the stem, and she holds this breadth for four frames aft.

We first made a level foundation, stretched the keel plank out, set up four frames and stem and stern post, sprung a ribbon plank around on each side from stem to stern, then we fitted the other eight frames into place.

Two parties camped near us finished their boat today, a much smaller one than ours.

May 12th: Got our boat all planked tonight and expect to finish her by tomorrow night. Johnny Reid and Jack Reynolds left here today in their boat; Harry Carter and his partner passed downriver this afternoon in their boat. They reported twenty new arrivals at the foot of Lake Laberge.

May 13th: Got our oars, paddles, and mast finished and completed our boat this evening. Two more boats passed down this afternoon. Weather fine all day.

May 14th: We hung up four good sleighs high in a large spruce tree, including the two belonging to Best and Manley. These cost ten dollars each at Juneau, Alaska. They had served us well, but we were not sorry to part with them.

Loaded all our supplies into our boat, including Best's and Manley's outfit, which altogether amounted to close to twenty-five hundred pounds; but we put our rockers, buckets, and other things on our raft, and Best and Manley came down on it in company with us in our boat.

Our boat leaked considerably at first. One was kept busy bailing water. Very cold and windy. Saw large flocks of young ducks, but were unable to get any as we only had rifles and no shotguns.

Drifted on down to Jack McCormack's Bar and found him and Ledger there just getting ready to leave. Went ashore there and had dinner, after which it was arranged for Ledger and McCormack to come down on our raft with Best and Manley. We prospected two different bars on our way down, but found only a few colors. The bars are mostly all covered with very thick ice, and are frozen for several feet in most places where the ice lies.

Arrived at Densmuir's Lower Bar at 4 p.m.. There we found about twenty-five men camped, including many of those parties who started ahead of us; they camped here on account of an ice jam one mile above Cassiar Bar.

Saw Buckskin Miller, who wintered here; also his partner named Criss. They reported very hard winter and shortages of provisions; partially provided with moose meat by the natives. About ten are made fast on shore here, also a number of rafts. Most of these men intend to leave for downriver tomorrow morning; several of them are bound for the Stewart River coarse gold diggings.

May 15th: Remained in camp here all day and put our copper plate in order. We first scoured it well with fine sand until it was very bright, then washed it off and let it dry. Next we rubbed a solution of cyanide of potassium on it, then immediately rubbed quicksilver on, which took well, and set it by till the verdigris appeared; then coated it again with quicksilver and acid.

A man came up from below and reported the river all clear of ice. Several parties left here for Stewart River.

Buckskin Miller gave me thirty dollars and forty cents in gold dust today to deliver to his daughter Louise at Victoria, B.C., also two letters to be delivered whenever I went outside again. Mr. Miller said we were correct in estimating that this past winter (1886) was the coldest known here for many years. He reported that it must have been between eighty and ninety degrees below zero. He said that his quicksilver froze although it was wrapped up in sacks and blankets and within three foot of a good fire.

It is now 9:30 p.m., and the sun is shining brightly on the surrounding hills.

May 16th: Got up at 6:30 a.m. Raining steadily but not hard. This is the first rain here since last October. All the men who were camped here left for Stewart River in their boats and rafts today. Two more parties also arrived from upriver. The four of us - Tom Manley, Billy Best, my brother William, and I - went down a few hundred yards to prospect Densmuir's Bar at noon. We washed fifty buckets of dirt and cleaned it up - but found only one dollar and fifty cents. The gold is very fine and light indeed. There was about three feet of ice on the bars, and another layer below, and then frozen ground and gravel below again. So we made up our minds that this prospect was not worth going to all the trouble and work of clearing and thawing the ice off the bar.

May 17th: Broke camp at 7 a.m. and started downriver again hoping now that we would not be held up by jams any more.

Called in at Cassiar Bar three miles farther down and found George Ramsey and his partners there, in a terrible way about some men who stayed in last winter and worked his bar clean out, also raiding his caches and taking out all his tools.

Started again, proceeded down about a couple of miles, when we saw a large male moose on the ice near the river about fifty yards from our boat. We had no rifle in the boat, so waited for Manley and Best to catch up with the raft; they had the rifle. The moose stood and looked at us a moment, then turned and trotted off toward the timber and disappeared. As soon as the raft caught up to us we all made a landing and tracked this moose for three hours but could not get sight of him again. He was very large, with a high hump at the shoulders and great breadth of horns.

Got started again, and on our way down we tied up to the bank just above the mouth of the Big Salmon River, while Manley and Best went up a slough on foot to look for a cache, the directions and description of which were given to them by the owner at Juneau. They found the cache buried about a foot deep in the ground. In it was a tank of quicksilver, still frozen.

The Big Salmon River comes into the Yukon on the right hand going down about five miles below Cassiar Bar. It is quite a stream. Parties have been up it about forty miles prospecting. Left again, and when about a mile farther down we ran across Bill Stewart, Jim McCarty and George McCue camped there.

They informed us that the river was blocked with ice three miles farther down, so we continued for a few hundred yards and camped for the night near Henry Miller's Camp. He had just followed a black bear for quite a distance but did not succeed in getting him. All the first parties are camped about a mile below here. The principal timber here consists of spruce, birch, cottonwood, black pine, willow, aspen, ash, balsam, and alder.

May 18th: Remained in camp all day. Took good bath, and changed clothes. Large quantities of ice are continually floating downstream to be halted and piled up against the jam below here. The river took a drop of one foot this forenoon, which indicates that the jam below is broken loose. Two more parties passed down today.

May 19th: Broke camp at 4:30 a.m. Had not gone more than four miles down when we saw all the boats that preceded us, high and dry, owing to another jam breaking loose a short time previously. Continued down for only about a mile and encountered another jam. Went ashore and camped at 7:30 a.m. This point was about ten miles below the Big Salmon River, or thirty miles above the Little Salmon River. Toward the evening the ice commenced to move out slowly. Here it was reported that the remains of a human being were found lying on a bar a little distance farther down.

May 20th: Got started at 8 a.m., proceeded on our way only about two miles, and found the river blocked with ice again. Camped again. Heavy wind blowing downstream.

May 21st: Heavy wind blowing upstream. Remained in camp all day. All the miners advocated keeping as much together as possible as a precaution against the hostile Indians at Stewart River.

May 22nd: Started this morning at 8 o'clock after repitching a couple of seams on the bottom of our boat. This time we made a run of eighteen miles before we came to another jam. The river along here is backed right up to highest watermark.

A couple of men (Criss and Reynolds) shot a fine black bear near the summit of the mountain yesterday and we traded a piece of bacon for some bear meat, which tasted very good.

May 23rd: Got under way at 6 a.m. and started down again with the crowd. The jam had broken loose at midnight last night, and the river fell about fifteen feet, leaving our raft and boat high and dry. Proceeded ten miles, and found another jam. Camped again. Saw three or four families of Tagish Indians. The river is now commencing to rise steadily.

May 24th: Got started this morning at 4:30. Ran down some eight miles above the bar where William and Holmes were last fall. The river here is beginning to widen out more; I judge it is about one-half a mile wide here. Tried to prospect a bar this morning. It looked very good, but was frozen hard. Counted sixteen boats and three rafts this morning, averaging three men on each. The weather was very warm all day. It is 9:30 p.m. now as I write, and the sun is still above the hills.

May 25th: Started at 6 a.m. and came down to a bar where William left Holmes last fall. Went ashore to prospect, but found fifteen feet of solid cakes of ice piled up, one on top of the other. Saw it was useless to remain longer, and came on down about eight miles farther.

The river along here has some sharp bends. The ice commenced to flow very thickly, indicating that another jam is not far ahead. So we made camp and took our rockers apart where the main parts were fastened with screws, and remodeled our outfits (which, of course, were not so heavy now as when we started to sleigh from salt water at Dyea two months and four days ago, for our appetites certainly were enormous), so that we four (including Manley and Best) could proceed downriver in our boat and abandon our (second) raft.

This afternoon a couple of men arrived here from Portland, Oregon, via Juneau. Reported having left Juneau the same day they arrived there, on April 12th, and had good glare ice all the way. Paid only ten dollars per hundred pounds for having their supplies hauled and packed from Healy's post at Dyea to the Chilkoot Summit. They came from the foot of Lake Laberge to here in three days; a trip which till now took us twenty days.

Two men coming over Bennett Lake had three sleighs coupled together with a large sail up. They ran into an air hole and lost all their outfit, and narrowly escaped being drowned.

All the streams deserving the name of river, putting into the Lewis or Yukon, thus far come in on the right-hand side.

We noticed fresh bear and moose tracks on the shore today, and rabbit signs everywhere, but have not seen a rabbit on the trip yet.

May 26th: Started at 6 a.m. from our camp some thirty miles above the Five Fingers run, until 10:15 p.m. Camped on an island one mile below Fort Selkirk near where the Pelly River comes in. The current coming down averaged about four miles per hour or more. We used paddles, making an average speed of some six miles per hour. Some portions of upper Lewis River are very crooked traveling - say ten miles or so to make one mile on a straight line; but from the Rink Rapids down the river is fairly straight.

We ran the Five Finger Rapids with all our stuff. There are two large rocks or, properly speaking, small islands, and three smaller rocks in the river here, and two boat channels. The right-hand channel, which is the one mostly used, was still completely blocked with ice, and we were forced to take the left-hand channel. The water runs quite swiftly here, and good care must be exercised in going through, especially with a heavily laden boat as was ours.

We covered some ninety miles today; the biggest run of the trip thus far. Six miles farther, or below the Five Fingers, we ran through the Rink Rapids, which we found quite easy. Sounded the water in these rapids and found it to be from six and one-half to seven feet. At the mouth of the Pelly River, or just below on the right-hand side going down, we noticed a long, high, straight, rocky bluff; and on the opposite side, on the left, we saw two tall, old chimneys - all that remains of the old Fort Selkirk, an old Hudson Bay trading post that had been burned down by the Indians many years before.

Lieut. Schwatka calls this great waterway on which we are floating down the "Yukon from the Lewis (Lewes) down"; but the miners and natives call it the Yukon (meaning "big water") from the junction of the Pelly down.

We kept on late tonight on account of the absence of other boats from our company. We found one-quarter inch of ice in our bailers this morning.

May 27th: Started this morning at 5 o'clock, and went five miles down and then ashore for six hours to wait for the rest of the boats. We were not sure if they were ahead or behind now. Started again at noon, and concluded they were ahead. Made a run of sixty miles by 10 p.m. and camped.

All along the river here, there are a great many islands and sloughs. The right-hand bank, for several miles, is steep and rocky, and the stream averages, I should judge, about one mile in width; the valley is about two miles wide.

May 28th: Started out at 6 a.m. feeling at last most thankful in the belief that we were not to be held up any more by tedious ice jams such as we had so often encountered on the trip. Saw great quantities of ice piled up on the islands, and in many places noticed large trees torn up by the roots, also large cakes of ice thrown up in the woods. About five miles farther on, hailed a couple of men camped with their boat; they were Charlie Munroe and his partner from Stewart River. We asked them about the Indian trouble. They reported there was no trouble at all but that the miners in there had run the man Leslie (whom we met going out with Dotey) out of the country for stealing, and that the Indians were all peaceable.

Munroe did speak very favorably of Forty Mile Creek, which is some one hundred twenty miles below Stewart River. The White River comes in on the left side going down, and is possibly eight miles above Stewart River. This is a grand waterway for steamboating. Arrived at Harper's and McQuesten's trading post at the mouth of the Stewart River at 1:30 p.m., the first place of permanent habitation. The chances of finding any replenishments were scant, though we did not need any ourselves.

The Stewart comes in on the right-hand going down. The little stern-wheel steamer *New Racket* was lying at the river bank with steam up in readiness to go below. The distance is about fifteen hundred miles from here to St. Michael's. Some men traded half a plug of tobacco for a foreshoulder of fresh moose meat. We also bought a piece of the same size for one dollar and fifty cents. Tea, sugar, and tobacco are what the natives seem to like very much.

May 29th: Left mouth of Stewart River, or Blowville, as the post is called here, at 8:15 a.m. Kept on till 6:30 p.m., after making sixty miles, then tied up for the night. Timber along here is rather scarce, and we saw no game of any kind. Sixty Mile Creek is sixty miles above Fort Reliance. Some of the portions of Rock Bluff show favorable indications for quartz. The average course of the Yukon thus far is about northwest.

May 30th: Started this morning at 6:30, and about 7:30 a.m. noticed a large clear-water creek or small river coming in on our right with quite a little valley extending back, and on asking Indian Bob and some of those who had been this far down and farther on previous seasons, we were told it was called the Klondike Creek. Here on the upper bank we also noticed several large smoking and drying racks made of poles on which the natives hang their salmon and moose meat to dry and smoke. This Klondike valley, we understand, is also a great hunting section.

At 8 a.m. we passed Fort Reliance on the right-hand side and three miles or so below the mouth of the Klondike, and there bought one pair of overalls for two dollars and one pair of moccasins for one dollar.

Arrived at Forty Mile Creek, our objective point some forty-seven miles below Fort Reliance, at 3:30 p.m. At last we have reached our goal, after two months and nine days since landing at the head of the salt water at Dyea, and, as can be seen from the foregoing pages, a hard, tedious, toilsome trip it was.

Found several men here who remained in during last winter: also most of those who came in this spring and arrived just in advance of us a day or two up the creek.

A couple of parties went farther down the Yukon to prospect. Some reports are very favorable of the diggings farther up this creek, and other reports are unfavorable. This creek is, I should judge, about a quarter of a mile or more wide at its mouth, and is a clear-water stream, with a canyon some seven miles farther up where it is necessary to portage boats.

From what we can learn, there are few very good claims on this creek; some of them paid as high as eighty dollars per day, and lots of eight dollar diggings. Some men are located eighty miles up the creek; it seems to be conceded by all here that very little can be done on the creek for about three weeks on account of high water, which is very discouraging. Those who wintered here during the past winter were very short of provisions.

May 31st: Remained here at the mouth of Forty Mile Creek all day waiting for Mr. Harper to come down from the post at Stewart River. Weather very warm.

The mouth of this so-called Forty Mile Creek up for about seven miles, is, properly speaking, named Franklin River after one of the discoverers. Met some men today who say that one hundred dollars per day has been taken out during favorable stages of the water in different places. There is a number of small streams putting into this creek farther up which, after being prospected, may turn out to be very good. I understand that this stream is about one hundred fifty miles to its head.

June 1st: Mr. Harper arrived here at noon today on the little steamer *New Racket*, accompanied by Al Mayo, one of his partners, who generally acted as engineer. The other partner, Jack McQuesten, was at this time outside in San Francisco for the first time in fourteen years, or since the time all three came into this country together. I did not feel exactly satisfied, as is often the case with a young tenderfoot on leaving home for the first time. So after consulting with both Mr. Harper and Al Mayo, I decided to join them on board the *New Racket* as assistant steersman, or pilot, and make the trip to St. Michael's, Norton Sound and

Bering Sea. She was to go for supplies for the miners up here at the post.

The thought of making this long trip by steamer to the mouth of the mighty Yukon gives me new interest, being quite used to stern-wheel steamers, besides seeing so much more of the country. The distance from here to St. Michael's, we estimate, is some sixteen hundred miles.

I turned over my interest in our boat and all our provisions and other supplies to my brother William and bade him, Billy Best and Tom Manley good-bye.

5. FROM FORTY MILE CREEK TO ST. MICHAEL'S BY STEAMER (June, 1887)

June 2nd: Pulled out in the stream and headed for the Bering Sea on board the steamer *New Racket* at 9 a.m. Passed a very remarkable looking rock a few miles below called "The Old Woman." It stands out in about the middle of the river, is over a hundred feet high, and the wash from the sea had formed quite a little island around it. Stopped at one of the Alaska Commercial Company's trading posts sixty miles farther down and took on some furs; also took on an empty lighter in tow of about ten-ton capacity. This lighter was not scow-shaped, but a modeled boat shaped much like a Columbia River fishing boat, only, of course, about three times the capacity. Left here again at 5 p.m., made a landing about three miles farther down, chopped wood for our steamer's furnace till 10 p.m., then ran all night.

June 3rd: The river commences to widen out very much about one hundred miles above Fort Yukon, and numerous islands appear causing many different channels which make it very difficult for a stranger to pick out the best and shortest route.

Passed Fort Yukon 66° north and 45° east at 9:15 p.m. The old fort is entirely deserted. Three large, hewn log buildings remain, with portions of an old stockade still in evidence. These buildings are well built, with rough plaster on the inside, and the roofs are of long, wide pieces of spruce bark so long as I could see. The stockade, with the exception of what still stands of it, has been all chopped down and used for steaming purposes on board the steamers. The Porcupine River comes into the Yukon about two miles or so below the fort near where the old steamer Yukon is now sunk and abandoned.

The country along here is low and flat; the river is some seven miles in width. It is quite light all night, for the sun is only out of sight for about an hour and a half at this time of the year. Sunset was at 10:45 p.m. tonight.

The river from Fort Yukon on the way down takes a long bend nearly due west for a considerable distance. Stopped to chop wood at 10:30 p.m.

June 4th: Got through chopping wood, loaded it on board, and got under way again at 4 p.m. Our steamer burns only two-foot wood. Stopped a couple of hours at an Indian camp where Mr. Harper did some trading, and while there we got news from the Indians that Bishop Seighers, formerly of Portland, Oregon, had been shot dead by one of his own men who traveled in here with him. It is said here that the man got up during the night and shot the Bishop through the breast while the latter was sleeping. The Indians report that the Bishop's remains and murderer were taken down from Nulato, where the crime was committed, to St. Michael's.

Left again, stopped at an Indian ranch a little further on to do some more trading. Here I saw six birch bark canoes, which are very light. Some of them carry four persons. Tied up for wind at midnight; blowing very hard.

June 5th: Started at 8 a.m. Tied up again at 10:40 a.m. to repair a joint in the steam chest. Indians along the river here use their dogs with large sleighs about eighteen to twenty inches wide and six to ten feet long, built up with side framework and handlebars at the rear. Great quantities of stuff including their camp outfits are lashed in these sleighs, and from four to ten dogs are in harness.

The natives often have from twenty to thirty dogs in a train with from forty to seventy-five pounds on each of their backs. This, of course, is during the summer season, and they walk right along with their loads. These dogs have to depend almost entirely on themselves for food, and during the winter they have a hard time trying to keep them from starving. Most of them are, of course, from necessity, excellent hunters, and they often dive into the swift-flowing river at the bank and bring out salmon in short order.

Stopped at a trading post at 7:30 p.m., where there are some mastodon remains buried in the ground. The chief of this section of the Yukon tribe took a ride with us today. He is now about seventy years old and was once of great influence among his tribe.

The Indians here use their bows and arrows principally, especially in wintertime, in order to save their ammunition.

Arrived at the head of what I understand is called the Lower Ramparts, at 11:30 p.m., where the river is considerably confined for a distance of some one hundred fifty miles. Had a sprinkle of rain today.

June 6th: Arrived at the rapids (fifty miles above a large Indian village called Nuklakiyet) at 10 a.m. The river here at the rapids is very confined, apparently only about five hundred yards from bank to bank, although the current does not flow, I should judge, more than about five miles per hour. But I understand it is more rapid during low water, for there is a bar near the middle composed of large boulders.

Sheffland's Gulch is about ten miles below the foot of the rapids on the right-hand side; it is said the Sheffland brothers had ten dollar diggings here.

6. THE KILLING OF BISHOP SEIGHERS (June, 1887)

Arrived at Nuklakiyet at 5 p.m., and learned more particulars regarding the killing of Bishop Seighers as follows:

It seems that previously there had been some misunderstanding between the Bishop and a man named Fuller, who shot him, prior to their leaving Nuklakiyet, and the Bishop asked Mr. Walker (a trader for the Alaska Commercial Company stationed at Nuklakiyet, and whom I also met and talked with personally on the subject), if he would accompany him (the Bishop) down to Nulato. But Mr. Walker could not leave his business. Then the Bishop asked a miner to go with him, but for some reason the miner could not go either. So the Bishop started out for Nulato with this man Fuller, and one or two Indians. No more was said by Fuller to cause any suspicion on their way down.

They made camp, had supper, and all went to bed, and at six o'clock (the) next morning one of the Indians was awakened by Fuller saying, "Get up, I am going to shoot you." Fuller was holding his rifle, and was addressing the Bishop. The Bishop, half asleep and not understanding, rose slowly, but before he had time to fully understand what was the matter, Fuller fired. The ball entered the Bishop's forehead and he fell back, dying instantly.

One of the Bishop's Indians, now aboard our steamer as witness, says the ball that killed the Bishop passed close to his ear, and also states that Fuller was trying to put another cartridge in his rifle when he (the Indian) caught hold of the gun saying, "Do you want to kill us too?" Whereupon Fuller answered, "No, that is the only man I want to kill," and pointed to the Bishop lying at his feet.

This man Fuller has been with the Bishop off and on for the

49

last four years. The Bishop always treated him very kindly, bought him anything he needed, and let him have his own way at everything, so says Father Tosey, who is now aboard with us.

All the white men here are in strong favor of hanging this man Fuller at once. Mr. Walker tells me that he received a letter from Fuller soon after the deed was committed, calling on him (Walker) as a law-abiding citizen to have justice shown him, and that he had good cause for killing the Bishop. Fuller also gave himself up and acknowledged the deed.

I was personally acquainted with Bishop Seighers, as was also every member of my family. We often saw him in Victoria, and we have in our possession letters written by the Bishop relative to one of his former trips into this country in 1882. These letters contain much valuable information.

Bishop Seighers was comparatively a young man when killed; a highly intellectual man, loved and respected by everyone whose good fortune it was to know him.

There seem to be good prospects found up the Koyukuk River which puts into the Yukon, for there are three men up there now, and we have four men aboard with us bound for there now who came down from Forty Mile Creek with us. The ice along here broke up on the 21st of May this spring, and was clear for navigation on the 28th.

Passed the mouth of the Tanana River at 3 p.m., a large stream coming in on our left. A whole fleet of Indians came down from up this stream to Nuklakiyet on rafts and in birch bark canoes to trade their furs in. There are about sixty Indians at Nuklakiyet now; they are all very friendly when one goes ashore. Every one of them in the camp comes up to shake hands. They find mastodon tusks farther down the river weighing one hundred fifty pounds and from five to ten feet long, I am told.

When a flock of geese comes along, these Indians start in to quack, making sounds just like the geese. The geese, hearing this and thinking there are other geese in close proximity, fly and circle around and alight near the Indians who are, of course, generally hidden if possible; then the Indians shoot many of them.

June 7th: Weather very windy and cold all day. Landed and took an English minister on board who came into this country by

50

way of the Red River. He had been wintering up the Porcupine River.

June 8th: Left Kokrine's trading post this morning at 4 a.m. Weather still cold and raw. Stopped to chop wood at 6:30 p.m.

June 9th: Landed three prospectors at the mouth of the Koyukuk River this morning at two o'clock, some twenty miles above Nulato, and the Indian witness who was with Bishop Seighers showed me the spot about ten miles above this where the Bishop was shot. It is some thirty miles above Nulato.

There seems to be gold found on most all the creeks and rivers putting into the Yukon. Arrived at Nulato at 6:30 a.m.; Left again at 7:30 a.m.

This river (the Yukon) would be a fine stream for good large stern-wheel steamers and possibly light-draft, twin-screw boats right from the mouth up to the Five Fingers Rapids, and no doubt pretty large steamers could be taken through there too. She could go right up to the mouth of the Hootalinqua without any trouble, and they could have smaller ones there up to the White Horse Rapids; then a line of still smaller and lighter draft stern-wheelers could be used above the canyon to the head of the lakes, but as yet there is nothing to justify an outside steamer to be put on the river.

There are four small steamers on this lower river now, namely the *New Racket*, sixty feet long and belonging to Messrs. Harper and McQuesten; the *Yukon*, seventy-five feet, owned and operated by the Alaska Commercial Company; the *St. Michael's*, and another one called the *Explorer*, about the same size as the *New Racket* and the *St. Michael's*. The latter steamer Lieut. Stoney had up here. It is now owned, I understand, by one of the missions in the lower Yukon. These steamers moved about nine miles per hour in still water.

Passed the Redout, an Indian or Russian fishing village about forty miles below Nulato, from which place there is a portage salt water of seventy-five miles or so, and by the river the distance is five hundred fifty miles.

June 10th: Stopped nine hours to chop wood. The weather is very fine today. Passed a place where coal can be found right handy to the river. Arrived at Anvick (Anvik) where the steamer Yukon is lying ready to go to St. Michael's. On board I saw Fuller, who shot and killed Bishop Seighers. He is to be taken to St.

Michael's, and from there to Sitka for trial. He is a Jesuit brother, I now learn, and a very powerful, tall man, and is constantly walking to and fro in the steamer's cabin praying. He wears a large cross suspended with a bead chain about his neck.

Left Anvik village, near which there is a river putting in of the same name. At 3 p.m. saw several large sealskin boats here about thirty feet long and five to six feet in width. These are called "bidrows." Villages become more numerous from Nuklaliyet down. It appears to be about high water here now. The salmon run has not passed up stream yet. These villages contain an average of about one hundred fifty inhabitants composed of Indians, Esquimaux (Eskimo), and Russians; the majority appear to speak the Russian language.

June 11th: Arrived at the Russian Mission at 8 a.m. Was introduced to the Russian priest here; had a look through their church, which was established forty years ago. Saw more sealskin boats or bidarkas similar to one in which, we now learn, a Swede left Alaska some years ago and arrived safely in San Francisco. All these sealskin canoes are put up without a nail or a piece of iron in them. They are laced and bound together with animal sinews and narrow strips of skin, and the main body of the boat is kept well oiled frequently, and the frames are made of thin pieces of bent young spruce and other saplings.

The natives here live in houses built half under the ground during the winter, and are called "barabas," a Russian name. The doorway is generally located about ten or fifteen feet away, and leads to the baraba through an underground tunnel. The top, or roof, of the baraba is covered with heavy timbers slanting two ways, to give it some pitch, and on top of this is a heavy thickness of soil with a square hold left in the roof for the smoke of their fires to escape.

I went into one of these barabas, creeping through the tunnel, and took in the situation. Many of these Esquimaux are quite fat and short, and some of them were sitting around the fire quite naked. The odor of their bodies is very strong. There were about ten in the family, including the little children and other relations. I sat and watched them eating great quantities of seal meat, fish and oil. They were quite friendly, but I could not converse with them much except partly through an interpreter who was there.

June 12th: Arrived at Andreafsky (now known as St. Mary's) at 5 a.m. An old Russian fort, this is some two hundred miles from St. Michael's, and about the last settlement going down.

Left Andreafsky at 6 a.m. Came down thirty miles and stopped to chop driftwood, for there is no other wood to be had after getting below the Russian Mission. Weather quite cold and foggy this morning. When we get twelve miles below Andreafsky, the last mountains are seen in the distance, and away off to our left a large lone mountain can be seen, called the Kinsilvak (Kusilvak) Mountain, which is cone-shaped and partially covered with snow. Proceeded on down and entered the Aphoon Slough, perhaps forty miles in length and which opens outright on the sea coast about eighty miles from St. Michael's. This slough takes a northerly course for the first half of the distance; then it takes an easterly course.

One of our Indian deckhands went out this evening and shot two large swans that measured nearly six feet from tip to tip. Stopped again to cut driftwood.

June 13th: Started at 1 a.m. Turned into a little river called the Kooklick (Kotlik) about six miles from the sea coast where there is a small village. Procured a few dozen wild goose eggs, laid up for the night, and chopped wood.

June 14th: Started out at 4 a.m. Ran aground several times in the slough, got out to within fifteen miles of Point Romanoff, where we sighted a large field of ice and icebergs. Could not find any opening through, so were obliged to run back to the mouth of little Kooklick River and tie up. Weather very cold today with northeast wind; freezing hard this morning. Our barge was sheeted with ice.

The steamer *Yukon* (which we left at Anvik on the tenth instantly preparing to leave there) passed down this afternoon with five small barges in tow, some of which are similar to the one we have. This steamer went on and managed to find a channel through the ice.

June 15th: Started this morning at 6 a.m., picked our way through the ice, and arrived at the mouth of the canal at 2:30 p.m., twenty miles' distance from St. Michael's. This canal is very winding and quite narrow, and the banks are very low; in many places only about two feet high. This route is considerably a cutoff for light-draft steamers, and they avoid going around outside the island. Arrived at St. Michael's, our destination, at 5 p.m. Weather still windy and very cold. Dropped anchor off shore, about a quarter of a mile.

The A.C. Company's steamer *St. Paul*, which we fully expected to find here, has not as yet arrived from San Francisco.

June 16th: Still here at anchor. Weather cold, raw, and windy. This place is very dismal; there is neither firewood nor fresh water on St. Michael's Island; these have to be procured from a distance of three miles.

June 16th, 17th, and 18th: Saturday. Still lying at anchor here at St. Michael's; heavy northerly wind last night, and snowing hard.

June 19th: Sunday. Weather fine all day; got one and a half tons provisions aboard for crew's use on return trip upriver.

June 20th: Monday. Weather still fine. The steamship *Dora*, direct from San Francisco, arrived here at six o'clock this morning but brought no supplies for miners.

The steamer St. Paul is expected in within five days, and is bringing the supplies. Jack McQuesten arrived on the *Dora*, making the trip in one month and five days, having left San Francisco on May 14th. Mr. McQuesten reports that some rich quartz mines were found by a Capt. Hague at Unalaska.

Mr. McQuesten also says that the Alaska Commercial Company is getting out plans and specifications for a light-draft stern-wheel river steamer for the Yukon River, to be sent up next spring in knock-down sections and put together here. This steamer is to carry two hundred tons of freight.

June 21st: Tuesday. Got our barge loaded up with some supplies that Mr. McQuesten brought with him on the *Dora*, also stowed some three tons on board our steamer, the *New Racket*, thus making in all some twelve tons or so.

7. THE RETURN TRIP FROM ST. MICHAEL'S TO FORTY MILE CREEK (June-July, 1887)

June 22nd: Wednesday. Left St. Michael's at 6:30 a.m. Arrived at the head of the canal, heavy south wind blowing. Stopped there and chopped wood.

June 23rd: Thursday. Got under way this morning at 4 o'clock. Blowing heavy. We were obliged to put in at the mouth of the Picmictalic River for shelter at 6 a.m. and laid at anchor all day.

June 24th: Friday. Left the mouth of the Picmictalic River at 6 a.m. Wind considerably moderated, quite a sea on. Rounded Point Romanoff, and on getting abreast of the Potaliac River, we got around and lay there until the tide came in.

June 25th: Saturday. Got off the sandbar at 3:30 a.m. and went into the Potaliac River to cut driftwood. Met the steamer Yukon returning from Andreafsky with the steamer *St. Michael's* in tow; she had been aground for a while. Stopped again for three hours, to wood up at the mouth of the Aphoon Slough, and started again at twelve o'clock. Passed the old burial grounds on the Aphoon Slough, where the natives of different tribes used to meet and fight years ago.

Stopped at 7 p.m. and chopped down a couple of Esquimaux barabas for wood for our steamer, which filled her up enough to last about twenty hours, and left again at midnight.

June 26th: Sunday. Stopped again for wood at 4 p.m. just before the mouth of the little slough, the head of which is about twelve miles below Andreafsky. Got under way at 8 p.m. Arrived at Andreafsky at midnight.

June 27th: Monday. Left Andreafsky at 5 a.m. Stopped to wood up at 9:30 a.m. and started again at 3 p.m. Weather pretty warm. Mosquitoes commencing to show up. Stopped to wood up at 11:30 p.m.

June 28th: Tuesday. Started at 5 a.m. Arrived at the Russian Mission at 10:30 p.m.

June 29th: Wednesday. Left the Mission – I now understand it is called Holy Cross (actually Holy Cross is upriver) – at 3 a.m.; took on board there a man by the name of Joe Goldsmith, who had been up the Kuskokwim River prospecting but found nothing there to justify his remaining there to mine. Stopped to wood up at 10:30 a.m. Got started again at 3 p.m.

June 30th: Thursday. Stopped to wood up at 11 a.m. Mosquitoes very bad. Started again at 5 p.m. Passed Anvick at 9 p.m. The natives are all very busy now getting their salmon caught and dried.

July 1st: Friday. Stopped to wood up at 2 p.m., and started again at 5:30 p.m. I took a swim in the river this afternoon; found the water very cold. Had a heavy shower of rain this evening.

July 2nd: Stopped to wood up at 11:30 a.m. Broke a screw in the donkey pump and had to lay up an hour and a half to repair it. Started out again at 4 p.m., and at 7 p.m., lost the oil cup of the crank pin overboard, and were obliged to anchor for a half an hour to fix a new one on. The wheel ropes chafed through; we put a splice in them and rove it over again. Stopped to wood up again at 11 p.m., and started at midnight.

July 3rd: Sunday. Raining heavy this morning. Arrived at noon; took on two cords of wood which had been chopped before. Saw two white men (Steve Custer and partner). They reported having been up the Koyukuk River prospecting where the other three men (Moffat, Powell, and Brown) went, but Custer and partner did not find anything up there. They were some five hundred miles up that stream.

Left Nulato again at 1 p.m. Stopped for an hour at a place where about six hundred natives camped temporarily, drying and smoking salmon; the run, of course, had commenced since we passed downriver.

July 4th: Monday. Stopped to wood up at 3 p.m. and started again at 8:30 p.m. Stopped again at a place one hour to give Mrs. McQuesten some provisions.

July 5th: Tuesday. Had a shower of rain today at noon. It

lasted for only ten minutes, but it came down in drops large enough to fill a tablespoon. Stopped to chop wood at 1 p.m., and started again at 8 p.m.

July 6th: Wednesday. Stopped to wood up at 2 a.m., and started again at 6:30 a.m. Arrived at a place called Noekocket (Kokrine's place) at 9:45 a.m. Took a man aboard here by the name of George Washington Barnes, who had been up the Noekocket stream prospecting but could not raise a color. This man was in serious condition from mosquito bites; his face was so swollen and poisoned and inflamed that his eyes could hardly be seen, and he could not see at all. He had previously resided at Juneau, Alaska. Started again at 11:30 a.m.

July 7th: Thursday. Stopped for wood just opposite Nuklakiyet at 4:30 p.m.; washed out the boiler and laid over for the rest of the day and night.

July 8th: Friday. Started at 7 a.m. Blowing very hard. Tried to cross the river with our steamer and tow, but she would not handle and broached to on us several times in the heavy sea that was running up against the stream. Our steamer rolled guards under several times in the trough of the sea, then broke our wheel ropes again. Managed to run in and tie up and splice the wheel ropes and unshipped the rudders, and laid over till the wind moderated some, then started out again at 10 p.m. The river here is several miles wide.

July 9th: Saturday. Stopped for wood at 10:30 a.m. Got a good load chopped up and stowed away on board, and started again at 6:30 p.m. Blowing very hard again. The barge was aground when we went to back off just above a strong current near a bluff: had to give a strong jerk which started the barge off, and she ran on the rocks in the swift water. Mr. Harper was thrown overboard by the shock, but was pulled out again. He suffered a cut on the hand. Our steamer heeled away over on her beam ends and took in a large quantity through the after gangway. This caused a great commotion on board, and all the Indians on board rushed to the weather side and started to climb out over the steam.

Found that one of our rudder stocks was bent so that our wheel kept striking the outer end of the rudder when same was put amidships. Had to land and put a new rudder stock on; the old one broke in the weld when being repaired.

July 10th: Sunday. Got through shipping the new rudder at 2 a.m. and started out. Passed through the rapids at 7 a.m. The rocks on the left side now show out of water in places about three feet. It took us half an hour to get through the rapids. Stopped for wood at 2:30 p.m.; started again at 7:30 p.m. From, say, twenty miles above the rapids, for a hundred miles up it is very good, easy water.

July 11th: Monday. Stopped to wood up at 7:30 a.m. Started again at 11:30 a.m. Passed Mastodon Bone Creek at 11 p.m. twelve miles below the head of the ramparts.

July 12th: Tuesday. Stopped to chop wood at 1 a.m. Mosquitoes very bad. Started again at 11 a.m. and pulled into the bank again to wood up at 9 p.m.

July 13th: Wednesday. Started again at 2:30 a.m. Weather very disagreeable today; raining and blowing and cold like fall weather. Stopped to wood up at 8:30 p.m.

July 14th: Thursday. Started at 4 a.m. Weather still raw this forenoon. Stopped to wood up at 4 p.m.; started again at 11 p.m.

July 15th: Friday. Met two men (Johnny Reynolds and partner) on their way to the Kuskokwim, just from Forty Mile Creek. They reported prospects are looking favorable up Forty Mile. Reynolds had some coarse gold with him, about three hundred twenty dollars. Some pieces weighed four and five dollars. He sold out up there to Dick Popland for three hundred dollars. Reynolds reported having taken this gold out in four days. Stopped for wood at 4 p.m. Started again at 11:30 p.m.

July 16th: Saturday. Arrived at Fort Yukon at 3:30 p.m. Stopped there and chopped out some of the logs of the old Hudson Bay Post buildings. Filled our steamer up, and started again at midnight.

July 17th: Sunday. Ran aground with both the steamer and barge this morning at 7 o'clock. After considerable work we pried the steamer off with long levers, and then took three and a half tons of freight out of the barge with the steamer in three different attempts, for we could scarcely get up to where the barge was aground. After four hard pulls the barge came off the bar at 4 p.m. Landed to wood up at 4:30 p.m., and started again at 11 p.m.

July 18th: Monday. Stopped to wood up at 11:30 a.m. Water very strong along here. Got partly filled up with wood and left at

7 p.m. Stopped at 10 p.m. to file the crank-brasses, which were brassbound. Started at 11 p.m.

July 19th: Tuesday. Stopped to wood up at 4:30 a.m., and started again at 1:30 p.m.

July 20th: Wednesday. Stopped to chop wood at 4 a.m. Got filled up at 2:30 p.m. and started again. The packing in the steam chest blew out, which delayed us one hour. Came through a slough tonight, and found it all split up with bars and shallow water at the head. We had a very hard time getting through. I had to get all the native deckhands out on the forecastle with poles to assist in keeping the steamer head on to the stream, for she barely crawled along and had hardly any steerage way, and scraped along over the bars, picking the deepest and best water.

To our left was an island, at its head a large drift pile, and beyond this the main river. Our barge was a heavy drag, and it was with the greatest care and exertion, with our men using the sounding poles on the forecastle, that saved us from drifting down broadside onto the drift pile at the head of this island. This would have been very serious, and might have caused the loss of at least our barge and its contents.

I was on watch in the wheelhouse when we entered this slough, and feeling that we would have easier water and considerable of a cutoff, I took it upon myself to try this channel. However, as was seen on reaching the head of this slough, I would much rather have not taken it, but it was several miles through and I did not like to turn back.

Al Mayo was standing alternately on the forecastle wiping the perspiration from his brow, and then disappearing again for a while in the fire room to shove more wood into the furnace. This was the hardest tussle we have had coming thus far, and when we got through and were well past the head of the island where the water was deeper, and we made good headway, all hands on the forecastle commenced to whoop and cheer with an intermingling of Russian, Indian, and our own language.

July 21st: Thursday. Stopped to chop wood at 6 a.m. Started again at noon. Entered what we call the Upper Ramparts at 1:30 p.m. Stopped to wood up at 11 p.m.

July 22nd: Friday. Started at 7 a.m. Met a Mr. Maiden at noon coming down in a boat alone to prospect creeks. He found a prospect at Charlie's Creek, not far from here, where he is going to work. He brought letters from home (in Victoria), also one from my brother William at Forty Mile Creek. Mr. Maiden purchased some provisions from Mr. Harper, and we took him in tow at two o'clock for the creek. Stopped at 11:30 p.m. and got partly filled up with driftwood.

July 23rd: Saturday. Started at 4 a.m. Stopped again to load up with wood at 6 a.m. Started at 1 p.m.

July 24th: Sunday. Stopped at a drift pile to chop wood at 5:30 a.m. Got half filled up and left at 1:30 p.m. Weather about the warmest we have had yet. Mosquitoes still pretty wicked and hungry, but not so plentiful as farther downriver. There are several large creeks coming in along this part of the Yukon which have a very favorable appearance as gold country.

At noon today we are just about one hundred miles from Forty Mile Creek. Stopped to wood up at 10 p.m.

July 25th: Monday. Started at 2 a.m. Weather very warm all day. Arrived at Fort Adams (one of Harper and McQuesten's old trading posts) sixty miles below Forty Mile Creek at 1 p.m. Started again at 2:30 p.m. Stopped to chop wood at 8 p.m. Started again at 11 p.m.

July 26th: Tuesday. Stopped at 4 a.m. to repair the broken rudder of the barge. Also chopped a load of wood there and left again at 9 a.m. The rudder of the barge broke again and she had a narrow escape from running up a bluff rock in an eddy. So we're obliged to lay over again and repair the iron eyebolt into which the rudder slips. Started again at 4 p.m. Had a heavy thunderstorm this evening, accompanied by heavy rain and lightning.

July 27th: Wednesday. Stopped at 4 a.m. to wood up. Started at 8 a.m. Arrived at Forty Mile Creek at 1 p.m. Thirty-six days since leaving Forty Mile Creek for the round trip; and as the foregoing record shows, running night and day excepting the time it took us to cut and load wood, and the six days layover at St. Michael's awaiting the arrival of the steamer from San Francisco.

Found several men here at Forty Mile waiting for us, or rather, the several tons of supplies we brought. We were indeed glad to get back, for it certainly had been a long, hard and tedious trip, to say nothing of fighting mosquitoes all the way up. We estimate that we have covered some thirty-three hundred

RETURN TRIP TO FORTY MILE

miles on this round trip from Forty Mile to St. Michael's and return, and as noted herein, we cut all our wood except at one landing.

8. "POLING OUT" UPSTREAM FROM FORTY MILE CREEK – ENCOUNTER OGILVIE PARTY AND CAPT. WILLIAM MOORE (July-September, 1887)

July 28th: Thursday. Lay here (Forty Mile) today, several parties left here with their boats and supplies just purchased for up the creek. There are three different parties going to start upriver in a couple of days or so. It is reported that one man took out twenty-six ounces in one day up this creek. I saw a nugget that Mr. Steel took out; it weighed thirty-five dollars.

Mr. Harper has a large packing case set up on deck on the barge for a counter, and a pair of gold scales and merchandise scales and is selling provisions, clothing and gum boots to the miners as fast as he can dish it out. All was sold out the second day after we reached here. The miners paid mostly all in gold dust.

Flour sold at $17.50 per hundred weight
Beans sold at 20¢ per pound
Bacon sold at 40¢ per pound
Sugar sold at 33¢ per pound
Butter sold at $1.50 per pound
Gum boots sold at $17.00 per pair

July 29th: Friday. I procured a boat here from a man by the name of John Burk, to pole out upriver in, but she is in a very bad condition. Her bottom planks were worn, and her seams all open, also some of her timbers split. But I gathered some pitch

62

from the spruce trees, melted same with bacon grease, and caulked and pitched her bottom seams, though after this she still leaked considerably. However, we had no nails or tools, and I could not build a new boat, nor did I wish to remain here any longer than I had to.

Joe Goldsmith, to whom I have referred before as having come aboard the *New Racket* on our way up, decided to go outside also by way of the upper river or "pole climbing route," as many call it here; so he and I agreed to go out together. Then, a man by the name of Jack Currier, who desired to get outside for the winter, came to me on hearing I intended to leave very shortly and asked me if he could not be the third party. Most all the men left here this morning for up the creek except a few who are going outside, and some who are waiting for the steamer Yukon to arrive from St. Michael's.

The steamer *New Racket* started again for St. Michael's at 5 p.m. Mr. Harper and Al Mayo wanted me to remain here for the rest of the season and winter, and go steamboating with them and learn the river thoroughly. But I was bent on going out home to Victoria, and made up my mind not to remain; and though I could have remained in longer, I knew by the time we reached the lakes it would be getting toward the first of September.

July 30th: Saturday. Went across the creek, or, as many call, Forty Mile River, for more spruce pitch to boil down for our boat. We repitched her seams, and finally got her fairly tight. A strong downriver wind has been blowing all day. We intend to leave here this evening. Three or four parties started to pole out upriver this morning. Got our poles and gear all ready, loaded our provisions and rolls of blankets, and a piece of duck canvas about twelve feet square called a "fly" used in place of a tent, and at 5 p.m. started upriver for the coast. Mr. Harper gave us a nice, large piece of meat from a bear that one of his men had just killed.

Poled about ten miles and camped for the night. Not one of us three had a watch to tell the right time, and had to guess the time as best we could. I took the center station in the boat, Jack Currier took the stern, and Joe Goldsmith the bows and alternately changed off with me. This was really my first experience at poling upstream, but we did fine.

Joe Goldsmith and Jack Currier proved very excellent

boatsmen. We worked hard and well together right from the start to get out as soon as possible. Strange to say, we were leaving good gold country, as many others were, and to which many men outside were trying to come; but this has been the case in many placer strikes -leaving, and coming. But the fact is, that in my case, I am homesick to get out, and I dreaded the long hard winter in here.

July 31st: Sunday. Made a start at about 5 a.m. Overhauled two of the head boats at noon. Old man Steel's and Hank Summers' parties camped opposite a creek sixteen miles below Fort Reliance. In poling out, we found it best to keep to the right-hand shore all the way from Forty Mile Creek to Stewart River. We met three men coming down in boats to Forty Mile Creek. They had been up to the headwaters of the Hootalinqua River prospecting, but could not find anything much worth remaining there for, and reported a poor formation there for gold.

August 1st: Monday. Passed Fort Reliance at about 5 p.m., and camped two miles above there for the night. Some places are very heavy poling, but we are keeping right up to Hank Summers' party; they have a smaller boat than ours, a very good model for upstream work, and three men in it. My arms and joints are becoming very stiff and sore from the heavy straining and reaching with the poles, but this will pass away, my partners tell me, in a few days after becoming accustomed to the work.

The water runs down from the pole to our elbows and continues down our legs to the knees, especially while poling in deep water. We average, I should judge, about eighteen to twenty miles per day against the current, but these are long days, working early and late, as is seen by our approximate time of starting and camping.

August 2nd: Tuesday. Started out this morning at about 5 a.m. Passed the mouth of the Klondike Creek where a number of Indians were fishing on our left-hand side a short distance above Fort Reliance. Met four men in a boat coming down, bound for Forty Mile Creek. Made between eighteen and twenty miles today, then camped for the night.

August 3rd: Wednesday. Made the usual early start this morning and worked very hard poling until about 7 p.m. Had some very strong ripples and bluff to get over and around. Met a man named Axle in a small birch bark canoe on his way from Stewart River to Forty Mile Creek.

Our boat is taking considerable water, so we unloaded all our stuff this evening and caulked her up a little; then camped for the night. Killed a fat porcupine today on the bank; it tasted fairly good to us after being cooked.

August 4th: Thursday. Covered about twenty miles today. Started early and worked very hard all day. Came around some very dangerous drift piles where the swift current sweeps under them, making it necessary to put out our line ahead. Camped on an island. We judged it was between three and four miles above Sixty Mile Creek.

August 5th: Friday. Experienced very strong water mostly all day. Reached the mouth of Stewart River, crossed over to the left bank at about 6 p.m., making the trip from Forty Mile Creek to Stewart River - a distance of some one hundred twenty miles against an average current of four and one-half miles per hour - in six days. Found several Chilkat Indians camped one mile above the post.

August 6th: Saturday. Left the Stewart River post at about 5 a.m. Had some very hard poling, crossed back to the right-hand shore just after leaving the post and kept to that shore until within two or three miles below White River; then we crossed over again to the left-hand shore. Camped early, at about 5 p.m., three miles above the mouth of the White River or seventeen miles above the Stewart River. We are having good weather, though occasionally we have a light shower of rain.

Mosquitoes are not so numerous up here, but those pests are being succeeded by sand flies or gnats which are about as wicked as the former.

The stream became clear on the left shore before we came opposite the mouth of White River, and on getting above there it was all clear water. This is about the time, I understand, for White River to swell on the rise; it is only navigable for poling boats about eighty miles up, where it becomes very rapid, with several canyons.

August 7th: Sunday. Had quite a frost last night and early this morning. Camped about sixteen miles above White River. Caught another porcupine swimming in the river this morning.

August 8th: Monday. Started bright and early, and was

making very good headway when Mr. Kennedy, Old Man Steel's partner who was in one of the other boats, took all his belongings out of Steel's boat and asked to come into ours to work his way out. So we took him in. This made four of us. Old Man Steel had with him his native wife and another man. At noon a good stiff upriver breeze sprang up so we rigged a sail and made good headway covering about twenty miles today.

August 9th: Tuesday. Traveled early and late today, and in fine weather; made about twenty seven miles. Our boat still continued to leak pretty badly, and has caused and is causing considerable annoyance, to say nothing of the several gallons of water we are continually pushing upstream, and the delay it causes us in bailing and stopping to endeavor to tighten her up at different times.

The wild geese are commencing to fly south now.

August 10th: Wednesday. Started this morning at five o'clock, and camped for the night at the foot of the lava bank about fourteen miles below the mouth of the Pelly River. Had good towing, or as some call it, "tracking ground" most of the day. On these occasions one or two, depending on the number of men in the boat, takes a rope, say five-eighths or three-quarters of an inch thick and about fifty to seventy-five feet long over his shoulders and walks ahead, while one man remains in the stern of the boat with a pole to push and steer; and often one man is in the bow. One end of the line is fastened to the extreme point or stem of the bow, and another short line is fastened four to five feet back from the bow and joins the longer rope about five or six feet from the boat, forming a bridle. This, during towing, keeps the boat's bow out from the shore. Many river men have traveled alone with their boats in this way for long distances, and when coming to swift portions of the river, where there were no tracking or towing beaches, they would cross the river by using their oars where easier water or towing ground is available. This is what we are doing on this trip.

The Yukon along here is fairly low at present.

August 11th: Thursday. Weather quite cold this morning; white frost and thick fog, but nice and warm as soon as the sun comes out. Arrived at the mouth of the Pelly River at about noon.

Numerous small islands appear along here and above Pelly

River, and very poor towing beaches; but there are drift piles which make traveling by boat difficult. Met a party of men who came through the country by Cassiar and down the Pelly River; they are on a survey, and reported having come up from Victoria, B.C. at the same time that Mr. Ogilvie, the Canadian surveyor, came with his party.

Camped six miles above the mouth of the Pelly River this evening.

August 12th: Friday. Made about twenty miles today. Met the Canadian track-survey party in charge of Mr. William Ogilvie, with their scow, *Peterborough*. Canoes were camped at the left-hand bank on their way in from Victoria, tied up alongside their large scow in which they came down through Miles Canyon and White Horse. Here, with this party, I found Capt. Wm. Moore, my father, who had come to assist in the building of their scow and boating downriver, etcetera. Capt. Moore decided to return upriver to the coast with us, so I took him into my boat with nearly four hundred pounds of his outfit. This made our boat set very low in the water and harder to handle, and caused her to take considerably more water.

Here, forwarded a little batch of provisions down to my brother William at Forty Mile Creek, with Mr. Ogilvie. We then bade the survey party good-bye and tied up to the river bank; and the survey party, with their large scow and Peterborough canoes, gathered together and left for downriver. We remained in camp rearranging our bulky load so that it would stow as well as possible in our boat.

August 13th: Saturday. Started at 6 a.m. Camped at 4:30 p.m. (We had a watch in our party now). Made about twenty miles.

August 14th: Sunday. Weather rather cold this morning; made fair headway and camped at 4:30 p.m., five miles below Rink Rapids.

August 15th: Monday. Started at 5:45 a.m. Passed through the Rink Rapids at 9 a.m. on our left hand. Here we had to put out our towing line and haul her through. Two men remained in the boat to assist with poles, one in the stern and one in the bow. Met with some very strong water this afternoon coming around a bend where there were many long trees (swashers) reaching and leaning way out from ten to thirty feet over the river, on a level with and a little above the water, whose roots had been undermined by the current, causing them to lean and fall over. This necessitates keeping the boat out from the bank so far that we cannot get bottom with our poles.

In these instances, we are obliged to chop our way through the lower branches and haul our boat through under the tree. On other occasions, where the main body of the tree is down on a level or below the level of the water, we have to either go right out to the end of it or cut the upper branches off and haul the boat over the tree - if it is below the water far enough to allow her to pass over. In some instances, if the tree is not too large, we chop it off nearer the bank.

I have found that such places as these, and drift piles, gave us much annoyance on the trip, as coming around rocky bluffs where the swift current sweeps against us and then is off again. It necessitates two and three attempts sometimes before we succeed in getting around, for in these places the water is generally deep and poling ground unobtainable.

The bow of the boat must be kept close in against the bluff all the time, and the stern out. To do this, a short pole about five to six feet in length with a good steel hook at the end is great help, in fact almost necessary. This the bow-man should have to reach out and catch hold of any little crevice available in the bluff, haul the boat ahead and hold her there until the stern-man with his longer pole gets a set against the bluff, if possible, and leads astern; then he holds the boat steady, if he can, till the bow-man with his hook pole reaches ahead again for a new hold.

In many instances where it happens that neither one or the other man can get a fresh hold with his pole and the bow swings out from the bluff, the boat is carried downriver again, sometimes several hundred yards, before a new attempt can be made.

Unfortunately, on this trip we have no hook pole and are obliged to do the best we can by reaching out with our hands, often tearing off pieces of our fingernails and scratching our hands badly. In getting around many of these bluffs, especially with deeply laden boats, the utmost care has to be used to avoid getting the boat swamped completely and losing the whole outfit and one's life besides.

I found Jack Currier and Joe Goldsmith both excellent

boatsmen, however, and although this, as I said before, was my first upriver poling trip, I had become as efficient as they were after a few days out from Forty Mile Creek, having been in and around boats and water all my life. It therefore came naturally to me.

August 16th: Tuesday. Unloaded all our stuff and turned up our boat bottom this morning to caulk her again, but it did not seem to diminish her leaking very much.

Started from camp at 6 a.m., made about twenty miles, and camped at 3 p.m. Hauled our boat out again and recaulked her; also ran some hot moose tallow into her seams. Sand flies and gnats are becoming very thick and annoying. They interfere with our progress very materially, often causing us to miss a set with our poles in order to brush them off our faces and bare arms.

August 17th: Wednesday. Started at 5:45 a.m. Found that our boat leaked as much as ever, and were obliged to bail her out every fifteen minutes. Had very strong water today. Made some twenty miles and camped about fifteen miles below the Little Salmon River. Saw two red squirrels swimming the river where it is nearly a mile wide.

August 18th: Thursday. Started at 5:30 a.m. Passed "Eagle's Nest," a large bluff rock with holes in it, at 7:30 a.m. Passed the mouth of the Little Salmon River at 1:15 p.m. Had a very good water and poling ground today. Camped at 5:15 p.m. about eight miles above the Little Salmon River. At 7 p.m. a strong breeze sprang up with indications of rain.

August 19th: Friday. Started this morning at 5:30. Had very fair water all forenoon, then quite a heavy shower of rain at 12:30 p.m. Camped at 4:15 p.m., one mile above Chapman's Bar.

August 20th: Saturday. Ate our lunch at the mouth of the Big Salmon River at noon; camped at Cassiar Bar at 4 p.m.

August 21st: Sunday. Started at 5:30 a.m. Camped eight miles below the mouth of the Hootalinqua River. Had a sprinkle of rain during the night.

August 22nd: Monday. Made a start at 5:40 a.m. Very foggy and cold this morning. Had very strong water to contend with all day. Crossed the mouth of the Hootalinqua River at 9:30 a.m. Stopped for a while at 10:30 a.m. in a huckleberry patch and had berries for dinner. Camped at 5 p.m. fifteen miles below the foot of Lake Laberge. Saw a scow with three men in it pass down this evening.

August 23rd: Tuesday. Started at 4 a.m. Quite cold with thick fog. Had fairly easy water nearly all day with only a few heavy ripples. Entered Lake Laberge at 3 p.m. and camped at 4 p.m., three miles up the lake. Weather calm and still on the lake.

August 24th: Wednesday. Started from the foot of Lake Laberge this morning at four o'clock, weather frosty with fog. Kept to the port shore until abreast of the island, then crossed over to the starboard shore. Quite a fresh breeze sprang up while making the crossing. Camped three miles above the head of the lake in the Thirty Mile River (section of the river between Hootalinqua and Laberge) at 5:30 p.m.

It was a relief to lay aside our poles for a while and take to our oars and paddles while crossing the lake. We all enjoyed the best of health and had big appetites. Joe Goldsmith did the bulk of the cooking on this trip, and his sourdough bread was fine. We had no Dutch oven but just used two gold pans, first digging a large hole in the ground and then making a hot fire in it, generally with birch wood. Then when there were lots of hot ashes and cinders, we greased these gold pans well and put a lump of sourdough sponge in one and covered it, placed it in this hot hole in the ground, and covered it all up. After leaving it there for two or three hours, we would find our large loaf nicely baked. Sometimes, if it was scorched too much, we would just trim the outside crust.

I have baked bread in this way without any pans at all by wrapping the dough in a piece of ordinary paper and then shoveling the hot ashes over it quickly before the paper could ignite. Of course this was not quite so good, for the paper would scorch and stick to the loaf. This sourdough bread baking we usually do about three times a week on a trip like this, and on the evening after camping we often would leave the loaf in the ground all night. Occasionally we baked yeast-powder bread in the frying pans.

Often we also cooked beans and bacon in a hole in the ground, but a good Dutch oven is a very good thing to have on a trip like this.

August 25th: Thursday. Started this morning at six o'clock. Came through a slough leading to the right-hand - which we found cuts off about five miles - passed the mouth of the Takhini

River at 10 a.m. and tied up to the bank there to eat our lunch. The current most all day was not very strong. Two men passed downstream in a boat this morning, bound for Forty Mile Creek. One of the men was a Mr. Burns from New Westminster, B.C., whom I used to know there and on the Fraser River. Camped at 4:30 p.m. about a mile below the foot of the White Horse Rapids. Weather very cloudy all day and threatening rain.

For long stretches, both below Lake Laberge and above, our poles would slide down into the soft clay for four and six feet and almost stop the headway of the boat in extracting our poles.

August 26th: Friday. Started at 4:30 a.m. Towed our boat up through the White Horse after portaging all our luggage. Took the boat through our right-hand side. The water appeared to be fairly high. The boat swamped on us once, but we got her through all right and loaded all our outfit aboard again and poled up through about two miles of very swift water, or, what many call, rapids; then reached the foot of the Miles Canyon. Here we portaged all our outfit again over the hill on our left-hand side for a distance of about one mile. We also portaged our boat here, for it was impossible to tow or line a boat through this canyon.

We lashed two poles about ten feet long across the boat, one a few feet from the bow and the other a few feet from the stern, and by taking out all the oars, paddles and her inside bottom boards, we walked and dragged her right along. We made use of an old wooden windlass with rope rove through a purchase block to haul our boat up over the steep pitch at the foot of the canyon.

Arrived at the head of the canyon with all our stuff and boat at 4 p.m. and camped there for the night. Saw some Frenchmen there who had just arrived and were about starting upriver. They reported having left the mouth of the Stewart River six days before we left Forty Mile Creek. Also met four men on their way down in a large canvas boat. With them was Father Tosey, two other priests, and one miner. The priests had been with Bishop Seighers prior to his murder, and Father Tosey left St. Michael's about June 25th of this year with the Bishop's remains, bound for Victoria, leaving the latter place again for the Yukon on August 8th. So it will be seen from this that Father Tosey must have lingered little, since he and I met and parted on the Yukon a little more than two months ago.

71

August 27th: Saturday. Left the head of the canyon this morning at six o'clock, overtook the Frenchmen's party again at 9 a.m. Had considerable rain during the day and last night.

Arrived at the foot of Marsh Lake at 4:30 p.m. Here we had a good fair wind and made fine headway, and it felt good to be able to lay back in our boat and let only one of us do the steering and feel her skip through the water without having to push on our poles as we had to do on the river.

August 28th: Sunday. Started from the foot of Marsh Lake this morning at 4:30, and camped on Taku or Tagish Lake about one mile above Taku Inlet or Big Windy Arm at 4:30 p.m. On this lake it was very still and calm.

August 29th: Monday. A strong head wind sprang up before day broke this morning; got up and hauled our boat up away from the surf and turned in again.

The Northern Lights are shooting and streaking the whole sky with much brilliancy. The wind abated considerably by 5:30 a.m. Here my father and I parted company with Joe Goldsmith, Jack Currier, and Kennedy went into Hank Summers' boat. We bade our companions good-bye, and my father and I started out for the head of Little Windy Arm to see if there was a stream of enough depth to pole up with a boat, and, possibly, a route to get out that way.

I will explain here that on our way upriver, after bidding the Ogilvie survey party good-bye, my father told me of his trip through a pass leading from a little bay called Skagway, about four miles or so south of Dyea, through which pass he and an Interior Indian called Stick, or Skookum Jim, picked their way through to Lake Bennett in the month of June. It took them seven days, however, for there was no trail of any kind and traveling was very hard most of the way.

This pass was at once named the White Pass by Mr. Wm. Ogilvie after my father reported to him at Lake Bennett. The name was in honor of the then Minister of the Interior at Ottawa, I understand. My father reported this White Pass, about one thousand feet lower in altitude than the Dyea or Chilkoot Pass, and he confided to me his great desire to locate on the coast at Skagway Bay on the shore of Lynn Canal.

His object was to bring this route to the front, and divert the early spring travel through this pass to the interior over the ice and snow up through the canyons and chain of small lakes on this side of the Summit, a route which he reported would be easier going by early spring or winter travel with hand sleighs than the Dyea or Chilkoot route, though a few miles more travel to reach Lakes Linderman or Bennett.

My father also stated to me that Skagway Bay was accessible by large ocean steamers at all times of the year and that safe anchorage was there for them, and his idea was to exert all endeavors toward getting a trail of some kind blazed through this pass and to take up some land at salt water on Skagway Bay, and as soon as possible erect some kind of landing or small wharf in a suitable location.

It was with this idea in mind that we both struck out to explore the head of Little Windy Arm, to see if there was some fair-sized watercourse leading from the vicinity of the White Pass into the head of Little Windy Arm which we thought might be utilized for small boating in the summer and sleighing during the early spring and winter months.

I will state that when my father went through this pass last June with Skookum Jim, he was limited as to time and expense by Mr. Ogilvie. My father paid out twenty dollars toward the expense of his trip though. It was hard work getting through; mosquitoes were very bad, all the streams were swollen, there was dense underbrush, and traveling over and around rocky bluffs way above the canyons; but on nearing the summit and after reaching it, the going down to Lake Bennett was much better.

Arrived at the mouth of Little Windy Arm at 10 a.m., by which time the wind had increased again and kept on increasing; until 6 p.m. it was blowing very heavy and quite a sea running up on the beach. So we watched our chance, made a quick landing in the surf, hauled our boat out, and made camp for the night. Saw a large black bear running along at some distance up the beach in the opposite direction from us.

August 30th: Tuesday. Started from the mouth of Little Windy Arm at 5 a.m. Still blowing pretty heavy dead ahead and considerable sea on. We are heading straight up the arm. We rigged a bridle on our boat with our towing line and towed her up most all the way. Arrived at the head of the arm at 5 p.m., about fifteen miles, we estimate, from its mouth.

August 31st: Wednesday. Took a look about the country

here. There was considerable fog hanging on the mountains, and it was also raining and we could not see much, and were convinced that we came up the wrong arm. As there is no watercourse flowing into or in the vicinity of the head of this arm, and no trail or signs of camping grounds whatever, we concluded that we should have explored the head of the Taku Lake inlet or what some call the Big Windy Arm farther down which we passed on the same side of Tagish Lake. It seems to us that the heads of Big Windy Arm and Little Windy Arm cannot be more than five or six miles apart.

Our stock of provisions is now beginning to look rather scanty, so we decided to return and proceeded on out over the old route by way of the Chilkoot or Dyea trail.

Left the head of this arm at 8 a.m. and carried a very strong breeze dead astern all the way down to its mouth, and portion of the way up to Caribou Crossing (Carcross) where we camped at 4 p.m.

September 1st: Thursday. Left Caribou Crossing this morning at six o'clock with a light head wind. At 11 a.m. it increased too much to allow our making but very little progress, so we went into camp fifteen miles from the head of Lake Bennett, which we estimate is twenty-six miles long.

September 2nd: Friday. Started at 5:30 a.m. Kept on till 10:30 a.m., when it commenced to blow very hard head wind. Lay over for a while, then started again at 4 p.m., and camped for the night at 7 p.m. about eight miles from the foot of Lake Lindeman. The southerly winds coming right down off the snowy summits are quite cold even at this time of the year.

September 3rd: Saturday. Remained in camp all day. Blowing a gale all day without intermission.

September 4th: Sunday. Started this morning at 7:30. Head wind still blowing very hard with quite a sea running on the lake. We were obliged to tow our boat all the way up, which was a hard, tedious undertaking. The boat is still leaking badly and shipping water continually over her bows, which necessitated stopping often to bail her out. Arrived at the head of the Lake Bennett at Payer Portage at 5 p.m. and camped for the night here. Found some Chilkat Indians there also, getting their canoes ready to go to the lakes to trade calicoes, blankets, and so on, for furs, with the Interior (or as they are called by many) "Stick" Indians. A great deal of this trading between the coast and the Interior Indians has been done for some time at Caribou Crossing, where the Interior Indians have a large house.

We have made arrangements with two of these Indians to help us portage our boat over to Lake Lindeman, a distance of about one mile, laying skids down and dragging the boat along.

September 5th: Monday. Left the upper end of Payer Portage or foot of Lake Lindeman at 11:30 a.m. Still blowing hard head wind. Arrived at the head of this lake at 5:30 p.m. and camped there for the night at the end of our long, tedious six-hundred mile poling and rowing trip from Forty Mile Creek.

9. CROSSING THE DYEA OR CHILKOOT SUMMIT (September, 1887)

September 6th: Tuesday. Today is my birthday. I am twenty-two years old.

Got together all such articles of clothing, bedding, cooking utensils, and so forth, we could not pack with us over the summit, made a large bundle of it in a large canvas and lashed it up well, then cached it about twelve feet up in a good-sized spruce tree here. Then we got our packs and packstraps ready, and hired an Indian to take one pack of one hundred pounds for us, and my father and I took a pack each of about sixty pounds, including our

blankets, some provisions, a couple of cooking utensils, a pot of cooked beans and bacon, our axe and gun; and after hauling our old boat out on the shore we started at 8 a.m., although our Indian packer advised laying over to await the storm's abatement, for it was blowing a gale from the southwest with heavy rain.

We got wet to the skin before we were out two hours, and had no wood to build a fire because we were then above the timber line.

Overtook five men at 11 a.m. – Tom Manley's party on their way out. They advised us that it would be impossible to cross the summit and that they had lost their way.

I will state that along here, after leaving timber line and for a considerable distance beyond the summit, there is in fact no trail whatever, for our route lay through and over bare rocks and large boulders, running water, gullies, and small glaciers. At intervals there are a few stones piled up, placed there by Indians as guide marks. But these are a long distance apart, and, of course in the early spring and winter, the whole surrounding country is covered with deep drifts of snow.

This summit is certainly a place one must be very careful to cross during even a moderate storm at those seasons of the year, as I have before stated. We kept with our Indian in advance of us, and the Manley party followed.

Arrived at the summit at 4:30 p.m. with fog, sleet, and strong wind; got down to within half a mile of Stone House (a pile of large boulders and overhanging rocks) and there found with much discouragement that, owing to the swollen condition of the stream leading from different parts of the summit down to the canyons and into the Dyea (Taiya) River, we could not ford it and get to camping grounds, and attempt it meant drowning. So there was nothing to do but wait for the morrow, by which time we hoped the rain would cease and the creek go down.

Darkness was about upon us now, and we were cold, hungry and wet to the skin, and all our blankets were wet except one roll of bedding that my father had wrapped in a canvas covering which was partially dry. We lay down in the rain, in a clump of willows on the wet soggy ground near the creek, and shivered and partially steamed ourselves till morning, without fire or hot drink. This is the hardest night I have yet experienced thus far in my life, to say nothing of its being my birthday, and coincidence will no doubt always keep fresh in my memory the date of crossing the Chilkoot Summit on this occasion.

September 7th: Wednesday. Started this morning at five o'clock and forded the creek, which had gone down some, for the rain subsided early this morning. In making this first fording, the swiftly rushing water drenched us nearly to the hips. We advanced with a pole some eight to ten feet long setting downstream, with our packs slung well up on our backs. It was risky work for the large smooth boulders at the bottom of the creek proved unsafe footing, and if once one falls in such swift creeks as these, with a pack on his back, his time is surely come because he would be pounded to death against the boulders, perhaps before he had time to drown. We were obliged to reford this creek lower down several times, but the first ford was the worst.

Arrived at Sheep Camp at 9 a.m., worn out, cold, wet, and hungry. My buckskin trousers, after slopping through the water, had, it seemed, stretched half a yard.

Camped here at Sheep Camp for the rest of the day and night, dried out our clothing and blankets by a good, rousing camp fire, and ate what we had left -which was very little now: some hot coffee and a few hardtack biscuits.

September 8th: Thursday. Left Sheep Camp at 10 a.m. Found the trail down to the forks around the canyons very rough, continually leading up and down short pitches. We forded the creek often, and arrived at the forks at 4 p.m., where we got into a small canoe and came down the swift Dyea River to Healy's trading post, a distance of some eight miles, and arrived at 6 p.m. wet through again and with empty stomachs.

Took lodgings here and had a really good supper supplied by Mrs. John Healy, the miners' and travelers' friend. Never before has a meal tasted so good as this one. Mrs. Healy brought out some of her own preserves, consisting of red currant jellies and jams, which she helped to pick here herself. She and her husband, Capt. John Healy, made us very comfortable.

September 9th: Friday. Still waiting here for Capt. Healy's little steamer, the Yukon, from Juneau, for which he has sent word to get here as soon as possible.

Weather very disagreeable; rain, and blowing hard from the southeast.

September 10th: Saturday. A Mr. Lansing, French Joe, Michael Duval, and a man named Guss, arrived here today from Forty Mile Creek. They report a very hard trip from Bennett Lake. Mr. Lansing brought a letter and two hundred thirty-eight dollars from my brother for us. This party states that several men are on their way out and not far behind. There are ten men here now, including all of us, awaiting the arrival of the steamer from Juneau.

September 11th: Sunday. Still waiting for the steamer.

10. DOWN LYNN CANAL BY CANOE TO JUNEAU (September, 1887)

September 12th: Monday. No steamer in sight yet. Made up our minds at noon to start down Lynn Canal for Juneau in a canoe, bought some provisions, and left Dyea at 1 p.m. Passed close in to the little bay of Skagway on our left, about an hour after leaving the mouth of the Dyea River. Noticed carefully the low pass or valley through the mountains at Skagway, and could see at once this bay would afford good natural facilities for a wharf along the easterly side at the high bluff.

Arrived at Haines Mission at 5:30 p.m. Took supper there at the old Dickinson Store building and lodged there for the night.

September 13th: Tuesday. Left Haines Mission at 5 a.m. in a large canoe owned by an Indian named Phillip. There were six of us altogether, besides the owner of the canoe and another Indian. The other four miners remained at Dyea to wait for the steamer.

We pulled and paddled steadily all day and the following night except a quarter of an hour halt at a beach on our left-hand side a few miles above Berner's Bay. Here we noticed a man by the name of Lewis, who was doing some assessment work in that vicinity in a quartz mine and whose permanent interests and home were at Juneau. On his asking us how the Forty Mile Creek mines and other prospects were turning out in the interior, French Joe, one of our party, who had been mining on Forty Mile Creek, jumped up in the canoe and hollered loudly to the shore that the Forty Mile Creek was worked out. In fact, he ran the whole country down despite having with him at the time some fifteen hundred dollars in gold dust which he took out of Forty Mile Creek in two months' work.

Immediately, when the Frenchman sat down again in the canoe, my father rose up and said, "Mr. Lewis, the Yukon is not only NOT worked out, but it has not begun to be worked into yet," contradicting French Joe's statement. I then remarked, "I'll bet Joe will be one of the first men to return to the Yukon next spring." We then bade Mr. Lewis good-bye and proceeded on our way down Lynn Canal.

September 14th: Wednesday. Went ashore to cook some lunch and rest for a while at 2 a.m., two miles north of the old deserted Indian settlement named Auk Village about twelve miles from Juneau. Left there at 3 a.m. Raining hard, but luckily we have not had much head wind, and it was principally to avoid meeting with heavy head wind that we traveled all night; at this time of the year Lynn Canal is seldom free from strong southerly winds. We picked our way through the winding shallow channel over the bar between Douglas Island and the mainland and found the tide just high enough to allow us to get through, for when it is low tide here it is all mud and sand flat for three miles or more.

Arrived at Juneau at 11:40 a.m. Eighteen hours and forty minutes, including one half-hour stoppages from Haines Mission, a distance of ninety-five miles, making fully five miles per hour. What little wind we have had was against us, but we considered this making excellent time and we pulled at our oars steadily and hard. Took lodgings at the old Franklin Hotel. A strong north-westerly breeze sprang up this evening; too late to have helped us along on our trip down.

September 15th, 16th, 17th, 18th, and 19th: Still resting up here at Juneau, looking around. Made a trip to the Treadwell quartz mine at Douglas Island and secured work there.

September 20th: Tuesday. I started in to work at the Treadwell quartz mine this morning, pushing two-ton ore cars to and from the mine to the mill at two dollars per day and board. My partner in work on the cars, for a while, was Malcolm Campbell whom I found to be a fine, honest, good-hearted fellow. The steamship *Idahoe* from Victoria and the Sound arrived here early this morning, and later proceeded on up to Chilkat and Haines Mission with supplies for George Dickinson's store.

September 21st, 22nd, 23rd, and 24th: Still working here at

the Treadwell mine and traveling about fifteen miles per day pushing ore cars.

September 25th: Sunday. The steamer *Idahoe* returned from Chilkoot and left here at noon today for Victoria with about sixty of the Yukon miners, having gathered these men up on her way down along different points. Forwarded letters, money, and some furs down on the *Idahoe* to Victoria.

September 26th: Monday. Nothing of any interest, only that I find this a dangerous place to work in, to say nothing of the Swede straw boss's head becoming too large for his hat.

September 27th: Tuesday. Quit work here at the mine this morning, and returned to Juneau across the channel.

September 28th, 29th and 30th: Still here in Juneau.

October 1st: Saturday. Raining hard all day. The usual thing here. Morris Horton, Dutch Charlie, and two Yukon miners arrived here early this morning from Chilkoot, Haines Mission. They report twenty-two more men are on their way down from Healy's post, including Doctor (George) Dawson's Canadian survey party.

October 2nd: Sunday. Three canoes arrived from the head of Lynn Canal, including Doctor (George) Dawson's party.

11. FROM JUNEAU TO SKAGWAY BAY BY CANOE (October, 1887)

October 3rd, 4th, 5th and 6th: Remained here in Juneau with my father, arranging matters and getting a canoe, provisions, a tent, and some tools ready to return up Lynn Canal to the little bay of Skagway to locate there and take up one hundred sixty acres of land and a wharf site.

October 7th: Friday. Loaded our canoe with our provisions, cooking utensils, bedding, gum boots, sheet-iron stove, tent, and tools, the latter consisting of axes, crosscut saw, sledges, steel wedges, several bars of three-quarter-inch round iron, half coil of one-inch manila rope, pair of double purchase blocks, large spikes, nails, and several other necessary tools, and started from Juneau to Skagway Bay at three o'clock this morning. The gunwales of our canoe along midships are only about six inches above water.

Weather very disagreeable, blowing from the south and raining hard. Headed up Gastineau Channel toward the bar inside of Douglas Island, and camped about four miles above Auk Village or some sixteen miles northerly from Juneau. Remained here for the rest of the day and night, as we were nearly wet through, though we had oilskin coats on. Got our tent pitched well, made a large camp fire and cooked a large kettle of beans, and made a big loaf of bread in a Dutch oven we got at Juneau; and fell to and had a good dinner.

October 8th: Saturday. Obliged to lay over in camp here today on account of my being sick. Raining very hard all day.

October 9th: Sunday. Started this morning at six o'clock. Light, fair wind from the south. Pulled steadily at our oars until within half a mile south of Berner's Bay, where we camped at 4:30 p.m., shortly after which it commenced to rain again and kept it up all night.

October 10th: Monday. Still pouring rain, so we decided not to break camp.

October 11th: Tuesday. Started at 6 a.m. Still raining, with strong fair wind. Found the ebb tide making out just below the southernmost point of Berner's Bay, which created quite a riptide against the heavy sea, so we were obliged to put in again and camp for a couple of hours until slack tide.

Started off again and made the run across the mouth of Berner's Bay in one hour; six miles. Carried a fair wind all along, and camped on top of a high rocky bank twelve miles northerly of Berner's Bay. A heavy surf was rolling in on the shore which necessitated our carrying the canoe above the high tide mark. Camping grounds after getting north of Berner's Bay on the right-hand side of Lynn Canal going up are very scarce. No rain tonight.

October 12th: Wednesday. Started this morning at eight o'clock; no wind; rowed up to within seven miles of Chilkoot or Haines Mission, and camped for the night at 4 p.m. Raining hard all afternoon and during the night. It came down in torrents, which started a little creek running close to our heads where we lay in our tent. Had to get up, dress, and dig a trench to divert the water away from us.

October 13th: Thursday. No letup in the rain yet this morning. Found our canoe nearly full of rain water. At noon we thought of making a start. But about 12:30 p.m. the southerly wind increased to a gale, blowing straight up Lynn Canal with heavy capped sea on, and the surf rolling in on the beach.

About dusk or 4 p.m. we heard voices calling out loudly above the roar of the wind and sea, and looking out of our tent we saw two Indians in a fairly large-sized canoe coming up the canal before the wind, seemingly looking for a place to land. They signaled to us to help them beach their canoe, and one of them shouted that they could not attempt to reach Haines Mission, where they were bound. So we hurried down to the beach at the edge of the surf and stood in readiness to grab hold of the canoe.

The canoe was pointed fairly in-between, and on she came on top of a big sea. The two Indians jumped out, up to their waists in water, making two of us on each side. But when she struck the beach she split from stem to stern. We hauled her away above the high-water mark. The Indians intend to repair her. We gave the Indians shelter for the night.

October 14th: Friday. Weather still very rough. High sea running with occasional rain showers, so we decided to remain another night here in camp. During the night, at 11:30 p.m., we were awakened by rattling among our cooking utensils, and on lighting our lantern we saw a stray Indian dog crawling out from under our tent which we thought we had pegged down to the ground pretty well.

In looking over our supplies we found that a two-pound can of roast beef, which we had opened that evening for supper, and of which we had used just a little, was gone. We rearranged our things and went to bed again, but before long were awakened twice again by this thief dog returning. He packed off, besides the opened can of roast beef, one whole large ham and ten pounds of bacon. We sat up all night on watch with our rifle for this dog, but he did not return.

October 15th: Saturday. Got a shot at the dog this morning but only wounded him. Weather moderated a little, so we packed up and made a start. After getting away from shore a short distance we found that the wind had hardly decreased, though looking out from shore we thought it had. When about one hour out, we found it would be impossible for our canoe to weather the gale, for she was taking in water over the stern and bows.

A little distance ahead of us, there is a long sandbar reaching two-thirds across the channel at low tide. We knew we could get around this, so we headed into the mouth of a little river just south of this sandbar and, keeping close-in to our right-hand shore, ran up into the river and poled up about two miles, where we put up our tent and camped.

Lynn Canal is now a foaming mass, and the gale increasing. Trees are being uprooted by the raging storm. Saw a large canoe with two people in it with a part of a sail up and heading for the Haines Mission shore, the same canoe and Indians, we think, that landed at our camp farther down the night before last. And while we stood watching this canoe, she disappeared before reaching shore. There is no doubt in our minds that the two occupants were drowned.

October 16th: Sunday. Rained hard all last night and this forenoon, but as there seemed to be quite a lull in the wind we made a start at 9 a.m. However, on nearing the bar we found there was not much abatement in the sea and wind, so we ran back up into the river and made camp again. By 11 a.m. the southwest gale was more fierce than ever.

October 17th: Monday. About 1 a.m. wind eased up a little, and it rained hard for a couple of hours; thought surely the storm was going to ease up enough to allow us to venture out with some degree of safety, but before daybreak we had to rush out of our tent to an opening at the edge of the river and away from the standing timber, because many trees were falling, torn up by the roots and some breaking in two, and within an hour the gale had increased to a hurricane, whirling into our faces. This is certainly the fiercest wind I have yet witnessed.

October 18th: Tuesday. Wind moderated pretty well during last night. Got up at 5 a.m. The weather looked pretty good, with all indications for a fine day. We broke camp and at 6 a.m. got started down the mouth of the river. Found the sea beyond all calm, with no wind, but as the tide was low we were obliged to wait for two hours until the tide backed up into the river sufficiently high to allow us to pass out over the bar.

Shortly after getting out of the river into Lynn Canal, the southerly commenced to spring up again, and increased steadily; and before we got around the point of the long bar, which extends out into Lynn Canal a mile and a half or more, it was blowing a pretty fresh breeze. We made fast time with our sail up. These canoes skip lively through the water, for they are finely modeled fore and aft.

Crossed over to the port shore quarterlingly, and doing so shipped considerable water at different times. Got above Haines Mission and had it very rough, especially in a riptide off a point there. The wind kept increasing all the time until we had to take in the sprit from our sail, and came near swamping several times in crossing the mouth of the Chilkoot Inlet just north of Haines Mission. Past this inlet there are really no harbors of any kind for even small boats or canoes till either Skagway Bay or Dyea is reached.

We kept on our way, however, hugging our port shore, watching for a place where we could run our canoe in, for we were now shipping water over the stern and bow. Our object was to make Skagway Bay, if possible. We were now only some three or four miles away, and could see the mouth of the bay and the line of the cottonwood trees along down near the mouth of the Skagway River.

But we were now, of course, on the opposite shore of Lynn Canal from Skagway Bay, and it would mean disaster to us to try to make the crossing in the trough of the sea to reach the opposite shore. We ran our canoe into a small nook in the rocks, jumped out, and quickly hauled her up halfway out of the water and then hauled or rolled our bedding, tent, and other things necessary for a camp up on top of a point with a rope, where we found about enough level ground to place our tent. Then we hauled our canoe clear out of high tide and camped here in sight of our destination.

October 19th: Wednesday. Wind moderated a little about 5 a.m. Commenced getting ready to start, but at 6 a.m. it was blowing harder again, and by noon the wind had again assumed its original force from the southwest and kept up this lick all day.

October 20th: Thursday. The gale died out this morning before daybreak. Commenced getting ready, loaded up our canoe, and got started at 8:30 a.m. Indications now showed for clear frosty weather. Arrived at Skagway Bay at 10 a.m. and ran our canoe up in the creek about a quarter of a mile, then put up our tent and camped at the foot of a little bluff on the beach, where a small creek comes down and joins the large creek on the right-hand or east side of the bay.

I have never forgotten my father's words to me. "Here," said he, "we will cast our future lots and try to hew out our fortune," as I struck my axe into our first tree. Later we reconnoitered up the valley a way and put up notice of location for one hundred sixty acres upland, and measured off six hundred feet for a wharf site and placed our notice on the same. We ran across numerous old deadfall traps for bear and other animals, a short distance up the valley. My father also said on this occasion: "I fully expect before many years to see a pack trail through this pass, followed by a wagon road, and I would not be at all surprised to see a railroad through to the lakes."

12. THE FOUNDING OF SKAGWAY AND MOORE'S WHARF (October-November, 1887)

October 21st: Friday. Found thin ice in the bay this morning, and a quarter inch of ice in our bucket in our tent. Sounded the bay with a long cod line and heavy weight for the most suitable location for the wharf, and eventually chose the easterly side of the bay at the foot of the high steep rocky bluff, and got out a few short logs.

October 22nd: Saturday. Weather still clear and frosty. Got out a few more logs and commenced building a crib to be filled with rock and brush at our wharf site.

October 23rd: Sunday. Got out a few more logs today, which were all we could handle, and built up our crib about three feet. We laid the logs in a square, notched in the ends, and drift-bolted the ends. These logs run from twelve to twenty-nine feet in length.

October 24th: Monday. Found snow on the ground this morning; built up about two feet on our wharf cribbing. One of the logs we placed in position today is eighteen inches in diameter.

John J. Healy came down in a canoe from his post at Dyea, with an Indian, to look at his schooner, called the *Charlie*, which had broken adrift at Dyea and drifted into this bay and grounded at high spring tide a little beyond our camp on the creek. We named this creek, where our camp now is, Mill Creek. We arranged with the Indian named Nan-Suk, who came down here with Healy, to work for us at two dollars per day and board.

Later, George Carmack and Mr. Wilson, the latter Mr. Healy's partner at Dyea, came down to repair the schooner *Charlie*, putting in some new bottom planks, caulking and refastening.

October 25th: Tuesday. Found about six inches of snow on the ground this morning; continued to snow off and on all day. Got two binder logs or stringers on the crib and one heavy front log on today. The latter log was very heavy to handle, being sixteen inches through at the butt and twenty-nine feet long. This first square crib is about twelve by fifteen feet on the inside and is constructed on the rocky beach. The first logs in it were laid at about half-tide mark. We piled spruce boughs inside of this crib, then a layer of large stones and rocks, then another layer of brush, with smaller poles to bind it all together and keep it from washing out at high tide.

Along the beach here it was all a mass of large boulders and stones covered with slippery seaweed, which makes our work very hard and tedious. It took a large quantity of brush and rocks to fill up this crib. The top logs are now some two feet above highest tide-mark.

October 26th: Wednesday. Weather turned soft. Rained all forenoon, and then came on to blow from the southward very suddenly and increased to a gale by 5 p.m. Got four good braces fastened to the upper logs of cribbing, and piled a quantity of rocks on them to hold the crib from being washed away during the high tides later. Our crib is about twelve feet high from the lower outer log to the top, the long or fifteen-foot side facing the water. The snow is about all gone again.

October 27th: Thursday. Wind died out again by daybreak, and it rained steadily all day. Got three more logs out and piled more rock in the crib.

October 28th: Friday. Commenced raining very hard before daybreak this morning and continued until 8:30 a.m. Then a strong southerly wind sprang up. I have never seen a place where the wind springs up so suddenly. Looking out from Skagway Bay here, we see Lynn Canal sometimes calm and undisturbed, then next we hear a far off rumbling sound, like surf rolling on a beach far away, and we know what to expect, because a few minutes later the strong southerly wind is chasing the white-capped seas up Lynn Canal. Then, in a few moments more, the wind sweeps around the high protecting point or bluff below our wharf site and our little bay is disturbed, though not as much as in Lynn Canal owing to the shelter of this high bluff. Lynn Canal is a dangerous stretch of water during the fall and winter time for small boat and canoe navigation.

October 29th: Saturday. Wind partially lulled down at 1 a.m. Piled quite a lot of rocks on and around the crib and placed two more long binders, or stringers, leading from the top logs of the crib into shore. Started to rain again, and continued all day. We have to walk around the shore back and forth from our camp to our wharf site, and at high tide we have to climb over and around many high rocks, some of which are as large as a small cabin. We use our canoe sometimes to tow logs, but the beach is so rough and rocky here, and there being some twenty-seven feet of rise and fall in extreme tides, that we find it safer to keep our canoe in our camp at the mouth of the creek.

October 30th: Sunday. Very high tides now. Got four more brace and stringer logs on the crib today, and also placed a large, heavy log down in front, at the foot of the crib on the rocks, and piled a large quantity of brush tree tops and rocks on and all around it to form a breakwater and protection for the crib.

October 31st: Monday. Rained hard all last night, and commenced blowing hard again this morning from the northwest. Made good progress on our cribbing. Tide very high about noon.

November 1st: Tuesday. No moderation in the wind yet. It increased at 6 p.m., tearing our tent, and obliging us to place extra braces to support the ridge pole to keep it from breaking in two in the middle. Placed considerable rock on the cribbing and got some more timber.

November 2nd: Wednesday. Ceased blowing at 3 a.m. and remained calm until 5 p.m., when a strong southerly wind sprang up and by 7:30 had increased to the usual thing - a gale. It became necessary for us to rig up a large wind-break out of spruce boughs and tree tops to save our tent from being torn down. The tide was even higher today than yesterday. In these long, narrow channels like Lynn Canal, during full and new moon tides, or a day or two after, these heavy southerly winds force the tides up somewhat higher than usual.

November 3rd: Thursday. No moderation in the wind yet, but made worse by an unusually heavy rain all last night and today; the rain beat right through our tent. We did not turn out to work at all today; the tide was still higher again today.

November 4th: Friday. Wind died out at 6:30 p.m. Very little rain today. Placed some covering logs on our cribbing, also one large corner brace or binder in position. At 8:30 p.m. a southerly wind again commenced blowing up the channel heavily.

November 5th: Saturday. Wind moderated at 1 p.m., and by 6 p.m. died out again and was succeeded by a heavy downpour of rain, very cold and raw. Made good progress with our work on our little wharf, or cribbing.

November 6th: Sunday. No wind all day until 7 p.m., when the usual wind sprang up from the southward. Snowed a little also. Stopped work today and rested, and did some extra cooking and bread baking.

November 7th: Monday. Weather calm until 7 p.m., when the southerly wind started up again. Had a light fall of snow, but made fair progress on the wharf.

November 8th: Tuesday. Wind calmed down at 10 a.m. Had a very good day to work. Got a large quantity of rock out on the cribbing and moved or rolled over some large boulders down the beach (we estimate these weigh more than a ton) with long levers and our kant hooks. These large boulders we placed as near as possible at the back and front of the crib structure.

November 9th: Wednesday. Weather very clear and calm until 3 p.m., when the southerly wind started up again. We have been daily expecting wind from the north and a freeze-up for a few days at least. Put in a lot more breakwater material such as rocks. boughs, and tree tops in front of the cribbing.

November 10th: Thursday. Wind drawing around more to the eastward. Had another light fall of snow. Weather getting colder. Did good work on our structure, and expect to finish this first little starter of a wharf by tomorrow night.

November 11th: Friday. Light northeast wind all day and clear frosty weather. Skim ice making in the bay. Finished all the work we intend to do on the wharf site this evening, and cleared away a foundation among the large boulders for a little log house, twelve by sixteen feet, on the beach, in line with and to connect with, the inner logs of binders that connect the crib to shore above high watermark.

November 12th: Saturday. Clear frosty weather still, and northeasterly wind blowing. Very cold. Laid the foundation logs for our future cabin measuring sixteen by sixteen feet on the bank, about twenty feet from the creek where it forks, and about a quarter of a mile farther up the valley from our present camp on the left-hand side of the creek going up.

High tides are making again, and in two or three days more we should have the highest tides of the season.

November 13th: Sunday. Still clear, frosty weather. Worked all forenoon getting out more logs for our cabin some of which we float and haul down this creek.

Mr. John Healy's schooner *Charlie* drifted partially out from her former position where a trench had been dug to allow her to float more readily. Mr. Wilson, John J. Healy and George Carmack came down from Dyea in a canoe, hauled her out into deep water, and moored her in the bay here abreast of our wharf site. They also made preparations to leave here for Juneau, so we decided to go on the schooner to Juneau also.

We cached our tools and so forth well up above the high tidemark at our wharf site on top of the cribbing, which we now felt sure would withstand the winter storms. I think we handled and turned over nearly all the loose rocks and stones on the beach in the near vicinity of this cribbing, and have experienced many slips and falls in climbing around this rough, rocky, seaweedy, and barnacled beach. We feel that we would have liked very much to have got our cabin either completed or further along before leaving here, but it is time to get away from here because winter is close at hand in earnest, and there will be no steamboat communication up here till next March.

Paid our Indian Nan-Suk off, and he paddled up to his home and family who camp just above the upper point of the bay. After paying this Indian forty dollars for his twenty days' work, we had barely enough ready cash left to lay aside for our fares from Juneau to Victoria.

Mr. Healy returned to Dyea with his partner, Mr. Wilson, and George Carmack, in their canoe for Mrs. Healy and all his furs from his post up there, amounting to some three thousand dollars.

November 14th: Monday. Lay at anchor here. No wind.

13. LEAVING "MOORESVILLE", DOWN LYNN CANAL TO JUNEAU IN THE SCHOONER *CHARLIE* (November, 1887)

November 15th: Tuesday. About 7 a.m. a light, northerly wind sprang up as we had expected. We weighed anchors, and bidding Mrs. Healy, Mr. Wilson, and George Carmack good-bye, we two and Capt. Healy hoisted our sails and glided out of Skagway Bay, or as we now often call this place, Mooresville, or Moore's Harbor, first having hauled our canoe up on the schooner's deck and lashing her down securely.

We had not gone far when we ran into baffling light head winds, which beat down to within five miles of Haines Mission, where we ran into a heavy snow storm at 8 p.m. It was very dark. The flood tide commenced to make up the canal, and the southeast wind kept freshening all the time. So we lowered our mainsail and jib and headed back for Moore's Harbor (Skagway Bay) under the foresail alone, making about seven miles per hour, with a big sea running and trying to curl up over the stern of the schooner.

By this time the wind had increased to a gale. We made our way cautiously in the bay and anchored off our wharf site abreast of the crib structure, and here rode out the storm all night. Old *Charlie* jumped and tossed around throughout the long hours like a bucking bronco.

Not a wink of sleep, and worst of all, we found that the *Charlie* was making water very freely. Try as we did, we could not account for this. She had just recently undergone a thorough overhauling, as I have stated before. The consequence was that we were obliged to take turns continually bailing and pumping water, and it became quite apparent that there was a pretty free leak in her bottom or sides below the waterline somewhere; but where, of course, we could not locate. The schooner was tightly sealed over her timbers, but as we had her trimmed well astern we could keep the water from coming up over the cabin floor into her hold by bailing from the cockpit away aft.

The stuffy cabin, and the bilge water odor that invariably ferments schooners' holds, together with the kicking about she did, made us all seasick. My father vowed that he had not actually been seasick for forty years, and I have good reason to believe this was so. I had never seen him seasick before during all the steamboating and sailing we did together.

We all gave freely to the fishes.

November 16th: Wednesday. Wind moderated a little at 8 a.m. Went ashore and got some wood and water aboard with our canoe. At noon the southwester had again reached its full force, and we put down another anchor. We experienced another very rough, miserable night. Our little vessel heaved and strained at her cables, so that every moment we thought she would part one or both of them. But we did not drag anchors, for this bay has certainly excellent ground for safe anchorage.

At about 2 a.m. we found that our rudder was missing. It had been jumped clean out of its sockets. This, we think, was caused by the lower end of the rudder striking bottom during low tide last night. The *Charlie* draws some six feet of water partially loaded, and is some forty feet long with a fifteen foot beam amidships.

November 17th: Thursday. Wind moderated a little at 7 a.m. Went ashore in our canoe to look for our rudder, which we found on the beach near the creek at the head of the bay. It was quite a heavy one, with several iron bolts and fastenings in it such as are usually used in the construction of these rudders. We had entertained some fears that it had sunk and was lost for good, so we were mighty glad to find it. We got it into the canoe, reshipped it again, and fastened it in place with extra cleats and the like.

A good fresh breeze kept up all day, and at 10 p.m. calmed down altogether for the rest of the night.

November 18th: Friday. A light northerly wind sprang up at 9:30 a.m. Have shortened our anchors and got all ready for our second start, and sailed out at 10 a.m., after which it kept on blowing a moderate steady breeze from the north.

Arrived at Haines Mission at 3 p.m. and anchored there abreast of the Dickinson store. At 4 p.m. the wind calmed down, and it started to snow heavily.

November 19th: Saturday. Blowing a good breeze from the north and snowing and freezing hard. At 10 a.m. it ceased snowing. Got ready, heaved up our anchors, and taking George Dickinson and Mrs. Wentworth aboard as passengers for Juneau, we left Haines Mission at noon. Kept a good fair wind down Lynn Canal.

As we look back astern and see the snow-capped mountains surrounding Skagway Bay and Dyea inlet fast fading away in the distance, a strange feeling comes over me and I wonder and ask myself, "Will I surely be back there again this spring?" It seemed, somehow, that perhaps I would not. It seemed desolate up there. The only person in that neighborhood, besides Mrs. Healy, George Carmack, Mr. Wilson, and a few Indians, was our Indian Nan-Suk, camped at a small bay (Smuggler's Cove) on the right-hand shore going up about a mile above the northernmost point of Skagway Bay.

Anchored in Berner's Bay at 9 p.m., but experienced a hard time making into the bay. It was pretty dark, and we had to beat our way into the anchorage, for the wind here was drawing out of the bay. Our ropes were frozen, the decks iced up, flow ice was making out of the bay, and we all felt very glad indeed to get into anchorage for the long night.

During all this time we dared not neglect our turn at the pump and buckets, for the leak in our vessel did not diminish. George Dickinson was also pressed into service, which he, of course, willingly took to.

From Berner's Bay down to the head of Douglas Island there are numerous islands and reefs to pick a way through; but from Berner's Bay to Haines Mission, or to Skagway and Dyea, almost a straight course can be held all the way, except for a little deviation on passing Eldred Rock. Therefore we did not think it prudent to keep on under the existing circumstances and pass by Berner's Bay, a good anchorage at this time of the year; nor did we at all wish to, especially at night.

November 20th: Sunday. We all took our hot coffee and

buttered hardtack by our stove in the cabin as usual, and at 4:30 a.m. hove up anchor, made sail, and headed out of this (Berner's) bay. Of course it was pretty dark; the days are pretty short here in the winter time, and it behooves those who are traveling, especially by water, in this country during the late fall and winter months to make early starts and early harbors if at all possible. It is far better and safer to remain in a good safe anchorage in Lynn Canal than to leave it and not to be sure of making the next safe harbor before nightfall.

We carried a good, fair sailing breeze all the way to the lower or southernmost point of Douglas Island. The *Charlie*, of course, drew too much water to allow of us taking the course over the bar between the island and the mainland even at highest tides.

Saw the steamer *Idahoe* headed for Juneau on her way from Sitka. Signaled to her for a tow in but got no recognition. I was anxious to get to Juneau in time to take passage on the *Idahoe* for Victoria, for I felt she would not lie long at Juneau.

Rounded the point and headed back northward to Juneau. Now, of course, the wind was against us and ebb tide was running. Tried to beat up against it, but the wind was not strong enough to beat with and make any progress against the tide, and we were obliged to anchor. So my father and I launched our canoe and bade Capt. Healy and the others on board good-bye and started for Juneau.

Arrived at Juneau at 11:30 p.m. and there got news that the *Idahoe* had just left for the south, but that the steamer *Sardonyx* was expected at any moment. Received letters from home in Victoria in Juneau.

November 21st: Monday. Waiting here at Juneau for the steamer *Sardonyx* from Victoria, B.C. Capt. Healy arrived here today about noon with his schooner and unloaded his furs. Then we helped him to haul her on the beach at high tide near the Carroll or Pacific Coast Steamship Company's wharf, and waited till the tide receded enough to allow our walking around the schooner's hull. And now came and explanation of the steady leak in her, which gave us all so unrest and hard pumping and bailing.

Down below her port bilge, about four feet out from her keel amidships, a stream of water was pouring out from a nice, clear-bored auger hole about three-quarters of an inch in diameter, into which, it is now quite apparent to all of us, Mr. Wilson and George Carmack forgot to insert a hardwood pin up through into her timbers and side keelson.

At all events, we felt more satisfied to know the cause of her leak. No doubt when she was first hauled out into the bay at Skagway there were some mud and auger shavings sticking in this hole which later washed out, therefore she did not leak so badly when first anchored in the bay up there.

While awaiting the steamer *Sardonyx* to arrive here at Juneau, we were reticent as to our expectations and intentions at Skagway, but often talked matters over regarding our undertaking and fully made up our minds to return next spring to Skagway and resume our work on the wharf, so as to at least get some kind of a small landing constructed there even if it only reached down to extremely low tide mark; for to build out into any depth of water, a pile driver would be necessary, and this we could not think of getting because we had no funds to procure one.

The time waiting here seemed long, and my thoughts often revert to my long weary trip into the interior of the Yukon, partially by ice and water, and then all the way upstream again, and so on till the present time. And I wonder, as I realize how many changes and experiences I have seen and the long distance I have covered since leaving Victoria last March, that after all, there is certainly some unaccountable fascination about this rough Alaskan life, both on the coast and in the interior, which I do not quite understand.

As can be seen from my record, my home has been wherever we camped; and often when the weather permitted, the starlit canopy above was our roof. Both Captain Healy and Mr. Wilson do not seem to think that Skagway will ever amount to anything as a route for supplies or traffic for the interior, and seem to feel sorry for us, as they say, for wasting our time there.

Capt. Healy has often entertained us with stories of many of his wild, rough, and adventurous experiences back along the Missouri River, Fort Benton and Montana in the early days, where he was widely known among the Indians and fur traders, and headed several vigilante committees that captured desperadoes and fought the Indians. Capt. Healy has now with him a beautiful, large, long, curly, silken-haired buffalo overcoat made from the hide of one of the buffaloes he killed on the plains.

J. Bernard Moore (right) poses with his daughter Gertrude and pet moose "Carnation" in front of the Moore family home. *Dedman's Photo*

J. BERNARD MOORE'S
SKAGWAY SPEECH
and the
MOORE FAMILY
PHOTO JOURNAL

"Skagway In Days Primeval"

The following speech was delivered by J. Bernard Moore, at the Pioneer's Banquet, at the Fifth Avenue Hote in Skagway on August 2, 1904. It was printed in the Skagway Daily Alaskan on August 4, 1904.

Ladies and Gentlemen, I feel rather out of place in being on your program this evening. As you all know, I am not a speaker, or even a good reader, so I will handle the subject given me, that of Skagway in primeval days, in my own plain way as best I can. But I will have to touch on an early trip to the Yukon in order to show how I got here. My old logbook has furnished me a few of the memories recalled in this paper.

While poling my way up the Yukon River in the early part of August, 1887, in company with two men who joined me at Forty Mile Creek, after a trip thus far of about seventy days – or two and a half months from Forty Mile Creek to St. Michael's and return – I noticed on one Sunday morning a large scow moored to the left bank of the river and about five miles below the mouth of the Pelly River and Fort Selkirk. There were three or four Peterboro canoes tied to the scow.

The weather was very hot, and the mosquitoes thick and furious, which made poling against the swift stream all the more difficult. We had to knock a swarm of these pests off our faces every few seconds. Through the overhanging willows I soon perceived several men among whom was Gov. William Ogilvie, who at that time was in charge of a track survey into the Yukon for the Canadian Government. Pyramid Island, on the Chilkat Inlet, was his starting point.

I next noticed someone along the verge of the river, hurrying toward my boat and fighting mosquitoes with both hands. On a nearer approach I saw that it was my father. I ran the bow of my boat into the bank, where we talked matters over, and he concluded to return with me to the coast. Rolling his blankets aboard and bidding Gov. Ogilvie adieu, we continued upstream.

After some twenty-five days more of poling and rowing over the lakes we arrived at the head of Lake Lindeman, and thence went over the Chilkoot Pass to the little trading post of Healy & Wilson, at Dyea. After recuperating for a couple of days and enjoying the change from the usual miners' food - which was not so varied then as it is now - by partaking of the fine meals set up by Mrs. John Healy, and which included jars of rich red currant jellies like that our present campers enjoy so much to pick and eat. Mrs. Healy was a friend of all those entering and coming from the Yukon, in those days.

James Bernard Moore as a youth in Victoria. *Don Gestner Collection*

We left Dyea for Skagway in a canoe, and remained there about four days to look over the situation. This was my first visit; but it was my father's second, for he had passed through Skagway on his way into the Yukon by the way which afterward was called White Pass, in the month of June, 1887. My arrival in the country at Dyea dated from

Skagway, Alaska in 1895

A view of the "Mooresville" beach in 1895, before the stampede.   *Dedman's Photo*

March 21st, having arrived on the little steamer *Yukon*.

I found ice three feet thick, in a solid barrier, clear across Lynn Canal, from Smuggler's Cove to the opposite shore, the winter of '86 being the hardest and coldest known in the country. The little steamer's miner passengers and their outfits were put off on this big ice wharf, and we sleighed our outfits for about four miles to good camping timber. Strange to say, not one of the five hundred men who went into the Yukon that year had any sleigh dogs. Forty Mile was then the objective point.

After remaining four days at Skagway, as I said before, we proceeded in our canoe to Juneau. There we built a good, strong. flat-bottomed boat, twenty-five feet long, and rigged her with a leeboard and sail. This took us a week. After loading her with provisions and other material such as ropes, blocks, iron bars, tools and the like, we returned to Skagway, arriving about the last of September.

We remained there for two months, cutting timber and taking soundings of the entire bay to ascertain the depths of the water, with a view of putting in a wharf. We also paced off and made notes for a location of one hundred and sixty acres of land.

Our tent was pitched near the creek, on a little elevated point between the bluff and the present electric light plant, where salmon trout could be caught at our tent door and where, ten years later, ground was broken for the present railroad tracks.

The entire land in this valley between the mountains, on both sides of the river, was thickly covered with spruce, hemlock, cottonwood, pine and birch. The three first-mentioned varieties of timber were the most plentiful, averaging ten inches and seldom reaching three feet in diameter. There were many beautiful little park-like areas where the underbrush was not so thick. From the upper line

Klinget-sai-yet, Minnie Moore.   *Don Gestner Collection*

Bernard Moore and son Bennie. *Don Gestner Collection*

of Fifth Avenue to the bay, and from Broadway to the bluff on the east, was the edge of the timber. In many places along there, and down where the Ross-Higgins store now stands, and up Broadway for a short distance, the ground was seamed with little gullies from three to four feet deep; through some of these water flowed, and others were dry.

Along from about the upper corner of Broadway and Fifth Avenue, where Kalem's store now stands, the timber was more scattered but grew denser; and farther toward the bay, on nearing the river, were clusters of young spruce and many towering cottonwoods. All along the verge of high-tide line, from the east bluff to the river, we found a great lot of driftwood that covered a large area; and among it grew coarse high grass in abundance.

There was no sign of a house of any kind ever having been built in this vicinity nearer than Smuggler's Cove, which we, at that time called Wausuck Bay, after the native who lived there with his family in one of the huts that are there today.

I found places where camps had been made long ago; also very old axe blazes on trees, judging from the way the bark had grown around the cuts and the quantity of pitch surrounding them. I also found quite large spruce trees in which knots had been tied many years ago, while they were very small and pliable, but which did not seem to interfere with their growth except to make double the diameter of the tree at that place.

I found half a dozen wooden fox and bear deadfall traps between the edge of the timber at the bay and where the railroad shops are now built. They were made of round spruce poles five or six feet long and were driven into the ground about two feet in a V-shape very close together. These traps were about two and a half or three feet wide at the entrance, and the same in length and height.

About three feet above this structure, on a line with their entrance, had been fastened with a twisted native-made rope a heavy log some six feet long. The rope at one time led down into the trap and connected with a little lever upon which the bait seemed to have been fastened so that when the animal tried to crawl in to eat it, the lever would spring and the animal was killed or held under the falling log. The Indians had evidently covered these traps with leaves and vegetation to make the surroundings look natural. But when I arrived there, Nature had mantled the old traps with a covering of her own.

In the early days the native family of Smuggler's Cove set their heavy steel traps on both sides of the river and made a round of inspection about every two days. On many occasions they caught cross and red foxes. Several times Mr. Fox's front foot alone was found in a trap; the wily little animal had gnawed himself loose from his cruel fetter. Porcupines were very numerous and could be heard whistling in the trees every morning.

On the west side of the river, about two miles up the stream, I found an old half-finished cottonwood canoe, decayed and covered with moss. I saw one of these canoes made by a stormbound Indian on his way to Haines Mission. It took him about three weeks of steady work to finish it. It was close to sixteen feet long by four feet wide. All he had to work with was an axe and a small native-made adze - an old file fastened to a Z-shaped stick. This tool was used for the finishing

Capt. William Moore shows off his dog team on Broadway. Riding with the captain

touches before the canoe was spread by filling with water brought to near the boiling point with heated rocks. There were no worn trails on this side of the river except those made by animals.

Saltwater ducks were numerous in the bay. We often saw mallards swimming in the creek back of my present residence, and where the courthouse now stands. We frequently dined upon them. This creek is

shewing his six dog team
car Seat + hired man with Revolver

rs. Harriet Pullen, Miss Frances Rogers, and the man Moore hired to guide his team.
J.B. Moore Collection/Rasmuson Library/University of Alaska Fairbanks

a small branch of a stream that has since been filled but which in those days flowed where the barracks are now built and on around the back of my dwelling. Through its waters, during the freshet, we floated most of the logs for my first cabin - which I have since raised and moved some fifty feet west.

We remained there about two months in the fall of 1887. After locating a wharf site - abreast of where our present wharf office now is, and where the slide down the mountain appears down along the shore six hundred feet - we built two log cribs, twelve feet square and fifteen feet high, filled with rock and brush and bolted together. The outer one was at low watermark; both were connected by long spruce stringers. This was our very first starter for a wharf.

By this time winter was upon us. Not having our log house completed we took passage on the schooner *Charlie* with Capt. Healy, who was taking a bale of five thousand dollars' worth of furs to Juneau. Aboard were Mrs. Healy and Mrs. Wallace, a friend from Juneau, who had been visiting Mrs. Healy at Dyea.

It was the most stirring trip in my memory. The schooner had been hauled out and repaired by George Carmack, one of the original discoverers of the Klondike placer claims, who at that time was in Healy's employ at Dyea. During the whole trip we had to take turns, night and day, bailing water and pumping. It took us four days to reach Juneau. We battled a whole night lying off the head of Berner's Bay during a heavy snow storm, while ice floes from the rivers were bumping against and threatening to smash our boat.

On arrival at Juneau, the schooner was beached at high tide. Later we found that a bolt had been left out of one of the auger holes through the planking, and a steady stream of water was pouring in. My father, who had not been seasick for fifty years, as he said at the time, was good and sick on that trip.

We then took passage for Victoria on a steamer called the *Sardonix*, of which my brother-in-law, Capt. Meyers, was master. We returned to Skagway on May 26, 1888, having rowed up from Juneau in a large flat-bottomed boat with more supplies and gear to carry on our work. After finishing our log house, we commenced extending our little wharf. This season we were able to hire two natives, at two dollars per day, to assist us.

We cut piling from thirty to forty feet long and built out from our rock-filled cribs, setting them every ten feet apart and hoisting them straight, by hand, with a Spanish windlass of our own make. We strapped heavy rocks to the piles about five or six feet from the lower end at extreme low tide, after first digging a hole a couple of feet deep in which to set them. Then we bolted the camps across the three; then the stringers, and then we covered the whole with small round spruce poles, for lumber was out of the question this side of Juneau.

In this way we eventually got a structure thirty feet wide by some sixty feet in length, the outermost piles standing in about a foot of water in dead low spring tides. But it served our purpose during the

Capt. Wm. Moore (seated left) built this beautiful home in Skagway. He later sold it to Harriet Pullen, who operated it as the popular Pullen House hotel.

J.B. Moore Collection/Rasmuson Library/University of Alaska Fairbanks

intervening years till we were able to interest my present associates in assisting financially to carry out our plans. This structure stood for six years without repair.

One evening, while sailing into the bay bound from Dyea to Juneau with thirty Yukon miners aboard our large scow-shaped sloop, the *Flying Dutchman*, we saw that our little wharf had all collapsed except for the rock-filled abutments. The piling had been destroyed either by tornadoes or shattered by heavy driftwood.

But to return to the experiences of 1888:

After midnight of July 3rd, or early on the morning of the 4th, our sleep was suddenly disturbed by the barking of dogs that belonged to our native help. Hurriedly dressing and running out of the cabin toward the creek, we were surprised to see a herd of about twenty spike-horn mountain goats, including three or four little lambs. We hurried back, I for my Winchester and my father for a great long Smith and Wesson revolver he had carried all through the Cassiar gold excitement some twenty years before; and then, with one of the natives, we opened fire.

The goats were bewildered at first, and did not run away immediately. In half an hour we shot six large goats and a little lamb; the rest made a wild stampede through the willows and underbrush, across the creek, and up the mountain. The day was the Fourth of July, so we quit work to dress the goats. After salting a lot of the meat, the weather being very warm, we took the balance to the Healys at Dyea. They were then our nearest white neighbors; none others lived within fifteen miles at Haines.

We have always believed that the wolves had run these goats down from the mountains to the flat, though I have since understood that there are times of the year when these goats come down to eat a certain seaweed on the beaches. On a subsequent occasion, when returning from a trip across the channel, we saw many goat tracks on the beach before the tide had come in.

I have also seen bear up the river but none on what is now the town site, though from the enormous tracks I have seen, I could tell they had been over near the river catching salmon.

One day in the summer of 1892, while bound for Haines Mission with two men, one named Murphy, and the other "Skookum Jim" of Klondike fame, the latter succeeded in getting two bears; a tremendous brown one, and the other a two-thirds grown black.

Jim killed them about two miles up in the gulch, where the creek flows from Lake Dewey into the canal. He got back with nearly all his clothes torn off. After killing the black, and wounding the brown bear, he ran out of cartridges. The brown beast turned on him, and Jim, after running the muzzle of his gun down the beast's throat, fought him to a finish. He showed me places on the bear's head where he had hit him with heavy stones and the butt end of his rifle.

Since that day I have always felt as though I had never lost any live bear. It took the three of us to roll and drag the brown bear's carcass to the water and load it into the boat. Then, with both bears in the boat, at Jim's request, we ran up the Chilkoot Inlet, about four miles from Haines Mission, to dress them on the beach and stow the hides under the foredeck of my sloop.

Jim explained that because he was an Interior Indian, the natives of the coast would make him either pay the value of the skins or give them up. We landed them at Chilkoot instead of Haines during the evening. Jim sold them for forty dollars to Mr. Wilson, who ran a branch store there for Healy of Dyea.

For three seasons I took a position at Poindexter's Cannery at Chilkat as fireman during the fishing, and storekeeper and general caretaker of the works during the winter months. Meantime, I visited and worked at my home whenever I could. In the fall of 1892 I went to Juneau, Berner's Bay and Douglas to work in the quartz mines and sawmills. On February 2, 1895, I returned here and remained

Edith Gertrude Moore as a young girl. *Don Gestner Collection*

permanently with my family - which at the time consisted of my wife, and Benny and Gertrude - who had accompanied me on many winter trips in small boats, though the children at that time were very small.

On this return trip I induced seven young men from California - the first party of miners ever to cross the pass with seven tons of freight - to take this White Pass route into the Yukon instead of going by Dyea and the Chilkoot Pass, by assisting them up to the mouth of the first canyon about four miles from here. I hauled their outfit up the canyon with two horses which had been brought over from Dyea on a raft for that purpose. I also cut a trail some two miles in length over a ridge to avoid the falls at the junction of the upper and lower canyons.

In the spring of 1896 I engaged men to work here, and brought in horses, wagons, cows, pigs, fowl and lumber. Later on I had an official survey made of my location of a hundred and sixty acres by Charles Garside, Deputy United States Surveyor of Juneau.

In July of the same year I carried the mail from Juneau to Dyea by sailboat, thence to Forty Mile Creek by way of Chilkoot Pass, and past the mouth of Klondyke River on my way out a few days before the great placer mines were struck. I returned after this second trip to the interior early in September with out-ward mail, which I conveyed to Juneau by sailboat, making the run down there in fourteen hours.

From the spring till the fall of 1897 we employed about fifteen men to construct the old packtrail along the left bank of the river and canyons, crossing and recrossing farther up by bridges and fording the river about half a mile above here. We also made more improvements on the homestead, including a sawmill. We commenced to build our wharf with a hand pile driver, at first, and later got to use a steam driver.

Many of the first stampeders, some of whom I believe are still among us, assisted and worked hard on the old trail in completing it from where we left off to Bennett.

On July 29th, I induced Capt. Carroll to run back here from Dyea with the steamer *Queen*, and he landed about two hundred passengers and one hundred twenty-five tons of freight on our - at that time - small dock. This was the first large steamer and crowd of passengers with freight landed here. Next came the ill-fated *Islander*, in August. Later the *George W. Elder*, *Willamette*, and other steamers, as many know, also landed passengers by the hundreds on lighters and in small boats. The *Willamette* brought the largest list of all, having left the Sound, I believe, with some twelve hundred passengers, and reached here with not many less. No doubt there are many of us who remember the burning of the steamer *Whitelaw*, out in the bay, and the loss many sustained when their entire outfits were destroyed.

S-k-a-g-u-a - Skagua, used to be spelled on all the old maps and charts without the "w" and "y" subsequently inserted in the official way of spelling. It is, of course, an Indian name the meaning of which would take too long to explain in detail. But the name, or at least the explanation of it, would require our English word called "wind" to be used frequently. Skagway is a name very typical of a place where the same air is never breathed twice.

I remember, however, when this place used to be known as "Mooresville," and was referred to by the first newspaper, The Free Press, edited by Mr. Sylvester, who at one time was in business at Skagway.

My father and I were the first residents that Mr. E. C. Hawkins and Sir Thomas Tancrede called upon on their arrival here early in 1898, in the interests of the present railroad company before the first preliminary survey was made. Even after quantities of railroad ties and rails were landed here and piled up near the sawmill, and after track-laying had commenced, there were many people who would not believe that the railroad would ever be put through.

Many boatmen at that time made as high as a hundred dollars a day by inducing stampeders to take their outfits to Dyea, and another crowd to return here, and so on back and forth. Later, the Dyea tramway and Stikine River route proved quite a menace to this route until the former was taken over by the railroad company, and the latter abandoned after several hundreds of thousands of dollars were expended at Wrangell and for the river steamers to ply on the Stikine.

If John Laumeister, our first butcher, were present I would ask our toastmaster to call on him to tell about the moving of our old bunkhouse to the mill site, and about the crowbar and his torn trousers - for which he charged six dollars on my father's meat bill - and with the circumstances with which several of you are familiar.

On our very first visit here and, subsequently many, many times over, my father would tell me and numerous other people in Juneau and elsewhere, how he pictured to himself the future of this place. He never tired of predicting how roads would be built through here; of a little city built here; of steamers on the upper Yukon; and of large steamers, loaded with freight and passengers, docking at the waterfront.

He at times became so enthusiastic in talking to and writing me letters from below that I came to believe in his prophecy. He realized that the summit of the pass was a thousand feet lower than the Chilkoot. I decided to remain here, though in those days, when we mentioned Skagway as likely to be of some importance, the idea was ridiculed by many.

I quite distinctly remember calling on Charlie Dunlap - who, I believe, is present this evening - at his drugstore in Douglas City. I think it was in the fall of 1894 that I talked to him about our location here and of my intention to make an effort to turn the travel every spring and fall this way instead of over the Chilkoot. Mr. Dunlap

Edith Moore (foreground) married Mack A. Gestner and had three children. The youngest, Don, is being held by his father during this picnic scene in Haines in the 1920s. *Don Gestner Collection*

seemed to be favorably impressed with my views, and I believe he felt like coming here with me at that time.

I hope I have not bored you with the length of my paper. It has not dealt with the better-known and more stirring events most of us have experienced in this changing place, but merely with a few stray recollections of a settler on a lonely homestead in the wilderness. Except for a few trips in the spring and fall for the purpose of taking miners to Dyea, steamers rarely came to the head of the inlet in those days. – J.B.M.

Each one of us would put it on when we went to relieve him at his watch at the tiller on our way down to Juneau; by turning up the collar of this great coat to reach way above our caps, we could feel quite comfortable in the coldest weather.

November 22nd and 23rd: Tuesday and Wednesday. Steady rain, steamer Sardonyx has not yet arrived.

November 24th: Thursday. Steamer *Sardonyx* arrived at the Knowles quartz mill across from Juneau and came up Gastineau Channel a short way with a cargo of lumber and coal at 8 a.m.

November 25th: Friday. Cold, frosty weather again and northeaster blowing.

November 26th: Saturday. Took a trip across the channel to the Knowles mill just being completed, to ascertain about what time the *Sardonyx* would be ready to leave for the south. This new mill had steam up for the first time today and worked the machinery, but they do not intend running this winter.

14. FROM JUNEAU TO VICTORIA ON THE *S.S. SARDONYX* (Winter, 1887-1888)

November 27th: Sunday. Bought our tickets at reduced rates from the purser, and got our baggage aboard at the mill. The *Sardonyx* left and steamed across to Juneau, and hove to there for only twenty minutes, while Captain William Meyers, her master, cleared the vessel uptown. Left Juneau at 2 p.m. Encountered a very heavy breeze crossing the Takun Inlet which careened the steamer way over her starboard beam ends.

Passed the big-wheel steamer *Ancon* at 9 p.m. on her way up. Ran at half-speed all night in order to reach Wrangell Narrows by daylight and at the right stage of the tide.

November 28th: Monday. Entered Wrangell Narrows at 8 a.m. Half-tide strong against us. Arrived at Fort Wrangell at noon. Snowing lightly, weather mild. Left Wrangell at 1 p.m.

November 29th: Tuesday. Arrived at Fort Simpson at 9 p.m. Lay there an hour and took on some barrels of fish, also took on board two passengers: Judge Wooten and a Mrs. Anderson, for Victoria. Arrived at Port Essington above the mouth of the Skeena River at 2:30 p.m. and anchored off the wharf there.

The steamer *Boscowitz* was alongside the wharf. Took aboard a Mr. Cunningham and another passenger, also two live cub bears, and left again at 6 p.m.

November 30th: Wednesday. Crossed Millbank Sound at 8 a.m. Comparatively smooth water. Passed Bella Bella at 11 a.m. Entered Queen Charlotte Sound at 3 p.m. Strong easterly breeze. Got off Fort Rupert at 10 p.m.

December 1st: Thursday. Anchored at the entrance to Seymour Narrows at 8 a.m. Strong tide against us. Started again at noon. High water. Had fine water down the Gulf of Georgia.

JUNEAU TO VICTORIA

Arrived at Departure Bay at 8:30 p.m. December 2nd: Friday. Commenced taking on coal at 7 a.m. (one hundred twenty tons), and left again at 11 a.m. Arrived at Victoria, B.C. at 7 p.m., making the trip down from Juneau in a little over five days, including the several stoppages at out-of-course places.

The steamer *Sardonyx* is about a twelve-knot vessel, steel hull, long and narrow beam, and always had to carry a great deal of ballast; if she did not, she would flop over on her beam ends. She was purchased at Liverpool, England, and brought out here for Henry Saunders of Victoria by her present master, Captain William Meyers, my brother-in-law, who married my oldest sister, Henrietta. This was the steamer's first trip since her arrival on this coast.

I remained in Victoria for five months and seven days, which brought us to May 9, 1888. During this period I sketched some maps of the Yukon and lakes and routes, and assisted my father in getting out a report on Upper Yukon and routes into the Interior, for which we were afterward paid two hundred fifty dollars by the provincial government of British Columbia through its chief Commissioner of Land and Works at Victoria, B.C., the Honorable Mr. Vernon.

Our ready cash at home had, by this time, dwindled very low, and this two hundred fifty dollars helped us out greatly. But it was like pulling teeth to get even that much from the government. We also wrote letters to the Ottawa government, setting forth our idea of the important future of the great Yukon territory; its great future as a gold-producing country; its valuable fur-bearing animals; its thousands of miles of navigable waters for large and small light-draught river steamers; the White Pass as a good feasible route for either a pack trail or wagon road, and Skagway Bay as being a good safe harbor and a place for wharves where large ocean steamers could discharge big cargoes. But neither the Ottawa government nor the provincial government of British Columbia seemed interested.

We also tried hard to interest private individuals, offering them, in the way of inducements, an interest in our locations at Skagway, if they could just furnish us a bill of provisions, tools and supplies, and so on, so that we could return and continue our work on the wharf location, and also do some work on the one hundred sixty acres of land we took up there, in the way of putting up some fencework and a couple of houses. But our repeated appeals for assistance from our friends, among whom were several prominent businessmen in the best standing with quite considerable means, were listened to readily enough, but we received no assistance whatever. They all seemed to think that the Yukon, and Alaska, were too far away, and that we were too enthusiastic over the matter and looking too far ahead. No, they could not see it at all as we did.

Meanwhile, time was slipping away, and spring would soon be upon us, so I made up my mind to take out my declaration papers to become an American citizen. I took passage on the steamer *North Pacific* for Port Townsend, went before Judge Swan there, and took the oath, and got my papers. I returned to Victoria the next day on the steamer *George E. Starr*, and had to pay the purser my fare with a small gold nugget I had, for I had no cash left.

Now, having my declaration papers with me, this gave me the lawful right to take up and record locations of land in Alaska. So my father and I began to make preparations to start back north again, then left Victoria.

15. BACK NORTH TO SKAGWAY BAY VIA JUNEAU (May-June, 1888)

May 9, 1888: Wednesday. At 11:30 a.m., we are on the steamship Ancon bound for Skagway Bay, or Mooresville, with a summer's provisions; also purchased blocks, ropes, iron, spikes, nails, iron for splitting shapes, timber dogs, axes, broadaxes, a grindstone and other tools to continue work and extend a little wharf out from the crib we had built, and finish our log cabin. This bill of provisions, including the outfit of tools, tackle, and the rest, cost us one hundred fifty-four dollars, including the freight on same to Juneau City. We should have liked to take up much more stuff, like a good rowboat and a little lumber, but we had no means to do so.

May 14th: Monday. Arrived at Juneau at 9 p.m. after a pleasant and uneventful trip. Took lodgings at the Franklin Hotel. Wrote letters home to Victoria.

May 16th: Wednesday. Got lumber out and commenced building a boat on a foundation near where Charlie Young has a little shop and store, and worked steadily on it for long hours.

May 20th: Sunday. Finished our boat this evening and launched her. Found she was good and tight throughout. She is twenty-seven feet in length overall, five feet in breadth of beam on top, with flaring sides and shovel-nose bow.

Steamship *Ancon* arrived at noon from Sitka and left again for Victoria at 7 p.m.

Up Lynn Canal again from Juneau.

May 21st: Monday. Loaded our boat with all our supplies and started at 1 p.m., taking Mr. Pope and two other men along with us who were bound for the Yukon country.

Took course up Gastineau over the bar as usual; rowed until

midnight in order to reach good camping beach at the old deserted Auk village and camped there.

May 22nd: Tuesday. Got a good early start and made good progress with our oars. But no fair wind. Our boat was pretty heavily loaded, having some two and a half tons of deadweight in her.

May 23rd: Wednesday. Crossed Berner's Bay. Calm weather.

May 24th: Thursday. Rigged up our sail and put down a lee board which we made for the boat to be used in place of a center board. We were now carrying a good, fresh, southeast breeze, but our boat was loaded so deep that we put into shore, cut two good dry logs about two-thirds long as our boat and lashed them securely, one on either side of the boat, which made her ride the sea much more steadily, and we made good time running before the wind with our square sail up. This certainly felt good to us after the heavy rowing.

May 26th: Saturday. Arrived at Mooresville, Skagway Bay, at 9 p.m. Found our wharf as intact as we left it last fall. Hauled our boat up the creek as far as the tide would allow, unloaded her and made temporary camp for the rest of the night.

May 27th: Sunday. Spread our tent and fixed up a comfortable camp, and laid off for the rest of the day.

May 28th: Monday. Commenced cutting and getting out more logs for the log house we started to build up above near the creek last fall, just before leaving here. Also located some trees for wharf logs and short piling. It is difficult to get timber out here because we have no horses, and on the steep side hill in the vicinity of our wharf site, the trees are scrubby and short and taper to a point very quickly, though we have gotten out quite a few logs along there for cribbing, and rolled and slid them down the hill to the beach.

May 29th: Tuesday. Left here at 4 a.m. with our boat to take Mr. Pope and the other two men up to Healy's place at Dyea, where they intend to go inside over that route. Wrote letters home and forwarded them down to Haines Mission by a canoe with Indians, there to be reforwarded to Juneau, thence to Victoria.

Took dinner with Mr. and Mrs. John Healy, and left Dyea again at 1 p.m. Returned Skagway Bay at 4 p.m.

May 30th: Wednesday. Got several small logs out for our

house.

May 31st: Thursday. Chained off and relocated one hundred sixty acres of land reaching from ordinary high tidemark back up along the high bluff on the east side of the bay and toward the Skagway River.

June 1st: Friday. Placed one square of logs in position on our house today.

June 2nd: Saturday. Hired an Indian to work for us at thirty dollars per month and his board; after we furnished him with about three dollars' worth of provisions, he took his departure without commencing to work.

June 3rd: Sunday. Worked all day; got out four large logs for the wharf. Had to use our blocks and tackle to haul them out of the woods into the little creek back up a way from where we are building our house.

June 4th: Monday. Did not get to sleep until one o'clock this morning on account of the pestering mosquitoes. Arose at 9 a.m., got out more logs and gathered them all together in the creek, awaiting the high tides to float some of them down to our wharf site, and some to keep here for our house.

Some of the interior or "Stick" Indians, who came out by way of Dyea, told us that the ice on Lakes Lindeman and Bennett broke up on the 25th of May this spring.

June 5th: Tuesday. Started in to get out a few logs along the high bluff in vicinity of the wharf site.

June 6th: Wednesday. Made up a small raft of logs in readiness to take up creek for our house tonight when the tide comes up. Saw Healy's schooner, *Charlie*, sailing down Lynn Canal along the opposite shore. We could not understand this, as the Healy's had not intimated to us any likelihood of sending the *Charlie* on any trip.

Shortly after this we saw several canoes, with Indians paddling swiftly down the channel, headed for Haines Mission... We could not understand the reason for this also.

June 7th: Thursday. Got out several fairly good logs for the wharf today.

June 8th: Friday. Hauled some house logs up the creek today and placed a couple of squares on. Wearing gum boots, caught twenty small trout in the creek with my bare hands in back of our unfinished house; made a good dinner out of them. They

103

averaged about seven inches in length.

June 9th: Saturday. Saw a small steamer which we made out to be the *Lucy* (we had formerly seen her around Juneau and Douglas at Treadwell's), passing up the canal today at noon and headed for Dyea. Thinking that she was taking miners up to the Yukon, we hurriedly launched our boat, and rowed up the channel heading for Dyea; also we wanted to see if there was any mail for us, and to forward some mail down by this little steamer.

16. THE INDIAN BATTLE
AT DYEA (June 4-5, 1888)

After rounding the point of the bay above here and nearing the *Lucy*, where she was at anchor off the sand flats at Dyea, we noticed that her decks were crowded with men armed with rifles. Pulling up along side of her in our boat, we recognized several citizens whom we had met and known at Juneau before, and on inquiring as to what was up, we were informed that there had been a big fight near Healy's Post between several members of the Sitka tribe and the Chilkats. And while we were lying there, an Indian named Kosko, who had been shot in the leg, was brought out in a canoe and placed aboard the *Lucy* to be taken to Juneau later.

The following describes the occurrence:

Quite a number of Indians from Sitka had come to Dyea to pack there for miners going in over that route. This was strongly resented by the Chilkat tribe, as natives of Haines and Dyea are called; and the second chief of the Chilkats, named Kla-Naut, about thirty-eight years old, demanded that the Sitka Indians should either desist from infringing on his people's rights there, or pay him thirty per cent on all goods packed by the Sitka Indians over the Chilkoot Summit to Lake Lindeman. This would amount to four dollars and fifty cents on every hundred pounds, for the miners were paying fifteen dollars per hundredweight from Dyea to the lake.

This the Sitka chief absolutely refused to do, and put Chief Kla-Naut of the Chilkats at defiance, and ordered his own men to proceed to strap on their packs. Sitka Jack's son was also there with his father, a boy about sixteen years old, and was about to strap on a hundred pound pack, when Kla-Naut went up to the boy and slapped him in the face.

At this time, there were about one hundred Indians (men),

all told, assembled a few hundred feet above Healy's store and dwelling, which adjoined. Sitka Jack, on seeing Kla-Naut strike his son, jumped up and made a run at Kla-Naut, and a fierce hand-to-hand fight ensued between these two. Both were wounded by each other's knives. When separated, the Sitka chief was escorted and half-carried to a little house nearby and placed in the attic, and a guard of several of his followers was stationed around and near the cabin.

Chief Jack lay up there in the attic all night (This was on June 4th). He was attended by several of his men and women who did all they could for him in helping to staunch the blood from his wounds, and kept him posted continually on what was going on outside.

Chief Kla-Naut was also wounded severely, but not as badly as Chief Jack. There was a great to-do all night long, and many fights between members of these two tribes took place. Later, toward morning, it was decided by the majority on each side to have the matter settled by both sides, forming in line with their respective chiefs at the head, and force the issue by fighting it out.

The news of this proposition was carried to Jack and Kla-naut, and a few hours later Chief Jack and Chief Kla-Naut appeared at the head of their respective followers in front of Healy's post, a hewn log structure about twenty-five feet by forty feet wide and two stories high. Each one of the chiefs was painted up with his war paint and otherwise decorated, and they advanced toward each other with drawn knives, followed by their men, some of whom had rifles, besides their knives.

A fierce battle took place. Many were severely wounded, and several killed on both sides. The Sitka forces were considerably less in number than the Chilkats.

While the fight was in progress, the two chiefs, Kla-Naut and Sitka Jack, closed with each other in a desperate struggle, slashing at each other with their knives, and the blood from their previous wounds started out again from under their bandages.

Capt. Healy, Mrs. Healy, Mr. Wilson, a sailor, and a young man called White and his wife were in the store. Healy stood near the front entrance and the rest of them at the rear of the store, when it appeared that the Sitka chief was getting the best of the fight. The rest of the Indians, at this time, had for some reason or other let up in their fighting - no doubt they were too interested in the outcome of the fight between their chiefs, for those two were off to one side, more to themselves.

All at once Kla-Naut staggered, and made a rush to enter the store but did not succeed in gaining entrance, for Chief Jack's forces demanded of Healy that Kla-Naut should not be given protection in the store and threatened to burn down his post and buildings if he sheltered Kla-Naut in the post, so Healy gave up Kla-Naut.

Then the two chiefs went at each other again, both losing blood freely now, but bent on getting the other's life. All at once, Chief Jack dealt Kla-Naut a finishing blow over the head with the butt-end of a rifle that one of his men handed him, braining Kla-Naut, who fell to the ground. A second later Chief Kla-Naut's son, a youngster about seventeen years old, slipped behind Chief Jack and drove a knife into his vitals to the hilt.

Both chiefs were carried off to nearby shacks by their respective followers and died there a short time afterward. Then there was a great to-do: neither side had a chief or leader.

17. THE CHILKATS THREATEN TO BURN HEALY'S POST BUILDINGS AND DWELLING (June, 1887)

The followers of Chief Kla-Naut now went to Healy and demanded a large number of blankets and other things in payment for the life of their chief, saying that had Kla-Naut been allowed to remain in his post, protected and not given up again, he would not have been killed. Healy barricaded all the doors and windows and refused to accede to their demands, whereupon the Chilkoots threatened to set fire to the post buildings.

Healy at once went to the sailor, whom he had on his schooner of late, and made arrangements for him and Mr. Wilson to proceed on the following morning to Juneau, with all haste, for assistance. This was the 5th of June and night was at hand, but it was still quite light at this time of the year. Healy, Wilson, Mr. White, and the sailor then proceeded to cut little holes through the hewn logs of the store building, commanding a range outside from all sides and ends of the structure, and kept watch all night with rifles at the ready. They noticed that the Indians came near often, and it was quite apparent that some of them wanted to fire the post, while others, more timid with fear of future consequences to themselves, would not agree to it.

This was a long, miserable night of suspense for the inmates of the post and cause of great fright to Mrs. Healy and Mrs. White, the latter lady being in a delicate condition at the time. At last, the night wore away without further serious trouble, and in the morning Wilson and the sailor set sail down the canal for Juneau with a good, fair wind, making fast time. This was the 6th of June.

When the Indians saw the schooner leaving with Mr. Wilson and the sailor, and heard that she was going to Juneau for assistance, there was a scurry among them and many piled into their canoes and put out down the canal for Haines Mission and some for Sitka, leaving but a few at Dyea. All this, then, explains our having seen the *Charlie* sailing down past Skagway, followed shortly afterward by a number of canoes.

To return to the arrival of *Lucy* at Dyea: when Wilson arrived at Juneau and called for assistance, the *Lucy*, being there with steam up, was immediately sent out with twenty-two sworn-in armed deputies for Dyea, and immediately on her arrival at Dyea many little white flags were to be seen stuck up on poles by the Indians as a sign of truce.

Mr. Healy afterward told us that he did not think it necessary to send (nor could he have very well sent) word to us at Skagway of the trouble.

The Indian Koskoe recovered from the gunshot wound in his leg, but walked lame always afterward, and some of the other Indians who were wounded died later. The *Lucy* remained over at Dyea when we left there for Skagway again, after seeing Mr. Healy on shore. We arrived back at camp at 6 p.m.

We learned afterward that the cause of the fight at Dyea was among the Indians themselves and was allowed to die out eventually; and the Sitka Indians, as well as the Chilkats, packed over the summit. But I do know that in many cases, they afterward paid a percentage of their earnings to the Chilkats.

I have often seen, and knew many of the Indians who had been in this fight, particularly Chief Kla-Naut, Koskoe, and Kla-Naut's son. The latter young fellow spoke English quite fluently, but was very tricky and unreliable in any business dealings.

June 10th: Sunday. Worked all day rafting logs for our house and placing them in position; have only had one shower of rain since arriving here.

June 11th: Monday. Weather cloudy, and a strong southerly wind during the forenoon.

June 12th: Tuesday. Had considerable rain this evening.

June 13th: Wednesday. Raining all day. The schooner *Charlie* anchored in the bay at 6 a.m. and landed a few pieces of casing lumber and shingles from Juneau. Mrs. Healy is to leave on the *Charlie* in a few days, bound for the new discovery of Black

Sand beach placers at Yakutat Bay to the westward.

Received a letter from my sister Minnie by the *Charlie* from Victoria.

June 14th: Thursday. Commenced putting rafters out of small poles up on our house this morning. Two canoes bound for Haines Mission put in here for shelter, it blowing a strong southwester.

June 15th: Friday. Cut a doorway in our log house and cased it up. Chinked some of the spaces between the logs. A large canoe put in here for shelter this evening, for it still blew hard up the canal. Most of the Indians are now leaving Dyea for Haines Mission, since the packing is about all over now.

June 16th: Saturday. Did not get to sleep until 4 a.m. on account of mosquitoes. Moved over into our log house this afternoon before it was completed, putting up our tent within the square of the log walls. Still blowing strong southerly wind.

June 17th: Sunday. Raining hard all morning. Rafted some more timber and poles to our house, and wrote letters to my brother Johnny and to the Minister of Customs at Ottawa. Hired two Indians at thirty-five dollars per month and their board, one of whom was Nan-Suk, the same one we had here with us last fall; the other is named Billy.

June 18th: Monday. Our two Indians started to work this morning. We finished putting up the rafters this evening. Received letters, papers and photographs from home in Victoria.

June 19th: Tuesday. Fine, very warm weather all day. Did considerable work at chinking the logs all day.

June 20th: Commenced working on our wharf again. Blowing hard, and rainstorms.

June 21st: Thursday. Fine weather in forenoon; afternoon storming and raining again from the south. Gave our two Indians a fresh supply of provisions.

June 22nd: Friday. Commenced placing our posts, or piling, one at a time in the wharf; three in a bent, nine feet apart, and twelve feet out toward the water from our rock and brush-filled crib, setting the foot of these posts down in the rocks and then bracing the three diagonally, and also bracing the whole bent to the crib. Then we piled quantities of rock around the foot of these posts.

June 23rd: Saturday. Got the second bent of these posts

placed in the wharf, twelve feet out from the first bent. The posts in this bent are twenty-seven feet long now, leaving spare end to saw off later.

June 24th: Sunday. Laid off today, washed our clothes, and took a bath.

June 25th: Monday. Hewed out a large cap for the first bent, made a plumb bob level, and nailed a straight across the three posts in the first bent, and sawed them off top. Placed our cap and bored it, cut a number of three-quarter round iron bolts, and bolted cap down on the top of the bent. Rained hard all morning. Afternoon fine weather.

June 26th: Tuesday. Some nails, and a few bundles more of shingles, and a padlock we had sent for, arrived today from Juneau. Also two letters.

June 27th: Wednesday. Got out some more timber for wharf.

June 28th: Thursday. Hewed out a cap about eight by ten inches and twenty feet long for the second bent.

June 29th: Friday. Bolted down the cap on the second bent and did other work.

June 30th: Saturday. Got one post, or pile, up in the outer and last bent. Mr. Wilson and his bride came down here in a little canoe today from Dyea to visit us. They were just recently married at Juneau.

My father was standing on one of the bents on some loose poles when Mr. Wilson and his wife started back to Dyea, and in bidding us good bye, Mr. Wilson said, "Well, I hope the undertaking you folks have started here will fulfill your expectations and turn out all right, but I am afraid you are losing time and energy here in this place." These were the same discouraging remarks we always heard about our Skagway Bay wharf and land location. And indeed, at times I really felt as those who spoke that way to us did, and often was sorely tempted to give it all up.

July 1st: Sunday. Laid off all day and took a good rest, which we needed, for this work in the rain and windstorms, and wearing oilskin coats, and heavy hip gum boots, and floundering in the water among the slippery rocks on the beach, is pretty hard.

July 2nd: Monday. Lashed three rocks, weighing about seventy-five pounds each, with large strands of new, heavy manilla rope, notching in the edges of the rocks first with a

111

sledgehammer, and then placing some gunnysacking around the rocks first, so that the rope lashing would not slip off or chafe through.

Then we tied these rocks with another strong rope, about five feet from the foot, or lower end of a pile, which was thirty-two feet long and eighteen inches at the butt, or lower end. We rigged up a Spanish windlass with our double blocks and ropes, and tried to place this pile out in about ten feet of water at extreme low tide, with heel ropes and top guys, but could not get it in position. So had to give up reaching out into the water to any depth with the crude equipment we had.

18. A MIDNIGHT VISIT FROM A BAND OF MOUNTAIN GOATS (July 3, 1888)

July 3rd: Tuesday. Was aroused from sleep this morning at one o'clock by the loud and fierce barking of the dogs belonging to our Indian Nan-Suk. On getting up and hurriedly throwing on our clothes to ascertain the cause of this disturbance, we were met at the entrance to our house by our Indian, Nan-Suk, who had rushed over from his tent right near our cabin. He asked for our Winchester rifle, saying, "Sheep! Sheep! Mountain sheep. Plenty!"

We handed him our gun, and my father snatched up his long ivory-handled Smith and Wesson six-shooter he carried all through the Cassiar country in 1873-1874. We all started for the rear of our cabin right near the creek, and were astonished to see there, perhaps thirty mountain goats, large and small, scampering through the brush and willows to within forty feet of our cabin; some were jumping into the creek, which was about three feet in depth. Nan-Suk had by this time fired several shots, and my father also was blazing away at the sheep.

Some of the animals seem to be dumbfounded, not knowing which way to run, and the dogs were barking and scurrying about and chasing them; when, all at once, a very large goat started across the creek past the house. It appeared to be wounded, and dropped not far from the front entrance.

My father and I went up to this monster male goat, the largest I ever saw, and stooped down to drag him to one side. All at once, having apparently recovered from being dazed by the shot, he sprang at us, knocking me down. My father blazed away at him again two or three times, then the goat fell dead.

By this time we could not see any more live goats in the close

113

vicinity, but could hear the dogs still barking farther away down toward the mouth of the little creek where we first camped about one-third way to our wharf site. We all started out then to reconnoiter in the vicinity of a clump of brush and willows across the creek at the rear of our cabin, where we first saw the goats, and found scattered around in different places, five full-grown goats and one little lamb lying dead, aside from the large one we had the tussle with close to the cabin. He weighed fully two hundred pounds.

We decided that this killing was not bad, all having taken place in the short space of not more than a half an hour, and congratulated ourselves on being so lucky as to get so much nice fresh meat.

Our Indian, Nan-Suk, was simply jumping with glee over it all, and started down with our rifle to follow the now far-off sound of his barking dogs. But he returned half an hour later saying, "Goats too far, too far. He gone up mountain." We then proceeded to drag and pack the five goats and the little lamb across the creek and placed the seven of them within the walls of our cabin.

Shortly afterward the dogs returned, completely tired out by their long chase up the mountain after the rest of the goats. We retired to our beds to sleep, and Nan-Suk went to his tent with his dogs.

These are regular, spike-horn goats. They have two black horns slightly curving back to a point, some eight to ten inches long with not much spread. They have long, shaggy, white wool or rather, more like wavy hair, and the males have a high hump between the foreshoulders, and their hoofs are cloven. We are strongly of the opinion that these goats were either driven down by the wolves, or that they came down to munch a certain kind of seaweed on the beach here for the salt in it, which we understand they do sometimes.

19. THE CHILKAT BLANKET AND WINTER STEAMING FROM VICTORIA (July, 1888 - April, 1889)

The wool or hair of these animals is used by the natives in this part of Alaska to make into yarn, which is afterward made into the noted Chilkat blanket. A great deal of the yarn is first dyed with native-made dyes, and afterward woven into the blanket in fantastic figures representing the legends of the different tribes.

These blankets are of different sizes, usually from four to six feet in width, straight across on top, and with a gentle circular shape at the bottom, or lower edge, with long fringes of this goat wool yarn hanging down about eight inches. The fringe is always of the natural color.

These blankets are tightly woven, and are thick and heavy; and it takes about four to six months and often longer to weave a good-sized one. There are only a few native women who know how to weave these blankets. The average price for a fair-sized Chilkat blanket is fifty, and often seventy to one hundred and fifty dollars for a large-sized, extra well-made one.

These blankets are highly prized among the natives, and always represent just so much money to them.

The U.S. gunboat *Pinta* passed up the channel today on her way to Dyea, and passed back down again this afternoon on a trip of investigation regarding the recent Indian trouble and fight at Dyea.

Worked half a day on the wharf. The rest of the day we dressed the goats and salted a quantity of the meat. Saw a stray lamb way up high on the bluff above the wharf site, but we did not care to take the time to hunt it.

July 4th: Wednesday. Worked all day and got the last pile in the outer bent placed in position and weighted with slung rock at the foot, and braced it temporarily.

July 5th: Thursday. Our two Indians wanted to quit work, so we went up to Healy and Wilson's post at Dyea and settled up with them by giving them orders on Messrs. Wheelock and Flannery of Juneau for their pay, amounting to thirty-eight dollars and fifty cents for which we had previously arranged.

July 6th: Friday. Wrote letters home and paid out three dollars for meals and four dollars for one of our Indians for boots. Gave Healy and Wilson a lot of our fresh mountain goat meat, then returned to our camp at Skagway.

July 7th: Saturday. Finished placing shakes on one side of the roof of our cabin. Very strong southerly wind blowing all day.

July 8th: Sunday. Was obliged to put in some extra pole rafters on the other side of the house in order to work our shingles in. House will be shaked on one side of the roof, and shingled on the other side.

July 9th: Monday. Still blowing. Heavy southerly gale. Went down to the wharf this forenoon to make secure the outer three piles.

July 10th: Tuesday. At about 1 a.m. the wind calmed down, but at noon it started up again as usual. Finished shingling and shaking the house today.

July 11th: Wednesday. Hauled a large hewn cap onto the inner part of the wharf this forenoon, filed two crosscut saws in the afternoon, and finished digging a trench around our house and banking up the ground al around the lower logs.

July 12th: Thursday. Put up more braces on the piling.

July 13th: Friday. Worked during the forenoon on the house, and in the afternoon on the wharf.

July 14th: Saturday. Sawed off the tops of the three piles in the outer bent, bolted down the cap on them, and laid two stringers on the top of the caps.

July 15th: Sunday. Laid off for a rest. Strong southerly wind still, but generally commencing to blow about noon or a little after.

July 16th: Monday. Made a platform of poles six feet wide on the wharf this forenoon. Raining heavily all day.

July 17th: Tuesday. Worked until 3 p.m. on the wharf, and then went to our house and did some chinking. The weather for the last three weeks or so has been almost a continual string of wind from southward.

July 18th: Wednesday. Placed more stringers on wharf.

July 19th: Thursday. Bored and bolted the stringers down to the caps with three-quarter-inch iron bolts, twenty-two inches long.

July 20th: Friday. Commenced getting out a few long fender piles and long side, or corner brace piles. Also started to rig up with guy ropes a pole derrick of two heavy poles twenty feet long, to which to attach our blocks and tackle and leading to our Spanish windlass to hoist these long sticks.

July 21st: Saturday. Completed rigging the derrick. Weather fairly good.

July 22nd: Sunday. Made a new windlass out of a heavy round piece of tree about four feet long and ten inches in diameter. Set in a heavy stand and crossbars to heave round on, to wind the rope up leading through the double block at top of derrick. Wrote some letters and forwarded them by Johnny Riley to Haines Mission on his way from Dyea down there in a canoe.

July 23rd: Monday. Got out some long fender braces for corners of outer end of wharf.

July 24th: Tuesday. Could not find our boat this morning anywhere in the bay. We had to build a small raft to cross the mouth of the Skagway River in order to reach the westerly side, and struck out with our rifles over hills and mountains and through and over masses of windfall timber and around bluffs to reach Healy and Wilson's at Dyea. Passed a night in the woods without covering or anything to eat.

July 25th: Wednesday. After making many signals in the way of fires, firing rifle shots, and waving a white rag high up on a stick from a high point where we were up the Dyea River, away on the right-hand shore of the bluffs near Dyea, Mr. Wilson came downstream in a little canoe and took us across the river and up to his post, where we got an old canoe and fixed it up.

July 26th: Thursday. Left Healy and Wilson's place at Dyea this forenoon. Our canoe leaked as fast as one could bail out the water. Arrived back at Skagway and found that the Indian named

George had found our boat way down toward Haines Mission and brought it back for us. We hired this Indian to work at two dollars per day and board.

July 27th: Friday. Placed two long fender braces in position, one at each outer corner of the wharf, with the butt ends out ten feet or so from the foot of the outer corner piles, and the small end of the fender piles or bracers bolted to the corner piles, and then lashed it well with manilla rope.

July 28th: Saturday. Hoisted another fender brace, placed it in position, and bolted it.

July 29th: Sunday. Commenced making preparations to start for Juneau again. Made two sails for our boat and fixed her up, and also made complete masts for her.

July 30th: Monday. Hoisted some heavy logs on top of the wharf for future stringers and to make weight to help hold the structure well down during high tides and next winter's gales. Also threw a quantity of brush around the foot of the fender piles and weighted it down with heavy rocks.

July 31st: Tuesday. Put some bolts in the fender braces and cleared our ropes and Spanish windlass and left them on top of the pole platform on the wharf.

August 1st: Wednesday. Packed our necessary gear-tent and other stuff- into the boat, locked up our log cabin with its few odds and ends, and left Skagway for Healy and Wilson's at 4 p.m., taking our Indian, George, with us. On reaching Dyea we paid him twelve dollars and seventy-five cents for labor and the recovering of our boat. Mr. Wilson advanced this amount to us, and in return we gave Healy and Wilson an order on Wheelock and Flannery of Juneau.

August 2nd: Thursday. Left Healy and Wilson's at Dyea at 9 a.m., bound for Juneau. Struck a head wind one mile south of our place, Skagway, and had to camp, anchoring our boat with a long trip line.

August 3rd: Friday. Got under way at 1 a.m. Carried by a very light northerly (fair) breeze for an hour, when it died out altogether. Took to our oars, then, and arrived at Haines Mission at 9:30 a.m. Left there again at 11 a.m. Anchored at 4 p.m. about eight miles below, or south of the Mission, the flood tide being against us, and light southerly head wind.

August 4th: Saturday. Got under way at 2 a.m. Carried by a

light northerly breeze down Lynn Canal to within twelve miles of Berner's Bay, when the wind sprang up again from the southward. Anchored again.

August 5th: Sunday. Started at a little after midnight. Head wind all day. Crossed Berner's Bay, rowing hard all the time, and anchored seven miles below (or south) of this bay at 7 p.m.

August 6th: Monday. Started at 1 a.m. on the ebb tide and rowed down to within nine miles of Auk Village, where we went ashore and camped for the night.

August 7th: Tuesday. Made a start at 1:30 a.m. and rowed to Auk Village, where we got light leading winds and were carried down all the way over the shoals of the bar to Juneau, arriving there at 7 p.m. We met several canoes and rowboats going to and fro over the bar at high water at 1 p.m.

From August 7th, the date of our arrival at Juneau City, up to and including August 16th, we remained here at Juneau after stowing away our stuff, tent and boat.

August 17th: Friday. Bade my father good-bye and hired out to Mr. F. H. Poindexter (a cannery man) to work at his fishery and cannery at Pyramid Harbor, Chilkat, Alaska, near the mouth of the Chilkat River, and a few miles south of Haines, or just across the peninsula, for forty dollars per month. Left Juneau on the little steamer *Lillian*, the cannery company's boat, for Chilkat at 11 a.m. Bill and Steve York, two brothers, also some other men hiring out, were taking passage at the same time.

August 18th: Saturday. Arrived at Mr. Poindexter's salmon cannery, called the Chilkat Packing Company, at 1 a.m.

I remained at the cannery for two months, working in different capacities: hewing timber for foundations for extensions to the cannery, setting posts for the same, and at odd times as boat puller on the fishing boats.

October 17th: Tuesday. I was paid off today with one hundred dollars, at the rate of fifty dollars per month instead of forty dollars. Mr. Poindexter seemed well pleased with my work, and after squaring up a little bill at the cannery store, my cash in hand amounted to ninety dollars.

October 18th: Wednesday. I left here (Pyramid Harbor) together with several other fishermen and cannerymen on the

Pacific Coast Company's steamship *Idahoe*, Captain Hunter in command, bound for Victoria. Having been hired at Juneau, my fare back to Juneau was paid by the cannery company. Mr. Poindexter and his wife also took passage, bound for California.

The Idahoe, on this trip, went around by way of Sitka first, thence to Juneau. Before reaching Juneau, I went to Captain Hunter and asked for a chance to work my way down from there to Port Townsend or Victoria, and he arranged it with Mr. Bradley, the first mate. And Capt. Hunter told me I could ship on the Idahoe as deckhand for the winter if I desired, and have a chance to work up shortly to quartermaster. This proposition I took under consideration.

October 21st: Saturday. Arrived at Juneau in the forenoon. My father dame aboard to see me and Capt. Hunter. At this time my father was engaged in building a sloop-rigged scow, fifteen feet in beam and some forty-five feet in length, with a large center board, which he called the *Flying Dutchman*. I handed my father thirty dollars out of my earnings at the cannery. This left me sixty dollars.

The *Idahoe*, after lying at Juneau for an hour, proceeded across the channel to the Treadwell mine wharf to discharge two hundred fifty tons of coal. This was where I came in, working my way down in the hold shoveling coal into the large wooden tubs which were then hoisted up and dumped on the dock. I was not aware that the steamer had this coal for Treadwell's.

At noon, four or five of us at a time would get into one of these large, iron-bound wooden coal tubs and were hoisted to the between decks for our dinner, where I and all the deckhands would stand around a long narrow swinging table and eat our meal from the customary tin plates, drink our tea from large tin cups amid the rattling of same and loud coarse talk and swearing and scuffing of these men.

Mr. and Mrs. Poindexter passed me on the upper deck today and did not know me. I was black all over with thick coal dust.

The *Idahoe* on this trip south called in to every cannery on the coast, I believe, and took on over eight hundred tons of canned salmon. There were salmon cases piled in every bit of spare freight room on the vessel. To me it was a well earned fare. I wore a black derby hat, and the deckhands made a football of it down in the hold.

It was the custom to scrub down the decks and play the hose on them every morning at five o'clock. So one morning, having tipped the steerage steward to allow me to sleep in a spare bunk in his room, I thought I would sleep a while, when I heard, just on the deck above me, two of the deckhands stop scrubbing with their brooms, and one remarked, "I wonder where that young fellow Moore is that's working his way down." The other deckhand remarked, "Yes, that's so. I'll go and look for him."

Presently, I heard the fellow coming, and soon he was at my door and then in the room. Whenever a man undertakes to work his passage on a freight and passenger steamer he earns his fare to the full extent, for the deckhands never give one who is working his passage any peace. I earned my thirty dollars steerage fare to the full extent of this trip.

October 28th: Saturday. Arrived at Port Townsend this evening. I went to Captain Hunter and told him I was ready to help discharge cargo, if that was the custom. But he said no, I had done all that was expected of one working his passage. So I bade him good bye.

October 29th: Sunday. Left here (Port Townsend) for Victoria, B.C., on the steamer *North Pacific*, and arrived home this evening. Remained in Victoria with my mother for a month, living over James Bay on Superior Street.

November 29th: Engaged as a deckhand at forty dollars per month on board the old steamer *Cariboo Fly*, owned by Henry Saunders, Capt. William Meyer (my brother-in-law), master. Left Victoria the same morning, after helping to load cargo, for the northern ports of British Columbia and Queen Charlotte Island.

Arrived back at Victoria on December 11th, discharged freight, loaded up again, and left on the second trip on December 14th, returning to Victoria on December 22nd. Continued my work off-and-on aboard the *Cariboo Fly*, during which time I made two more trips north; one through Skidigate Channel, where we heard the news of the total loss of the schooner Skeena, together with ten Indians and some white men, including young Jimmy Cunningham, son of Robert Cunningham of Port Essington, and a schoolmate of mine. The Captain and one Indian boy were saved. We found some good specimens of coal in a harbor where a location was taken up by Mr. Henry Saunders of Victoria for a black cod fishing station.

121

February 20th: (1889) The steamer *Cariboo Fly*, being laid up for the winter, I and the rest of the crew were paid off.

March 5th: Received a letter from Mr. Poindexter, my former employer, dated March 1, 1889, San Francisco, engaging me for the coming season at his cannery at Chilkat, at fifty dollars per month, and advising me to be in readiness to meet him and his son Theodore at the outer dock in Victoria on April 1st. My fare to Chilkat to be paid by the cannery company.

April 1st: Bade my mother good bye, and in company with my youngest sister, Gertrude, and my little nephew, Franky Moore, then about three years old, I walked down to Rithetts outer dock, where the steamer Carona, with Mr. Poindexter and son aboard, was just pulling into the wharf. Kissed my sister and little Franky good bye, and left Victoria once more for Chilkat, Alaska, at 10:30 a.m. during a strong southwest wind. Arrived at Departure Bay at 7:30 p.m. to load four hundred fifty tons of coal.

April 2nd: Left Departure Bay at 11 p.m.

April 3rd: Passed through Seymour Narrows at 6:30 a.m. Fine weather. Passed Alert Bay at 1 p.m. Passed the steamer Maude at 2:30 p.m., bound south off Fort Rupert, which is near the northernmost end of Vancouver Island.

Crossed Queen Charlotte Sound. Sea not very heavy. Entered Fitzhugh Sound at 5:30 p.m. Crossed Millbank Sound at 11:30 p.m.

April 4th: Passed up through Granville Channel. Weather very misty. Anchored at 5 p.m. off Fort Simpson for the night. Weather thick.

April 5th: Got under way at 5 a.m. Rounded Cape Fox at 7 a.m.; passed into Loring (or Nah-Hah) Bay. Put off some freight at a cannery four miles above Fort Wrangell.

April 6th: Our steamer ran ashore this morning at six o'clock when about halfway through Wrangell Narrows on the ebb tide, and in a short time Carona was left almost high and dry. This vessel is apparently hard to handle. Besides that, she has not been on even keel since leaving Victoria, but always carries a list to port or starboard. This is her first trip north.

Weather still raw and cold, with rain. Tried to back our vessel off at 6 p.m. at high tide, but could not yet move her. Put out anchors abreast, all ready for the morning high tide.

April 7th: Sunday. Succeeded in backing our steamer off at 6 a.m. and proceeded on our way again. Strong, fair wind now blowing. Arrived at Juneau wharf at 3 p.m. Put out some fifty tons freight there, then went across to Treadwell's dock and unloaded some two hundred tons coal.

April 8th: Monday. Left Treadwell's for Chilkat at 5:30 p.m.

April 9th: Tuesday. Arrived at the cannery at Chilkat at 3 a.m. This time Mr. Poindexter and his associates are located on the opposite shore of the inlet from Pyramid Harbor.

20. WORKING IN THE HAINES CANNERY (1889-1890)

I started working in and around this cannery in different capacities: building scows, repairing boats, building net racks, and assisting the engineer, Jim Cox, with the machinery. And when the actual fishing season commenced, I was boatpuller for a while; then later I was sent over to the mouth of the Chilkoot River with a stock of general merchandise and trading goods on board of our large schooner the *Flying Dutchman*, which my father had built below Juneau near Taku Inlet during the preceding winter. Here we anchored, and lived aboard the schooner.

My duties were to tally all the salmon caught by the natives and other fisherman and deposited on the deck of our schooner, and pay for same. The cannery company's steamer came from Chilkat once or twice per day to take the fish to the cannery. I remained here at Chilkoot till the salmon season (which is short here) was about over. Then I assisted in putting up a large foundation of heavy posts for a new cannery which, however, never was completed.

Our company put in three miles of nine-inch iron piping, connected up by short lengths reaching from tidewater up to the outlet of Chilkoot Lake, and built around the edge of the river with enough fall to run a good stream of water through it. In this way, large quantities of salmon were caught up there and deposited into this large pipe, and carried down to us at tidewater. A man named Bigelow, or Long Shorty, as he was most commonly known and called, was in charge of this pipe-flume system at the upper end, where he bought the salmon from the Indians.

Later, I was transferred back to the cannery at Chilkat, and after turning in my accounts to the company, I took the job of fireman, including the duties of attending to the large retorts. I continued at this work till the end of the packing season, after helping to load and check off what cases of salmon there were left on to scows, thence to the steamer that called for them. All our fishing nets and boats were now stowed away in the cannery for the winter.

I was then transferred to the company's store to take inventory of their stock of general merchandise, and offered the position of taking charge of the store and being caretaker of the company's whole cannery property. At this time, Mr. Poindexter and his associates had purchased a new and very speedy steamer called the *Puritan*, for she was too much of a fuel eater. Our schooner, the *Flying Dutchman*, was hauled up on the beach near the cannery at highest tide and moored there for the approaching winter.

Now came the point in my existence, as will be seen later, which had a great deal to do with my future life. I had promised the company to remain here in charge for the winter. But as I saw the preparations being made, and the fueling up of the steamer *Puritan* for her farewell trip below, I went to Mr. Poindexter and to my father and declared that I too wanted to return home to Victoria. This was the first week in October (1889).

Well, I was argued out of my desire to go below by both my father and Mr. Poindexter; the former saying that while there I could keep in touch, and be posted on conditions regarding our holdings and location at Skagway Bay. At any rate, the day was won against me. I agreed to remain at the cannery, and it was with a feeling of great loneliness and homesickness that I saw the Puritan steam out of the inlet at nine o'clock one clear, frosty morning. And as she disappeared from view way beyond Davidson's Glacier and headed down Lynn Canal, I turned and walked back up to my little cabin on the brow of the hill, just above the cannery.

At this time there were three white men occupying cabins near the cannery, and were to have the privilege of knitting fish nets by the piece at so much per fathom and of a certain size mesh, usually six-inch mesh. One of these men was Tommy Symons, nicknamed "Mouse-hole Tom" on account of his small, light build. Another was a big man named Nick Barbarazzo, an Italian; and a man named Heipe; and a six-and-a-half foot, good-natured Swede called Long Peter.

Further up the inlet, about two miles from our cannery, now lived Captain John Healy and his wife. They also had a trading store there, having moved down from Dyea where they left Mr. Wilson, the other partner, at their other post.

Aside from Mrs. John Healy there was no other white lady nearer than Juneau, a distance of one hundred miles, except the occasional visit of Miss Sarah Dickinson at Haines Mission - a very accomplished young, half-breed lady who had been a pupil at St. Helen's Hall at Portland, Oregon for seven years - and the wife of the Rev. W.W. Warne, who also resided at Haines Mission.

There were, I should judge, perhaps three to five hundred natives residing in and around this near vicinity, including those at Haines Mission, a distance of only three miles across the peninsula by trail. The outlook appeared dismal to me, and the time dragged heavily. My duties were not enough to keep me continuously busy.

Snow began to fall now. In a few days a howling southeaster would blow furiously up Lynn Canal and on up this inlet, then in one or two days the snow would be gone again. It was now nearing the end of October. Among the other instructions I had from the company was to have the natives cut a great lot of cordwood, and haul and pile it up close to the cannery during the winter, for which I was to pay three dollars per cord in trade tickets from the store, for the inventory showed us to have about ten thousand dollars worth of general merchandise-clothing, groceries, blankets, calicoes, and so forth. I was to pay the natives in tickets, of which we had a large quantity printed, ranging from ten cents to one dollar. With these, natives could buy stuff. In this way, the cannery really got its wood for one dollar and fifty cents a cord.

Soon it began to snow heavily. The rugged, saw-toothed peaks farther up in the valley of the Chilkat River towered high and snowclad, and across the channel beyond Pyramid Island rose the high, steep mountains, the base and foreland of which formed the snug Pyramid Harbor.

I visited Captain Healy and his wife at times, and was always made very welcome, and listened with much interest to many of his tales of hairbreadth escapes and adventures which he had experienced years before in Montana, Fort Benton and on the Missouri River.

At this time, there was also a man by the name of Silas Gibson. He was about six feet ten or seven feet in height, with shoulders in proportion. He claimed to be a grand army man and had taken up and located quite a number of acres of land (I think one hundred sixty acres) just beyond Healy's store toward the mouth of the Chilkat River.

This man Gibson had a long, large nose with a big hump in the middle of it like a ship's rudder; and often when the heavy winds were blowing, we around there used to see Gibson running for a while when going a short distance, and all at once turn around and walk backward for a few moments against the wind. And we used to say that he could not face the storm on account of the wind striking broadside against his nose.

Gibson kept a little saloon in the same building where he lived, but as may well be imagined, his trade was very light. He never acquired title to the acreage he had located, and afterward died at Juneau, where he was, off and on, engaged as floor manager in the dance halls there.

This was a long dreary winter. Later on, when the snow began to lie deeper, I began to stir up the natives to get the necessary amount of cordwood out for next season's use. But they seemed to be slow about wanting to start in to cut, saying that they wished to wait till the snow was more settled and firmer to haul the wood out on sleighs.

Christmas came, and I enjoyed eating dinner with Mr. and Mrs. Healy. Along in the early part of January 1890, the snow was lying very deep, four feet or more on the level, and in drift places six feet or more in depth. I got to work with several men and shoveled a large quantity of snow off the roof of one of the lean-to additions to the cannery to relieve the weight, for the weather was beginning to change and showed signs of thaw.

On the afternoon of January 11th, a heavy southeast gale sprang up, accompanied by hard rain, and at about 8 p.m. it was pitch dark. Sitting in my cabin on the brow of the hill, some two hundred feet away from the cannery, I heard a long and terrible crashing sound of falling timber amid the roar of the wind and deluge of rain. I knew it was the falling of the cannery building even before I opened my door to look.

The whole portion of the old part of the cannery, built several years ago by a cannery man named Spoohn, was laid low; but the new wing, including the store building that had been built onto it since the present company took charge of it, stood firm and undamaged. A good deal of the machinery was located in that portion that was demolished, but all the fishing gear, nets, boats, and so forth, had been stowed away in the new wing.

I took a lantern and went out to look around. The wreck looked bad indeed. There was not a speck of snow lying on any part of the roof at the time of its collapse; the heavy rain had swept it all off hours before.

The heavy wind and rainstorm continued for three days and nights before it abated. Then, on scanning the opposite shore in and around Pyramid Harbor where the other cannery was located, I noticed that the smokestack of that cannery was gone, and apparently quite a commotion had recently taken place on the steep mountain and foreground.

Along in the afternoon of January 15th, I saw one of the large fishing boats (Columbia River pattern) sailing across the channel and making for our cannery, and when it neared the beach I saw that its occupants were Steve York and his brother Bill, caretakers over there. Steve and his brother had both had a narrow escape, besides seeing much destruction at their company cannery.

On the morning of January 12, 1890, a snow slide of many hundred tons rushed down the steep mountainside, tearing large trees and boulders, and dirt and mud along with it, sending one tree out over the cannery and taking the smokestack out onto the beach beyond. The force, or pressure, of the air preceding the snow slide tore off shingles of many of the older cabins and badly moved a large wing of the store building a foot or more away from the main building. Bill York, who was about to enter his cabin, heard the fearful roar and caught hold of the header, or opening, of his door. His feet were lifted out from under him by the force of the wind preceding the slide, and he was thrown heavily against the walls of the cabin inside.

I took a trip over to Pyramid Harbor later, after clearing up the wreck at our cannery and covering up the machinery as well as we could, and saw what had taken place over there. The

WORKING IN HAINES CANNERY

Pyramid Harbor cannery was a much better and stronger structure than the old portion of our cannery which had blown down.

Needless to say, this destruction of my company's property made me feel very bad. I immediately wrote to Mr. Poindexter in San Francisco, telling him what had occurred. Later I was advised that the company would rebuild early in the spring, and be all in shape in plenty time to go right along with the coming season's packing.

I now made strong efforts to induce the natives to start cutting wood, but they seemed very reluctant, so long as they had money left from their wages of the previous fishing season. It was now approaching the time (along about the middle of February) when the wood should have begun to pile up around the cannery. I consulted George Shotridge, head chief of the Chilkat tribe, and explained to him the necessity of my having a large amount of wood on hand before the opening of the fishing season. Otherwise, we could not get it cut by the natives, or haul it out of the woods if we could get it out, for the snow would be nearly gone.

Shotridge understood the situation thoroughly, and within a week, all the natives started to chop wood and haul it on sleighs close to the vicinity of the cannery. And in a month's time, I had piled three hundred seventy cords of wood four feet high, and measured and paid for in trade tickets. Of course, there was a large portion of the natives in the vicinity who did not chop wood at all for our cannery, and there were several days that no wood at all was hauled into the yards.

Now, since the wood chopping commenced, there naturally was more trading in our store. Col. Sol Ripinsky also had a general merchandising and trading store about a mile above me, and a short distance from John Healy's store; there also was another store at the Pyramid Harbor cannery, and therefore the natives were not bound to one store. This wood cost the company in trade five hundred fifty dollars. The actual fishing season generally lasts three and a half to four months - from the middle of May to about the last of August or middle of September.

It was now the middle of March (1890), and some of the advance men, including a number of Chinamen (to make up

129

weeks, great preparations had been made among a few of the leading natives of means, including George Shotridge, their chief, to hold a large meeting and give a big potlatch and dance at the old native village called Yen-da-Stucka at the mouth of Chilkat River on the right-hand side going up, and about five miles away from this cannery. Invitations were sent out to other tribes including Fort Wrangell, Killisnoo, Sitka, Juneau (or Auk) Village, and to other natives.

All this excitement and enthusiasm now among the natives of this whole vicinity, including, of course, those who resided at Haines Mission, for the coming potlatch was to be a big event to be spoken of in the years to come by their children's children.

During the time I had been in this country on the coast, off and on I had acquired quite a smattering of the native, or as it is called, the Klinget (Tlingit) language, which also was necessary for me in order to trade with them at the store, though many of these natives could speak the English language fairly well; and some who attended the Mission schools at different places spoke it well.

I was cordially invited to attend this big potlatch, for many of the grown men and older ones had known of my father and seen him at Fort Wrangell years before during his steamboating days there, and quite a few of them remembered having seen me at Wrangell and on the Stikine River when a boy of nine or ten years of age, in company with my father.

21. THE BIG INDIAN POTLATCH AND DANCE AT YEN-DA-STUCKA VILLAGE AND MEETING MY LITTLE GIRL WIFE (March, 1890)

I had never witnessed a native potlatch and dance before. Should I go and see it or not? How could I know what the outcome of this would be, or what bearing it was destined to exercise over my whole future life?

The next day the potlatch and festivities were to commence. I walked up to Healy's store and had a talk with Mrs. Healy and her husband. I told them of my desire to witness the big doings at the village, and noticed that many tons of stuff were being taken up to the mouth of the river in large canoes, some of which came up from Juneau, and that considerable of these goods were purchased at Healy's store, at Col. Ripinsky's, and at the cannery stores. These goods consisted of many bales of brown vicuna blankets, many bolts of calico, quantities of leaf tobacco, barrels of sugar, clothing, and quantity of groceries and other stuff, all to be given away up at the village.

I will explain here, so that a better understanding may be gained of the reasons for these potlatches. There often are in one vicinity many members of two tribes, and in this vicinity of Chilkat, this condition existed. These two tribes, called the Eagles (or Chanks in the Klinget or Thlinget language), and the Ravens (or in the Klinget, the Yaelths), but through the intermarriage of many members of these two tribes, they have become so closely affiliated that they are hardly two distinct tribes.

Now, at times, a potlatch is given by the Eagles to the Ravens; at another time one will be given by the Ravens to the Eagles.

Then again a chief individually gives a potlatch, the whole cost of the expense furnished by himself; and they often try to go one better than the other regarding the cost. At other times when a large family, or tribal, house is being built or completed, or a Totem pole is to be erected, a potlatch is given to commemorate the important event. New vicuna blankets are the main staple article with these natives, and more of these are given away at a potlatch than any other goods. These blankets ranged from four dollars and fifty cents to six dollars per pair, and represent the same value as cash to these natives in trade among themselves. On the occasion of this particular potlatch, the Ravens (Yaelths) were the hosts.

Now to return where I left off. I walked up to talk with Mr. and Mrs. John Healy. Mrs. Healy strongly advised me not to attend the big doings, but Mr. Healy saw no reason why I should not go up and see it all. He, himself, could not get away; and besides, he had witnessed similar events before, both in this and in other countries. He said that I should by all means see the affair, for it would prove very interesting.

I hesitated, but finally made up my mind to go. Night was coming on. So, everything being safe down at my cabin, the cannery and the store, I accepted the invitation of the Healys to sleep upstairs in a spare room at their place, and retired for the night.

Next morning about six o'clock I was awakened by a coffee mill grinding in the kitchen below, and I knew it was Mr. Healy grinding coffee for breakfast; I had often heard him do this while at his store at Dyea. Healy always both roasted his own coffee and ground it every morning, just enough for breakfast; he said it was the only way to get the best results from coffee beans.

Well, I arose quickly, knowing that Mrs. Healy would have her favorite hotcakes and maple syrup for breakfast. But just as I was pulling on my trousers, the large six-shooter pistol I had left in my hip pocket fell to the floor, struck the hammer and went off, sending the bullet down through the floor and ceiling of the kitchen and into the floor below, only a few feet from where Mrs. Healy stood cooking the hotcakes. She, of course, was alarmed and cried out asking if I was hurt. On coming down, I explained the matter.

After breakfast, Mrs. Healy again asked if I still intended to go up to the village, and I told her I did, and shortly afterward I left the store and started out up the beach to Yen-da-Stucka- where it was my fate to go.

Mrs. Healy was a fine woman, a loyal wife and helpmate to John Healy, and, as I have said before in this narrative, she had made many friends among the rugged and big-hearted prospectors of the great Yukon, both before this time and years later. And as I shook hands with her and bade her good-bye in her little kitchen where she was clearing up the breakfast dishes, it was only with a strong effort that I kept from kissing her right there in the presence of Mr. Healy, for she was like a mother to me and for some reason did not want me to go up to the village. And long afterward, I wondered whether she knew more than she wished to say at that time. She spoke the Tlingit language well, as also did her husband, and knew every native within miles around.

I was twenty years old, with no great and serious thoughts of the future. I felt light of heart, though lonesome at times, living in and seeing only the present. I threaded my way along up the shore, skirting the tidewater and on around Jones Point and the head of the bay beyond, thence on up the shore to the village. I saw a great number of natives all around, also noted a few white men from the Pyramid Harbor cannery and one from our cannery.

Later, directed by a loud, weird shouting sound, I went over to the largest structure there - a great, hewn log building, but it was almost impossible to gain entrance. The large doorway was completely blocked by many natives, and a number of them stood outside. At last I got a little farther in. There appeared to be five hundred natives or more, in and around the building.

The potlatch portion of the festivities was in full swing. Bales of blankets were ripped open, and after being torn into two single ones, they were again torn into strips about six inches wide and handed out by George Shotridge, the Ravens' chief; at the same time he loudly called out the name of the native who was to receive the strip, then he passed it to other Indians stationed near him who in turn passed it on to the one who was to receive it.

This went on for hours. Then came the many different other goods passed around in the same manner. The tearing up of the givers care nothing for the expense and destruction of the goods, but generally the receivers of these strips of blankets sew them all together again later, with fine seams, and make good use of them for bed covering and clothing.

This big time, I learned, had started the day before I arrived at the village, and it was now noon of the second day. It kept on till toward evening, and the big stock of goods was distributed among all the members of the Eagle tribe.

Now their old, customary, time-honored war dance commenced. The interior of this large house was built with a raised platform about six feet wide and three to four feet high, extending all around and leaving a large square space in the center. The roof was supported with massive hewn timbers and posts.

The women folk wore fancy blankets made of fine heavy cloth of dark-blue and black with edges of red, four to six inches wide all around, trimmed with half a dozen to many rows of fine, small white buttons; there were many hundreds on one blanket. Their faces were painted and otherwise decorated with beads, ear and nose rings, and feathers.

The menfolk were decorated with paint, feathers, beaded jackets, girdles, moccasins, and raven's heads and wings. The latter were fastened on the heads of those who belonged to the Raven tribe, and the skins, head, and beak of eagles were fastened to the heads of many of the leading ones in the dance who belonged to the Eagle tribe.

Some of the natives were naked and painted to their waists. Very prominent among these was Billy Dickinson, a half-breed whose mother belonged to the Eagles, and the son of George Dickinson, storekeeper at Haines Mission and brother of Miss Sarah Dickinson, whom I have mentioned before.

Billy Dickinson possessed a good smattering education and was a very shrewd fellow, was fairly good-looking, strong, husky and well built. He could handle the pasteboards very well, and as a rule used to win considerable money away from the natives in their card games. He was also unreliable and tricky in business dealings.

I now had obtained a good location in the house and could command a good view of all of the proceedings. The womenfolk stood around and about the raised platform, chanting a weird slow song, and at the same time swaying back and forth and sideways in a swinging, rocking manner. The men were lined up in the center of the house, their heads about two feet above the top of the platform on which these women were standing. The male members of the two tribes held positions facing each other, shouting and jumping and going through a great many, and to me, inexplicable maneuvers of which all movements, however, meant something to them.

One Indian held a long, slender paddle-shaped batten, about four or five inches wide and twelve feet long or more, out over the main men dancers. This large batten had a large number of pieces or bunches of human hair fastened to it, which hung like fringes from each edge. Several other Indians, including Billy Dickinson, wore on their heads eagle skins with their wings and beaks; others had on the raven skins, wings and beaks for headgear. While facing each other, they would line up and rush at and bob their heads at one another to imitate real eagles and ravens fighting.

During all this time, the women never once sat down or stopped their weird chanting song and swaying movements, keeping time to the beating of tom-toms. I particularly noted that young Dickinson outshone all the rest in the dance among the men. He went into all kinds of contortions - shouted, chanted and jumped clean over the heads of some of the others, many of whom brandished knives.

During all this, the natives became much enthused and excited. The men who took actual part in the dance vied hard with each other to make the most impression among the large audience. While standing there taking all this in, and during a few moments' intermission in the men's maneuvers, I happened to glance up to a door that had just been opened from what appeared to be a room at the farther side of the house and which led onto the platform, and two young girls came out; one apparently fourteen or fifteen years old, quite light of complexion, of somewhat delicate appearance, and with long black hair. In fact she looked pretty, refined and modest, and in a way above any of her class I had yet seen.

She saw me at the same time I saw her, and after we held each other's gaze for a moment, she broke away from her chum (who was also fairly good-looking, and, as I afterward learned, was (who was also fairly good-looking, and, as I afterward learned, was her cousin), and ran quickly back into the room, which, I learned later, was used by the two girls to watch the dance and potlatch because they were not taking an active part in the proceedings.

I became immediately interested in this little girl and curious to know all about her. I was lonesome and yearning for companionship of the opposite sex.

About this time, or shortly afterward, the war dance commenced again and lasted for about another hour, when it was decided to take a rest till the next morning. It was now quite late, and dark, the weather was storming with a strong southerly wind, and many of the natives were leaving the house to go to other houses and cabins to retire - although many of them remained up all night, no doubt - and as I was about to leave the house too, deliberating with myself what to do about walking all the way back to the cannery in the storm at night, George Shotridge approached me. We shook hands and he welcomed me to his potlatch. I thanked him, and when I said that I thought that I would have to get back to my post at the cannery, he argued that it would be foolish to attempt a trip like that on a night such as this, and said I could share a cabin he had with his family.

I must state here that up to this time I had never met any of Chief George Shotridge's family, nor did I know he had a family. In fact I had only met and spoken to him on one or two occasions before. He and his family, as I afterwards learned, resided most of their time at Pyramid Harbor, when not upriver at Kluk-wan.

Well, I accompanied Chief Shotridge to his little house of two rooms, where things looked neat and clean, and where his wife and two little sons, Louis and Shotridge, about nine and five years old, and one daughter about eighteen or nineteen years old, were all awaiting the chief's arrival. I was introduced to all and made to feel at home. A good fire was going, and soon I was invited to have some supper, which was being made ready in the meantime by Shotridge's wife and daughter.

All this time I was thinking of the little girl I had seen up in the big house during the war dance. Just before we seated ourselves at the table, the mother called to the other room, the door of which was slightly ajar, for Klinget-sai-yet to come to supper.

136

Of course I did not know there was anyone in the other room, and on glancing up, I was indeed surprised to behold the little girl who had been in my thoughts for the past several hours. She also showed her surprise.

Shotridge introduced me, as he had to the other members of his family, and we all sat down to eat. The food was tasty. There were all kinds of good things to eat. I had my pockets full of cigars, and the chief and I smoked together and talked. But not once did either of the two girls speak, unless asked a direct question. This behavior is characteristic of these people.

The two sisters retired to their room, and a bed was made up for me in one corner of the room. I lay there thinking of this meek and modest little native maiden princess in the next room. No warning whisper came to me to flee and dismiss this child of nature from my mind.

Thoughts of home in Victoria and of another girl down there came to my mind but were chased away. I was in faraway Alaska, living in the present, and told myself, I will be going south to Victoria this coming fall.

Thus it was with me, and thus it was that lifelong unhappiness was brought about for her and for me, and which one's fault was it? Surely not hers, but mine.

Morning came, and the potlatch dance was resumed. About noon I started on my return trip to the cannery, where I arrived a couple of hours or so later. A week later, I went to this girl at her parents' house, where they were then living, about a mile from my place, or halfway to Healy's store. I took this little girl out sleigh riding with dog teams, and we went coasting, and in a short time became quite friendly and enjoyed each other's company very much. And unconscious of it, I grew to like and then love this little maid, and she in turn grew to think a great deal of me. But even then, I did not realize or think that she was destined to become my wife.

Time went on. The cannery hands and Mr. Poindexter arrived in due time; also his son Theodore, as superintendent. The fallen portion of the cannery was rebuilt, and everything was activity again. After turning in my accounts of the store satisfactorily, I again resumed my position as fireman and second engineer under Jim Cox, the chief engineer, whose wife and three young children accompanied him up to the cannery for the work pretty hard. We burned from two and a half to three cords of wood per day. But on Sundays, if there were not a great deal of fish on hand, we did not run the boilers and retorts.

In the meantime, needless to say, I saw the little girl often, and the Healys and others naturally looked upon the matter as a foregone conclusion that I would marry her, though this had not as yet come to me in this way. The girl had always lived with her parents and two younger brothers and sister, and had never before been seen in any other boy's or man's company.

Often, she and her two brothers would come down to my cabin at the cannery, at my invitation, while the snow still lay deep, and would spend hours in my little cabin and lunch with me. As time went on, I kept telling myself that I ought not to continue as I did, for I began to see plainly that the girl's parents looked upon the matter with more seriousness than I did. But matters drifted along, I being of an affectionate, generous, and confiding disposition, yearning for the society of the opposite sex.

Now about this time my little girl friend - whom I now called Minnie, instead of her native name, Klinget-sai-yet - and her father made a trip to Sitka and were away from Chilkat for about six weeks. And during this time I began to fully realize how much I really missed her.

Now, before proceeding further, I wish to narrate an amusing incident known and spoken of by quite a few even today. It happened at the cannery during that season.

22. JACK O---N AND THE HUDSON BAY RUM (Spring 1890)

At this time a great deal of liquor was regularly smuggled in by daring men to these parts of Alaska. The liquor was brought from Fort Simpson in Columbia River fishing boats, sloops and schooners, and quantities of it were brought into Juneau and Douglas. Some was also cached at the bar in the upper end of Gastineau Channel, later to be taken into the Yukon and to different villages or towns along the coast and sold in bulk, and often peddled by the bottle by these nefarious traffickers.

Mr. Poindexter was at this time Justice of the Peace here at Chilkat, and Johnny Healy held the position of Marshal. In some way or other, unknown to me or anyone else I knew, Mr. Poindexter seemingly had got wind of the fact that a heavily laden fishing boat was about due to enter the bay or inlet here with a full load of liquor from Fort Simpson, British Columbia.

However, one morning on going down to the cannery store to chat with Theodore Poindexter for a little while before going into the boiler room to resume my duties, on entering the store I noticed a very large cask set up on end outside the counter; also several ten-gallon kegs of beer, and several cases of bottled liquor.

When I asked young Poindexter what all this meant, he replied that his father and Johnny Healy had made a seizure late the previous night. Then he took me under the cannery and showed me a large Columbia River fishing boat - such as is now used at all these Alaskan canneries - chained up with a locked padlock at high tidemark to one of the foundation posts of the cannery. On my asking who was the recent owner of the boat and wet goods, he gave me the name of Billy L——k.

I immediately remembered this man very well. He had traveled into the Yukon country in company with me and my brother in the spring of 1887, over the Dyea Pass, and thence wet goods, he gave me the name of Billy L——k.

I immediately remembered this man very well. He had traveled into the Yukon country in company with me and my brother in the spring of 1887, over the Dyea Pass, and thence over the lakes by ice and on downriver by rafts and boat.

This liquor, in the meantime, was being held by Mr. Poindexter in his store preparatory to being shipped to Sitka by one of the large Pacific Coast Steamship Company's vessel due at Chilkat in about a week or ten days. As I said before, the large cask was standing up endwise on its chimes near the door leading outside from the store, and another door connected the store with the main cannery building.

Well, about six days later, one afternoon about a quarter to one, after finishing my lunch, I walked into the store to smoke and chat a while with the young Poindexter. There were several other employees in the store, also a number of fishermen and others, including some Chinamen and natives lounging around outside, talking, smoking and indulging in different games and pastimes, as is usual around these canneries during the noon hour before the men resume their duties.

About this time a man whom I knew, an engineer and a jack-of-all-trades well known by most people about here and those at Juneau and Douglas, walked into the store. He wore a gray and black checkered blanket jacket and a black slouch hat, and after passing the time of day and talking a while he remarked: "Hello! What have you here, a cask of liquor and a whole lot of other wet goods?" And addressing young Poindexter, asked, "How and when did you make the big haul?"

After being told more about it, he said, addressing me, "Ben, I'll bet you nor any other man in the store can tip or roll over that cask."

I replied, "Well, you want to bet on a sure thing. Why, that is full of Hudson Bay rum, and it would take more than one of us to move it very far."

Whereupon a great, good-natured fisherman called Long Peter offered to bet cigars all around with Jack that he would at least pull it over on its bulging sides. The bet was accepted, and the long, innocent Peter went up to it.

By this time a large crowd had gathered in and outside the store, blocking the doorway. Peter got a good strong hold of the cask at the upper end, and bracing himself with his knees on either side of it gave a horrible pull - and went sprawling on his back on the floor, with the great cask on top of him. I and one or two others jumped quickly to poor Peter's assistance, naturally thinking that he must be seriously hurt. But to our dismay we found that the cask was *empty*. Not a drop of rum in it.

Peter was not much the worse for his sudden precipitation to the floor, aside from receiving a good bump on the back of his head and bruising his elbows. After we resurrected Peter from under the cask and got him to his feet, he swore and fumed like a madman and commenced to flay around him right and left, cursing everything and everybody, gesticulating with long, lank arms and hands. The natives and Chinese and many others ran and tumbled over each other to get out of his way, for he was a powerful fellow.

Of course, Peter fully believed that it was really a put-up job by all of us. But in reality, none of us were aware that the cask was empty, except one man present whose identity no one knew, then or ever afterward, except myself; and for several years afterward, I did not know it happened, though I entertained strong suspicions that same day, which, as will be seen shortly, proved to be true later.

On rolling the large cask outside and examining it amid a horde of jumping and peering fishermen, natives and Chinese, we found a piece of five-eighth-inch gas pipe, about six inches long, sticking into the end cask that had rested on the floor, and a clean-bored hole in the floor of the store, immediately underneath the place where the cask had stood. And later, on examining the place under the floor of the store where the distance to the ground was about two feet, we found a wooden plug which tightly fitted the protruding end of the piece of gas pipe found sticking into the cask.

In the meantime the fishermen and other loungers outside were all rolling the cask around, trying to see if they could not drain a drink or two out of it, but there was not even a drop left, nor was there any moisture or sign of the liquor, either on the floor or the ground under the floor - showing that every drop had been successfully drained off and stolen.

We were all late getting to our work that afternoon. All was excitement and confusion. When Mr. Poindexter, Sr., appeared us. A hole was bored up through the floor of the store and into the end of the cask till within just an eighth or quarter of an inch of the burr was left, the person doing the boring being well enough posted as to the thickness of the end of the chime of this kind of cask. He also knew the thickness of the floor, and having the piece of pipe already cut and long enough to reach down below the bottom part of the floor, with the plug driven snugly in, the pipe was then driven through the floor and into the end of the cask, breaking through the thin remaining burr of the cask. The rest was simply to hold buckets or small kegs under the piece of gas pipe, pull out the plug, drain the liquor out till the receptacle was about full, then drive the plug into the pipe again till another bucket or keg was to be filled or carried away. It all seemed so simple to us now.

Mr. Poindexter was very much worked up over this matter; as also was Johnny Healy, for Poindexter was custodian of the rum for the government and now was unable to deliver it to Sitka. Rewards were offered and a strict watch kept for a long while, but no positive trace could be found of the rum or the man who stole it. But for all that, this same rum was dished out over the bar at one of the saloons at twenty-five cents a drink.

A few days later the steamer arrived from the south on her way to Sitka, and the remainder of the liquor, that is the case goods and kegs of beer, were forwarded to Sitka to the government authorities to be sold.

Five years or more later, on meeting Jack O——n, I said to him, "Darn you, Jack, I had at the time, and always have had since, a mighty good idea of my own that it was you who drained that Hudson Bay rum out of the cask at Poindexter's cannery store."

He admitted the whole thing, and gave me the entire details of just how it was done, which entirely agreed with our views and ideas at the time of the deed. Jack even said that he had to chase an old dog away from where he was lying asleep under the store floor, right under the cask, where it was necessary to bore the hole and insert the piece of gas pipe with the wooden plug.

He further told me that he made a good big thing out of the rum right there in the Chilkat, clearing in the neighborhood of twelve hundred dollars on it. He also said several times he had to lie very quietly when the cannery night watchman approached the store in his rounds, but there was a southerly wind blowing that night causing some surf on the beach, and this was in his favor and drowned what little noise he may have made.

He said he had bored the hole with a good, sharp extension bit - and didn't lose a drop of the rum. He got his bearings and the location of the cask during his many visits in and about the store and cannery previous to the night he did the job. All it cost him was the treat all around for the wager he made with Long Peter, for Peter moved the cask all right.

23. JACK O——N'S FIGHT WITH JOHNNY HEALY, I MARRY MINNIE (Fall, 1890)

This same season, after the above occurrence, Jack O——n, somewhat under the influence of liquor, walked into John Healy's store and some altercation took place between them; there not being very good feeling between these two in the past anyhow.

Healy was standing behind his counter and stepped up in readiness to wait on Jack, thinking he wanted to purchase something, when an argument started and Jack became very abusive to Healy and made a movement toward his hip pocket for his gun. In an instant, Healy had put one hand on the counter and leaped clean over it, and was on top of Jack in a flash. A fierce hand-to-hand fight took place between these two for the possession of the pistol.

They writhed and twisted around for several minutes until at last Healy succeeded in wrenching the pistol from Jack's hand and battered him over the head with it till there was blood all over the floor. But had Jack not been under the influence of liquor, this fight might have been either considerably prolonged, or one of them killed. They were both mighty good men in a fight, and fearless too. But Johnny Healy was quick as lightning and would as soon fight as eat anytime, despite his age, which I should judge was at that time in the neighborhood of fifty years.

I now accepted a position at Mr. Hugh Murray's cannery and remained there till the close of the season. Mrs. Healy had given company for me.

In the meantime, my little girl friend Minnie and her father, Chief George Shotridge, returned from Sitka, and I once more spent a good deal of my spare time in her company, and matters drifted on. At the close of the canning season, and on the eve of Mr. Murray's departure on his steamer, the *Chilkat*, for Astoria, he tried to persuade me to accompany him south. But I had become so attached to Minnie Shotridge that I declined to go back home. And matters continued to drift.

About this time I received word from Victoria, from my father, to turn his schooner, *Flying Dutchman*, over to Mr. Charles Young of Juneau. So I engaged a fisherman by the name of Heipe, who had been knitting nets for the cannery, to sail her to Juneau. We got out her large sails and bent them and pitched some of the schooner's seams along her sides, and in a day or two, one morning early with a freshening north wind blowing, Heipe and one Indian sailed out down the inlet for Juneau, crossed the bar near the head of Douglas Island at high tide, and arrived at Juneau that same night with only two or three feet of water in the hold, her bottom seams having dried out lying on the beach at Chilkat.

After settling up with Mr. Murray for the short time I worked for his company, the balance due me amounted to twenty-three dollars, which he paid me. A few days later, I married Shotridge's daughter, then proceeded with my little girl wife to Juneau on a small sloop, in company with my wife's mother and father. We arrived after five days, having been forced to anchor several times for shelter during some heavy storms. This was on October 20th, 1890.

After getting temporarily settled at Juneau, I went to the Reverend Eugene S. Willard at the Presbyterian Mission and had our marriage ceremony performed over again by him, at his mission residence in the presence of his wife, daughters and son, and two of his mission girls as witnesses.

Later I proceeded to excavate a foundation for a little three-room house. Working by myself, I had the house completed in a couple of months. It was situated so as to face the waterfront at Juneau, near the approach to the old first wharf, or as it was often called, the Carroll Dock, after Captain James Carroll, who was so long connected with the Pacific Coast Steamship Company, and who for the past thirty years or more has been in command of many of the best vessels plying Alaskan waters.

I remained at Juneau all that winter doing odd jobs, during which time my finances at times became extremely low. But I was happy with my wife in our small three-room house that I had built.

We used to attend Mr. Willard's church nearly every Sunday.

24. WORKING AT DOUGLAS ISLAND SAWMILL (1891)

In the spring we moved to Douglas City on Douglas Island, just across the channel; or in what was often called at that time, New Town, where I took a job working for Robert Pervis in the Treadwell sawmill. My job was to saw the large or small logs in two with a long crosscut saw according to the length of the lumber, orders in general allowing four inches over these logs.

Of course, as all those who are familiar with sawmills know, the lumber had to be sawed in two or three or four pieces, according to the length of the log and lumber to be cut, while lying on the incline slip on which they are hauled from the log boom into the mill. And when one man alone has to saw these logs, the long crosscut saw used wobbles very much at each stroke.

I could work and was used to it, and had done lots of it and never shirked my part. I started to work on the sawmill slip at 1 p.m. on a warm sunshiny day. My first introduction was to a very large log, six feet through and forty-eight feet long, which had to be cut into sixteen-foot lengths. It had stalled on the lower end of the slip, the large, heavy iron dogs having been pulled out several times already in getting it hauled up thus far.

I started sawing it alone, but it was a corker. However, I got the two cuts through by 6 p.m., but it was a tough job. I struck pitch and knots in my cuts besides.

I remained here at Douglas on the slip for a couple of months; then later got on the rollers taking slabs from the large circular saw. The head sawyer's name was Red. Then later I was put on the carriage setting, which I learned to handle well, and I thought that this beat the slip job all hollow.

My wife and I lived in a rented shack with one large room, for which we paid three dollars per month rent to Frank James. It was situated on the hill back of the Koehler and James branch store. I received three dollars a day in wages at the sawmill while on the carriage setting, and two dollars and fifty cents per day while on the slip and taking slabs on the rollers. These wages did not include my board.

One day, while Mr. Pervis was away after a boom of logs, I worked with one Jim Risdon, a young man who had succeeded Red as sawyer. We had worked a log down to a timber about six by eight and some sixteen feet long, and Jim Risdon was in a hurry to run another cut through quick.

I had dogged the stick well. But on the last cut, as often happens, one of the iron dogs was in line with the saw cut and Jim, not seeing it in time when I motioned to draw his attention to it, ran the saw plumb through the dog, cupping and ruining the saw and throwing its adjustable teeth right and left; and in backing out the saw, it threw the piece of timber clean out the length of the mill, tearing off a couple of boards, hurtling and twisting in its course, and looking for some(thing) to hit till it landed on the beach.

I continued working at the mill till the middle of November, when my wife and I moved to Juneau again and rented a little old log house on the hill up near the rear of the St. Joseph Hospital and St. Ann's Convent. The rent was three dollars a month. Our own house, which we had built, we turned over to my wife's folks.

The snow fell very deep here in Juneau this winter. The log house we lived in was covered only with shakes which lay very unevenly, and we had to shovel and sweep drifts of snow out of it every morning. At times we could hardly get out of the door on account of the snow piled up on the outside to a height of five feet where it had drifted.

25. CHEATING OF THE NATIVES BY STOREKEEPERS (1890-91)

During this winter of 1890-1891 I dealt with the firm of Koehler and James at their large store in Juneau, and had occasion to hear many stories of times before I reached Alaska.

It seemed that the natives were always charged more than the white people for what they bought, and were taken advantage of by the storekeepers whenever the latter had the chance.

It is a known fact that while a number of natives would be lounging about and sitting on the floor in some of the stores and trading or buying groceries, blankets, and other items for cash, one of these storekeepers in particular, whose name I will withhold, would take a scoopful of sugar off the scales and throw it back into the barrel under the counter after the sugar had been weighed – while the Indian who was buying it had his back turned for a moment, talking to one of his friends.

On other occasions, after Mr. Indian had closed a deal with the storekeeper upstairs for a number of blankets, and after they were all counted and loaded on the Indian's back, Mr. Storekeeper would innocently arrange for the Indian to get started down the stairs first. Then Mr. Storekeeper would whip a pair or two of blankets off the pile and throw them back on the floor upstairs before the Indian had proceeded below the level of the floor very far. Sometimes, of course, these storekeepers were caught. Then it was a great shame for the storekeeper, who, of course, would always offer some plausible excuse for the missing blankets.

Another unique little game – or rather steal – gotten up by one firm here in Juneau, which I always thought was a small, raw trick, was to have a false tin bottom in one-gallon syrup cans up from the main or outside bottom about three inches so that in this space there would, of course, be nothing at all.

149

This went on quite a while until one day it was found out; then there was "big shame" for the storekeeper again.

The above incidents have often happened at Juneau in the early days during my residence there on different occasions. I actually saw them myself, and have often talked about them with many old-timers who also knew the truth.

With the faithful fox terrier to which I referred before, a gift from Mrs. Healy, my wife and I went to Chilkat in April for a couple of months. There I worked, assisting one Henry Bodie to build some scows and caulking them. We made the trip to Chilkat in a small rowboat. During this time my father had returned to Juneau and built a large fishing boat a couple of miles above Juneau, in an old building that used to belong to one French Pete. And with this boat, which was similar to a Columbia River fishing boat with center board, and a large fish net, he fished for the canneries at Chilkat that season, receiving ten cents per fish.

26. CAUGHT ON A BAR ON A TRIP TO DYEA (1891)

One morning during two or three days' slack run of fish, I loaded up my father's large, sloop-rigged fishing boat with short lengths of one by twelve inch lumber to take to Dyea for Captain John Healy's post. He was sending the lumber to his partner, Mr. Wilson.

Leaving my wife with her mother, I took a man by the name of Murphy with me to assist me. Mrs. John Healy had expressed a desire to go along to visit the Wilsons and her old home at Dyea, so I told her to come right along, for the weather was nice and balmy.

We worked our little sloop down around Point Seduction or the end of the peninsula, and a little later we were sailing along nicely with a free sheet before a nice, freshening, mid-May breeze. Late the same afternoon we arrived at the sand bars at the head of Dyea inlet near the Dyea River, and first of all, of course, I prepared to put Mrs. Healy ashore right away.

I slipped on my hip gum boots, and she also had a pair on, and she holding her skirts up, we took hands and started to wade, my fox terrier swimming after us.

The tide, I knew, was on the flood, but only two-thirds in, for I had figured on this in order to run up into the mouth of the river as far as I could with the boatload of lumber in order to get it unloaded as close to the post as possible; though in order to do this it would necessarily take at least a couple of hours more to pole and haul the heavily loaded boat up against the main channel stream as the tide rose.

Well, as I said, we held hands firmly and started to make crossing through pools of water, running streams and over sand bars, leaving my man Murphy to look after the boat and keep her pushed close up to the edges of the bar as the tide came in.

We were making good progress, when we saw ahead of us quite a strip of water on the other side of the bar which we were crossing. The tide was flowing swiftly into this lagoon-like stretch of water, and there was no way to get to the uplands without crossing this pond-shaped piece of water; and I could see at once, as also did Mrs. Healy, that it was of mean depth. And behind us there were several places nearby now as bad as that before us, and we were a long distance from our heavily-laden boat and had no small tender or ship with the sloop.

We hurried on as fast as we could in the almost quicksand, with our heavy boots on, though I could see now that the longest gum boots ever made would be of no use in crossing this neck of water. Then we started to wade up to the knees. Then the water came higher and higher, till it came nearly up to my breast. Every once in a while one of us would step down into a hole, and we thought it would be all up with one or both of us.

However, we held hands and stayed with it; part of the time we swam and the rest waded and stumbled till we reached the uplands. Then we both sat down on the bank to rest and wring out our bedraggled clothes as best as we could, and emptied our gum boots. Then I started Mrs. Healy off up to the post. I then motioned to Murphy to head the boat in toward the main channel and pole her up to where I could manage to get back into her. After considerable time and gesticulating and shouting, I to him and he to me, I managed to wade out and get back into the boat nearer the main channel.

After considerable work towing and poling up against the stream, we landed our sloop in a bend in the river about half a mile up from the post, which was as close as we could get to it. Later I went up to the Healy post and got some dry shirts and overalls on, and unloaded a portion of the lumber. By this time it was dark, or as dark as it gets at this time of the year up here.

I might add that this wading and swimming and half-drowning affair could have been avoided had I insisted on Mrs. Healy waiting in the boat till the tide rose high enough to allow us to haul it up the main channel, as we always do.

27. SKOOKUM JIM'S ENCOUNTER WITH TWO LARGE BEARS (1891)

Next morning Murphy and I unloaded our cargo of lumber onto the bank, and bade Mrs. Healy and Mr. and Mrs. Wilson good bye. Mrs. Healy wished to remain on a visit a few days longer. When we were just about in the act of pulling out into the stream to float down, I noticed a lone Indian swiftly shooting down the current in a small canoe. On his paddling up alongside of my sloop, I recognized him to be my old friend Skookum Jim, or Stick Jim as my father used to call him; the same Indian to whom I referred before in these pages as having gone through the White Pass with my father in June 1887.

Well, Jim gave me to understand that he would like to accompany me to Chilkat. So we hauled his tiny canoe on board the sloop and started on our way again, calling in to Skagway for a few moments on our way down the Lynn Canal and seeing that our log house and everything there was all right.

We pulled out of Skagway Bay again, and proceeded on down the channel with a light, fair, northerly breeze, gliding along slowly. I was at the helm and Jim and Murphy were lying under the thwarts, napping. When we were down the channel about four miles below Skagway, near a waterfall, Jim awoke and sat up, and in a little while he was looking intently ahead toward our port shore a few hundred feet away. Suddenly Jim became very excited and remarked, "I see bear two."

Murphy and I looked intently, but could see no bears. But Jim, I could see at once by his earnestness, could not be mistaken, and knowing him to be one of the best hunters in the country, I believed that he did see two bears on the beach quite a distance ahead.

He begged me to land the sloop at the steep, rocky shore. This could easily be done, for there was no sea on at all. We moored our sloop, lowered the sail, and let Jim out with his little canoe to paddle quietly along close to shore for some distance to get nearer the two bears.

Before he started I said, "Now, Jim, I will remain here one hour. If by that time we do not hear from you or see you, I will hoist sail and leave."

Well, he left, taking his rifle and only four cartridges, and went skimming on down, paddling quietly and hugging the shore closely. Murphy and I then proceeded to cook our dinner on our little cannery charcoal stove, and after finishing dinner we smoked for a while. By this time I thought we ought to hear something from Jim. I unshipped the tiller and began to pound loudly on the gunwhale of the sloop to give Jim warning – if he was within hearing distance – that we intended to start again, or to get an answer by way of a gun shot or a shout from him. But no answer came.

We also shouted, with the same results. So we hoisted sail, let go our shore lines, and swung out from shore. Then, when we were just getting under way and while I was looking way up the mountain – for I knew that bears, if Jim really saw any, would make for the hills if he did not get them before they had time to do so – I noticed a moving object; but it was so far up the side of the mountain that I could not believe it was Jim.

However, watching intently, I could see the object bending over and stooping, then at times it would disappear altogether. But soon I could see that it was our Jim. He was rolling, pulling, and tugging at a jet-black object which then, of course, I knew must be a black bear, one apparently half-grown.

Murphy and I hurried up to assist him. The mountainside was quite steep, so that we could roll and drag the bear downhill especially now that there were three of us.

During all the time that had elapsed since Jim had left our sloop with his little canoe – over an hour – we had not heard a gunshot, and I noticed that Jim's clothes were badly torn in several places, and he had scratches on his hands and blood on them. I remarked on his condition, and he said that when the two bears sighted him, they at first made for the mountain. Not wishing to take any chances on firing at too long range, he followed them nearly to snowline and shot and killed the black bear first, and then shot and wounded a very large brown bear.

I said, "Well, where is the brown bear?"

"Down hill in bushes, but not dead yet," Jim replied, pointing toward a clump of underbrush a hundred feet or so from the water's edge. Then he told us about his hand-to-hand fight with the big brown bear, and showed us the claw marks on his hands from ramming the gun into the bear's throat and striking him on the head with heavy stones, and so forth.

Murphy and I could hardly believe all this could have happened, especially in only about an hour and a half. But the evidence was right there before us.

After considerable work, the three of us got the black bear down and loaded it into the sloop. We then followed Jim up the beach a way, after he first took a few more cartridges from the sloop, my little dog, Buck following at our heels, sniffing and barking excitedly. I took along a Colt revolver, the only firearm I had at that time.

On nearing a clump of trees and underbrush, I heard a great noise of snorting and moaning, and heard the bushes cracking and swaying. Jim quietly leaned forward, parted the bushes, took aim and fired just the one shot. Then the three of us stood still to listen, but the big brown bear lay there, within forty feet of us, still and dead this time.

We went up to it, and my little terrier jumped around and barked loudly and commenced to nip at and pull the dead bear's ears. I was surprised to see such a large bear. Both it and the black one had beautiful coats. Jim showed me places on the bear's head where he had bruised him with rocks and slashed him with his knife.

Eventually, by rolling, dragging and lifting the carcass over rocks and boulders, the three of us got it loaded into the sloop, together with the black one, hoisted sail again and proceeded on our trip down the canal. These brown or cinnamon bears are, as most people know, more precious than the black.

Jim, of course, felt that he ought to have the proceeds from the sale of the hides. So knowing that he had hunted and killed them and risked his life in doing so, I readily acceded to his request.

He now pleaded for me to run the sloop up into the Chilkoot Inlet north of Haines Mission and land there on a gravel beach to skin the two bears, quarter the meat and stow it all snugly away under the foredeck of the sloop. This we did. Jim asked this for the reason, as he explained, that he, being a Stick (meaning an Interior) Indian, the coast and Chilkoot Indians – if they found out that he killed these two bears in their territory on the coast – would make him pay them a royalty. This condition, of course, I knew before he told me of its existence among the natives.

Again we started on our way out of the Chilkoot Inlet without any of the coast Indians seeing our prizes and arrived quietly back in Chilkat late in the evening, Jim smuggled his two fine bear skins, one at a time, up to Captain Healy's branch store, where they were stowed away for a while till Jim could stretch and dry them.

Jim received forty dollars for the two skins. This was a cheap price, but under the circumstances Jim did not care to dicker too much and Johnny Healy, as we all knew, was not in Alaska for his health either. We all ate fresh bear meat for a few days. I also gave some to Captain Healy, and some to Mrs. Dickinson, a great friend of my wife's.

28. CANNERY WORK AGAIN, ACCIDENT ON THE SAW (1891)

I then went to work at the Chilkat Packing Company's cannery under one Jim Cox, the engineer. There I remained till the middle of October. Part of that time I ran a small circular saw to cut four cord of wood in two twice.

One day I was called to another job, and a man whose name I forget came to relieve me at the saw. I cautioned to him to be careful when he pushed the moveable table with the sticks of cord wood on it against the saw, not to lean over too far with too much weight, and to be careful not to fall against the saw, which turned very fast and was driven by the cannery machinery with belting.

This poor fellow had sawed up only a few sticks when he fell or slipped against the saw by pushing the saw table over too far, and he had his whole breast cut open for eight or ten inches, also two of his fingers were cut off; they were found hanging around the belting.

We brought him into the store, laid him on the floor, and sent for John Healy. He came down with a crooked flesh needle and sewed up the large, gaping wound. There was no doctor in this vicinity. Whisky was poured down the unfortunate man's throat in large quantities, and the cannery company's steamer was quickly gotten ready, and Mr. Poindexter took the man to Juneau to St. Joseph's Hospital. Few of us expected to hear that this man would live. But he stayed in the hospital only one month, then was out again on the streets of Juneau – having what he called a good time and drinking hard.

29. ROUGH TRIP FROM JUNEAU TO CHILKAT, MIllWORK, CHILDREN ARE BORN (1891-1894)

Shortly after this the cannery changed hands. I went to Juneau, and accompanied my father on a trip on his schooner, the *Flying Dutchman*, back to Chilkat with a load of lumber, bar fixtures, and other supplies belonging to one Joe Cooper. He later established a saloon at Chilkat.

On our way up Lynn Canal from Juneau we ran into a northerly wind and a snowstorm at the mouth of the Chilkat Inlet at about 7 p.m. It was pretty dark already, and the wind was increasing; and we felt that it would be impossible to make our way up to our destination that night, beating against the wind.

We decided to anchor off the beach, a little below Davidson's Glacier, till morning. The wind increased steadily and fiercely. My father and I, a young native man, and Joe Cooper, the owner of the cargo, comprised the crew. The weather was very cold and our schooner swung heavily and surged at our large, one hundred fifty-pound anchor and cable, rolling and pitching heavily. We were below decks, lying down but not sleeping. Pretty soon there was a lull in the wind. This was about 3 a.m. and, of course, pitch-dark. It had ceased snowing, and in another hour the sea had gone down considerably and the fierce northeaster had entirely subsided.

I felt the schooner swinging around and, as I thought, changing her position, and said to my father, "I'll bet we'll get a heavy southeaster, and I think it is coming now." We both hurried to the deck, and sure enough we felt the first whiffs of it already, and our schooner bow was heading southward.

Immediate action was necessary now, for this anchorage which we were obliged to take afforded no shelter at all from a

158

southeaster, but some, not much, from a north wind. Well, in less than fifteen minutes the gale was upon us, the sea breaking over our bows. And then we saw that we were dragging our large anchor, so we put out our kedge anchor. But, of course, before this could do any good at all, she dragged her large anchor another hundred feet before the cable on the small anchor we had paid out commenced to get taut. This checked the dragging for a little while.

Then the wind increased more and more. So, seeing that we either had to make a grand effort to get out of here and run before the gale up behind to a shelter point some five miles further north, or get dashed to pieces on the beach. We decided to slip our large anchor and cable, for it would have been impossible to get it aboard under these conditions.

We watched for a little lull, and managed to get the kedge aboard; then got four large pieces of cordwood from the dunnage in the hold, lashed them together, made fast the end of the cable and hoisted the jib half up. I took the wheel aft, Joe Cooper, my father, and the native boy went forward ready to let go the cable from the bits and throw overboard the cordwood buoy to which the cable was attached.

All ready – let go! was the word, and our schooner leaped ahead pointed up the Chilkat Inlet, running before the gale at great speed, the heavy seas curling up and trying to comb over our stern. Our jib, as I said, was only half-hoisted and it was a hard job to keep the schooner from broaching too, so we hoisted the jib up more – and it was blown to pieces. After this our large main boom, a ponderous stick, jerked the sheet cavel from its fastenings and swung about, and the sheet ropes caught our large heavy iron tiller, which measured one-half inch by three inches, and snapped it off.

By quick action and great effort we managed to get the boom sashed steady again, got out two large sweep oars and thus, only by exerting all our united efforts and strength, we eventually worked our way into a good sheltered bay and ran the schooner up on a sandy beach at about two-thirds high tide, and put out our kedge anchor. Then all turned in to try to sleep and rest, for we needed rest badly. We had considerable water in the hold, some of which had washed in from above, and we could not till now spare any time to pump or bail water. It was now 6 a.m.

We all got up at noon feeling pretty refreshed; got some dinner, cleared up the vessel, and pulled the plug out of the schooner's bilge near her bottom, and the water ran out of her for we were now high and dry.

Then we proceeded to rig ropes and blocks temporarily onto our large rudder until such time when we could have the tiller welded together either at Chilkat or at Juneau. The wind had now calmed down considerably. When the tide came in and floated us, we pulled out and sailed up to Chilkat, arriving there that same evening.

It is bad judgment for anyone to go into an anchorage on Lynn Canal that does not afford shelter from both northerly and southerly winds in the early spring, late fall, or winter; that is, of course, when it is possible to get into such anchorage, for I have seen the wind flop around often very suddenly.

We unloaded our freight for Joe Cooper, and next day took my wife aboard and sailed to Juneau. We arrived there on November 1st. This time I rented a little better log cabin than I had the previous winter, and we made ourselves more comfortable. Our little fox terrier, Buck, was great company for us and a faithful friend and watchdog, and we always allowed him to sleep at the foot of our bed.

My wife was now in a delicate condition, and I arranged for her mother to take charge of her at our first little house that we built and where my wife's mother, father, and sister were now residing again for the winter.

On November 20, 1891, on a Sunday at 4 p.m., our first little baby, a boy, was born. We named him Benny. No doctor or nurse was present; only my wife's mother and her sister. In due time my wife became strong enough to move back to our cabin with little Benny.

We passed the next five months here in Juneau, which brought us up to May 1st, when I procured work at the Knoll Mining and Milling Company through a Mr. Ross, one of their head men, and proceeded with my wife and little Benny, who was then just a little over five months old, to Berner's Bay, forty miles or more north of Juneau. We made the trip in a medium-sized, flat-bottomed boat with a small sail, taking a ten by twelve-foot tent and a sheet-iron stove along for camping on the trip if necessary, and to put up the tent to live in for the season after arriving at the sawmill at the bay.

I arrived there with my little family and faithful dog Buck in the course of two days, rigged up our tent with a board floor, frame for window, and lumber door, and fixed up our sheet-iron stove inside the tent, and in the course of a few days commenced to work in the sawmill under one Billy Rudolph, who was head man at the mill and operated it for the Knowell Company, and who, in fact built the mill for this company.

This man Rudolph was a fine mechanic and a very good all-around man, and good-hearted besides. The mill was practically built for the purpose of cutting timber for the Knowell Company's mills and mines at Silver Bow Basin near Juneau, and of course some of the lumber cut here was sold.

The mill was rigged for and run this first season by power from a very large overshot waterwheel. The water was carried by a large flume from a dam built across a creek up the hillside, about a quarter of a mile or more from where the mill stood near tidewater in a little nook about four miles from the lower or southernmost point (Bridget), and up in Berner's Bay about five miles across its entrance from Point Bridget to Point St. Mary. In and near the head of this large bay, there was at this time some good locations of quartz properties, and assessment and development on them were carried on every year.

The sawmill worked six men this year all told, and was rigged up with a muley or old-fashioned single, up-and-down saw which, of course, was slow business. Large timber was practically all that we cut.

There was a large wooden drum on one end of the shaft of the power or overshot wheel around which a five-inch hawser was attached to haul the logs up the slip from the boom, and when we got a good-sized log on the slip the muley saw had to be shut down till the log reached the deck in the mill. My job was alternately bearing off slabs (we had no live rollers), tending the hawser at the bull-wheel as we called it, and sometimes I cut the logs into proper lengths with a crosscut saw. We had no planer this season and no edger either, but we could and did cut some sixty-foot timbers with this muley saw.

There was a small wharf built at the edge of the creek and tidewater, connected with the mill by an approach some eight feet wide, with a track upon which we ran the timber out on cars to the wharf, from where it was loaded on to scows and towed to Juneau by a small steamer the company had chartered.

I worked here at the mill all season, while living in our ten by twelve tent, and got along very well; and our little baby boy throve. We were quite happy and contented, though the work in the sawmill was very hard, especially the lifting, handling, and loading the heavy ten by twelve, and twelve by twelve, and still larger timbers.

The mosquitoes proved to be very bad and tormented us all during the hot weather, and we rigged up mosquito netting to sleep under and also to protect little Benny during the day when he had his naps. And in one corner of the tent we rigged up a hammock swing for the little fellow and attached a cord to it which we could pull back and forth and swing him to sleep.

I remained here at the mill till it closed down for the winter in the early part of November, then moved with my family to Juneau again, making the trip down there in a small, open boat, camping one night in T Harbor, a nearly landlocked bay on the port side going down and about midway between Berner's Bay and Juneau.

I was paid off by Mr. Fred Knowell at Juneau at their head office, at three dollars per day. Of course there were some days of lost time at the mill. I then paid the firm of Koehler and James for our season's provisions, for we had boarded ourselves while at the mill and our groceries were sent to us at Berner's Bay.

My time check amounted to four hundred dollars after allowing for Sundays off and for lost time, and my bill for groceries, gum boots, and clothing for the season for myself and for my little family was about two hundred ten dollars. So out of my season's work of nearly six months I had one hundred ninety dollars left. This was not making money very fast, considering the length of time it took and the hard work and inconveniences we had to put up with.

There is a great deal of rainfall at Berner's Bay, especially in the fall; and while working on the slip and on other jobs outside the mill, especially when sawing logs in two in the creek at the foot of the slip, I often had to change all my clothes at noon and in the evening. After work my gum boots would be full of water, for half the time I stood in the creek up to my hips. I would often walk out on the gravel bar, pull off the gum boots, run the water out, then wring out my socks and put them and the boots on again. Then a little later I might step into a hole, and the water would run into the boots again over the tops.

Practically all the work done in this mill during the season was done by main force and strength. We had no canting gear, live rollers, or proper machinery for hauling the logs up the slip. Our power or bull-wheel was not able to haul the larger logs up onto the slip as it should, to be sawed into proper lengths. This necessitated our sawing them in the creek while standing in it up to our hips, often in ice-cold water.

One great source of trouble, delay, and danger of bodily injury in this mill was in tending the large hawser wrapped around the drum of the bull-wheel. I would drive the large steel dog hook into a large log, burying it as far as I possibly could; then take four or five turns around the overshot wheel, pull the lever and start the wheel, and often while the hawser would jerk that big hook away up into the mill. On several occasions it nearly struck me. On one occasion the hook flew out of a heavy log and came flying up into the mill hunting for someone to hit, and did strike one John Widmarl in the arm, breaking it and nearly cutting it off. This man was laid up for several months.

It was here, while at Berner's Bay this season, that we nearly lost our little child Benny. He got hold of some sugar-coated laxative pills one July morning and ate several of them, thinking they were candy. My wife came running to the mill, calling to me to hurry home, that our little Benny was dying. I dropped my work and ran over to our tent just about one hundred paces from the mill, and Billy Rudolph hurried along with me. We found the poor little fellow – then about eight months old – very ill, and he seemed to have convulsions too, and appeared about to die.

I was totally undone. My wife sat with Benny in her arms, tears streaming down her cheeks, holding him to her breast, eyes and voice pleading with me to save our little boy. Billy Rudolph and I placed hot applications of flannels wrung out of hot water to the child's stomach. We continued this for several hours; also we gave him some castor oil. And later that night our little boy was feeling fairly well. But this was a close call for little Benny, and we shall never forget it. Up there at Berner's Bay there is no medicine, and no doctor within forty miles.

I wintered in Juneau the winter of 1892-1893, where I did a few odd jobs of work occasionally, and lived happily with my wife and watched our little Benny grow and thrive. We took great pleasure in playing with him, and our little fox terrier Buck watched the little fellow jealously and would not let a stranger come near him.

In the spring of 1893, in May, I procured a fairly good rowboat from Mr. Ross of the Knowell Company, loaded all the belongings we owned into it, and we left Juneau again for the Berner's Bay sawmill, where I would work again for the season as before. Our boat was about eighteen feet long, with a round bottom, and it was much better than our old flat-bottomed boat.

Our bedding, camping tent, stove, cooking utensils, and so forth, made a fair load. We pulled up Gastineau Channel and over the bar and had a good trip up to the bay, camping only one night. A good southerly sailing breeze overtook us just south of Eagle River sand spit and carried us right into Berner's Bay sawmill nook the next day after leaving Juneau. My wife helped me to row and steer alternately, and often tended the tiller while we sailed, with Benny snugly curled up, sleeping or crowing in a comfortable place near the stern-sheets.

I remained here at the same mill, working and experiencing the various incidents that go toward making up sawmill life. Some improvements were made this spring in the gear and machinery of the mill, and we had a frame cabin about sixteen by eighteen feet to live in instead of a tent. This made us more comfortable.

I finished the season here, and again left with my family in the fall, in the rowboat we had borrowed from Knowell, for Juneau; and we spent part of the winter of 1893-1894 in Juneau and Douglas. On November 15, 1893, our second child, Edith-Gertrude, was born at Juneau. My wife was again under the care of her mother and sister.

In the spring of 1894 I left again with my family for Berner's Bay sawmill. The mill, this season, was under the management of a Mr. Finn, and a mess house was established for the mill hands who chose to board there. But I and several others who had families boarded ourselves.

The mill now had a planer, edger, and canting gear, and the power was supplied by an iron waterwheel placed at the bottom of a high reservoir built of thick timber into which at the top water flowed from our large flume.

The big old bull or overshot wheel was now only used to haul logs up the slip. Most of the improvements had been made by Billy Rudolph before Mr. Finn took charge. We also had top and bottom circular saws now; the old muley or up-and-down saw had been discarded. Our mill now cut on an average of about twenty thousand feet per day.

I left the mill when it shut down for the winter along the latter part of October, and this time my family and I went on the little steamer *Lucy* which towed a scow of lumber to Juneau.

30. OPERATING THE PETERSON SEALSKIN SLED TRAMWAY ON THE CHILKOOT SUMMIT (1894-95)

We wintered in and around Juneau. In the early part of March I met a man named Peterson, a Swede, who had had his wife and family in Juneau for some time and had been engaged in different pursuits. Among other activities, he used to run an open boat ferry between Juneau and Douglas, using a Columbia River fishing boat.

This man Peterson began to unfurl a great scheme he had which, he explained, would make big money. Eventually he talked me into going up to the Dyea or Chilkoot summit with him on wages. He even enlisted the help of Messrs. Koehler and James to persuade me to go with him, rather against my own judgment, for I tried hard to argue Peterson out of the proposition and really did not think that his plans would turn out satisfactorily at all. But I went with him.

This is what he had planned:

Peterson got numerous large hair sealskins, sewed them together in the shape of boats about six feet long and four feet wide in the shape of little boats, and then sewed heavy canvas sides on them with lashing cords. He made these sleds, of which he had ten, about two feet deep. Peterson had an idea, and was very confident and enthusiastic that by rigging up heavy poles along from the foot of the summit to the top of the Dyea trail, and having endless ropes and blocks and pulleys connected with these skin sleds, he could hoist freight up the steep mountain in them by loading snow into certain number of these skin sleds at the top or upper end, and that these would then have power enough to haul up an equal number or less of the other sleds loaded with the usual miners' supplies.

Well, as I said before, I argued with Peterson, and with Koehler and James; also told Peterson's wife that such an arrangement would never work at all, for I had been up there and knew the conditions and many obstacles there would naturally be against this, as it seemed to me from the first, crazy venture. The snow is very light, and even if conditions were good, it would take so much more weight in the descending sleds to haul even a very light weight up through the loose powdery substance.

Nevertheless, Peterson went into debt with Koehler and James to the extent of about three hundred dollars, and I went up to Dyea with him, taking my wife, little Benny, and our little Edith who was then about three and a half months old. We took passage on board a sloop called the *May Flower*, which was towed up by the steamer *Rustler*, with Captain Malcolm Campbell, a friend of mine to whom I have previously referred.

We had a miserable, uncomfortable trip up to Dyea in the cramped quarters in the hold of the sloop, where we had to sleep on top of sacks of beans, rope, boxes, and undergo the tossing and pitching of the sloop for three days and nights before we arrived at our destination, for it was a very stormy trip. But I had our large, flat-bottomed boat in tow too.

I worked like a beaver for this man Peterson, hauling with hand-sleds all the gear and provisions for this undertaking up from tidewater, along over the ice of the Dyea River, and on up through the canyon to what we called, and is generally known as, the Stone House, just above a rather steep incline.

We camped in a tent in the snow, which was blown down several times. We worked like horses. I thought right along that Peterson would see the futility of his undertaking. We rigged up a pole or station and loaded some of the skin sleds up with snow on the upper part of the hill and put a light load of miners' supplies in a couple of the ascending sleds but, of course, it would not work without both of us and several miners taking hold of the rope and pulling down hard. And this was just as much work, or more, than pulling up a medium – loaded, regular hand sled.

I told Peterson he could remain there as long as he wanted

and waste time. By this time it was early April, so I left him and after a month's hard work – for which I never received a cent. During this time my wife and two little ones remained at Dyea at the Healy and Wilson post.

I procured some light sail stuff from Mr. Wilson and made a sail preparatory to leaving there. Next day, when I went down to the bend in the river, about a mile and a half below the post, to see how our large flat-bottomed boat was, I found her frozen to the bottom and a solid mass of ice from stem to stern, flush with the gunwhales. The high tides backing up in the river had swamped her, and afterward the water had frozen solid.

It took me a whole day to partially chop out this ice, and then I had to pack salt water to thaw and loosen up the ice where a coating of some two or three inches still stuck all along her sides and bottom inside. And all this time it was still freezing hard.

About April 10th I decided to start down Lynn Canal, and got all our worldly belongings loaded into our big skiff. Just before we left, a lone Japanese man came down to the beach to ask if I would give him passage in the boat to either Haines Mission, Berner's Bay or Juneau, wherever I was going, for he had been stopped from going into the Yukon over the Dyea trail and summit by the miners. They had called a meeting about the matter because they did not want any Japs in there.

I took him along, and before arriving at our destination I was not sorry that I did so, as will be seen later.

We bade Mr. and Mrs. Wilson good-bye, hoisted our sail, left the bank of the Dyea River on half ebb tide, and went scooting down the stream out into Lynn Canal. We touched in to Skagway to look around, and found the creek still frozen. I found our log house intact, as were our other belongings. But the outer piling of our small wharf had given way, and not much remained except two large rock-filled cribs on the inner part. This did not surprise me much, because the piling had stood about six years, which was longer than we had expected to leave the work without making more improvements on the wharf in the meantime. But it was impossible for us to do this without funds, and no one would help us with money to improve the property.

I then headed our boat for Haines Mission, where we arrived

four hours later. We camped there overnight. Next morning a strong northerly wind was blowing, and freezing hard; deep snow and much ice was on the beaches. We took refuge with a Mr. Clark and his family, and were compelled to remain there for ten days during a fierce blizzard which we certainly did not expect to encounter at this late date, the 11th of April.

On April 21st the storm let up. We bade the Clarks good-bye, and once more got our rolls of bedding, sheet-iron stove, tent, provisions, and kitchen box loaded into our boat, first making Benny and little baby Edith comfortable in the after part of the boat. We rowed out of Haines Mission Bay and headed down the canal, hugging our starboard shore.

When about four miles down the canal, a northerly breeze sprang up again which, however, was not steady at first, but blew veeringly, flopping our boom over first to one side then to the other. This nearly capsized our overloaded boat, which only had about six inches of freeboard. I was at the tiller, my wife a few feet from me near the stern holding our little baby Edith and attending to Benny, and the Jap was forward near the bows.

On nearing Point Seduction, near the entrance to Chilkat Inlet, I decided to cross the canal diagonally over to Seward City and run down on that shore to Berner's Bay – our destination. So I headed the boat over, and in the course of an hour, and after much shipping of water over the gunwhales and much bailing, we arrived safely, made a landing to cook some dinner, and there camped for the night. There was no harbor, so we were obliged to haul our boat up above the high tide watermark.

Next morning we left Seward City beach and rowed and sailed on down to Berner's Bay, where we arrived at the sawmill early in the afternoon. We found about four feet of snow there on the level, and the creeks all frozen along the edges, with small strips of running water in the centers. It now started to rain hard, and before we packed our belongings from the skiff to the cabin we were all soaked through. We had to wallow through wet snow that came above our waists to beat down some kind of trail.

I split some wood and got a fire started in the house, and by evening we were fairly comfortable and mighty glad to get settled once more – even in a one-room shack at Berner's Bay without a soul, as yet, within thirty or forty miles, unless there were some men at Seward City. The latter place is called "city" but I have never seen or heard of a place that failed to deserve the name city as much as that place does.

In the winter, for weeks and months at a time, a vessel cannot make a landing to discharge a few tons of supplies, and there is no harbor whatever for the fierce seas that roll up on the unprotected beach. A small, narrow-gauge track leads up into the mountains from the wharf for about three miles to the quartz mines; on this track a small engine and cars are run back and forth to haul supplies.

I worked here at Berner's Bay sawmill about half the season, then commenced building a schooner thirty-eight feet long overall, four-foot hold, and a twelve-foot beam, with a large center board. I named the schooner *Gertrude*, after our little baby girl.

In the meantime my father came up to Berner's Bay and helped me to finish her up. I also had a Dutchman named Schwartz do some work on the schooner, principally putting on the cabin which extended some twenty feet, leaving space for the cockpit and companionway aft of about six feet, and a forecastle of about ten feet. The cabin reached about twenty inches above the deck.

My father arrived at Berner's Bay about the middle of June. For a couple of months prior to this time he had been at Skagway Bay doing some work on our location there, where he had a couple of natives employed. We built the hull of the schooner upstairs in the sawmill, then launched her down into the lower part of the mill to put on the cabin and caulk and paint her all over outside.

Because the season was getting late, and I had no sails or rigging and anchors and ropes for her, I launched her into the creek and floated her across the Nook a few hundred yards away and opposite the mill. Then I hauled her out high and dry at high spring tide and moored her well for the coming winter with two bow ropes and two stern lines fastened to deadmen dug into the beach.

At the end of the season, I went with my family to Juneau for the winter. Along the first part of January 1895, I went to work at the Mexican mine at Douglas for three dollars per day and board for myself, and moved my family over to Douglas where I rented a little house. My job was up high in a tower above the mill proper, at the rock breaker or crusher. A man named Jack Ross was also there. Our duty was to break up all the pieces of ore with a heavy sledge. They were brought in the cars from the mine and dumped on the floor or into the rock crusher. Anyone in Douglas familiar with these mines at this time knows whether he earned his wages or not.

I remained there for three weeks, then made up my mind that if I wanted to kill myself there were better ways than breaking ore rock for Treadwell's rock crusher. So I quit and built a flat-bottomed ski about sixteen feet long and with four-and-a-half-foot beam, got a bill of provisions of thirty-five dollars, and leaving my family at Douglas I left, taking with me a little man by the name of Peterson (but not the Peterson of Dyea summit sealskin tramway). Then I heard that seven young fellows from San Francisco were about to leave Juneau on the steamer *Rustler*, with Captain Malcolm Campbell, bound for Hootalinqua River in the Yukon. I intended to go in via the Dyea summit route, so I hurried over to Juneau and took passage on the *Rustler* with my man Peterson. Captain Campbell gave us a free trip up and also hauled my skiff on board the steamer.

31. FIRST PARTY OF PROSPECTORS WITH SUPPLIES GO THROUGH THE SKAGWAY OR WHITE PASS ROUTE (1895)

As soon as the *Rustler* cast off her lines at Juneau and headed down the channel, I got busy with Captain Campbell and told him I would like very much to induce this party of prospectors to go in by way of Skagway and the White Pass route. Captain Campbell said he would rather land them there, than to land at Dyea. So eventually, by strong arguments and agreeing to help these men lighter all their goods ashore at Skagway from the steamer, and assist them up to the mouth of the first canyon, they at last made up their minds to land at Skagway Bay and go into the interior through our route.

We encountered heavy weather up Lynn Canal, and it was very cold. Arrived at Skagway February 2, 1895, after a two days' trip from Juneau. These seven young men were from California, so they said; some were moulders and machinists, and one or two of them were quite young. And although they had told me on the trip up that they had quite a large outfit, I had no idea that they meant more than five or six hundred pounds apiece. But I really was surprised when we came to unload their stuff into my skiff and another large open skiff or lighter we hauled out at Skagway and now brought into service, that they had about fifteen hundred pounds each, or quite a little over five tons.

When we got all these supplies lightered ashore and hauled up with sleighs to camping ground in the shelter of the timber and piled up, they made a big bulk.

My man Peterson and I were camped in a tent a few hundred yards away from this party, in a sheltered spot among the tall spruce and hemlock near the edge of the creek and about five hundred yards up the valley north of our log house, because the log cabin was out in the open where the winds struck it hard. We were more comfortable in the tent. Besides, this log cabin was not completed as yet, it lacked a door, proper windows, and so forth.

I knew of an old man named Joe Fields who lived at Dyea for a while back and who did a little trading there with the natives. He had a couple of buckskin ponies, so I induced him to bring them down, and we built a raft at Dyea and floated them down on it to Skagway. And in the course of a few days we had helped the party of seven with their five tons of goods up to the mouth of the first canyon, about four miles up the valley from tidewater, hauling the stuff along on the river ice.

Then we cut a trail across a ridge from a point below the first falls, which are about ten feet high, from which point we went on northward to the second canyon. Sleigh load of supplies could not be hauled up over this point; hence we cut the trail across the ridge a mile or so, and connected with the second canyon farther above. These canyons closely resemble the one above Dyea, which I have described on my first trip to the Yukon in 1887.

We did not venture taking the horses up into the canyon for fear of losing them in some of the many big, open holes among the huge boulders into which we could look and see the water rushing in many places where there were openings in the ice.

I learned afterward that these seven young men got all their supplies worked through and over this Skagway route without having to pack any of it on their backs. Of course they were obliged to make many relays but got in all right, and went up the Hootalinqua River. But I believe they did not meet with much success in finding any placer diggings to pay worth staying for, and later that same season they headed farther down the Yukon to more promising locations.

The winter and early spring of 1895 was certainly a hard one. One of those young men had a thermometer hanging on one of their tents while camped at Skagway, and it registered 30 degrees below zero on one or two occasions, during which times we stopped sleighing upriver. The frost vapor caused by the heavy north wind rose for hundreds of feet out on Lynn Canal.

32. THE LONG SHORTY AND BIGELOW-SEELEY PARTY ARRIVE AT SKAGWAY BAY TO EXPLORE (1895)

It was now early February, and one morning the steamer *Rustler* steamed in and landed one Bigelow (usually known as Long Shorty) and a noted character; his nephew, a stout, heavy man by the name of Seeley; an old Indian named Schwatka after Lieutenant Schwatka, the guide; and another Indian by the name of Henry. Old Man Fields had by this time returned to Dyea, leaving his two horses with me at Skagway to run loose and forage for themselves by pawing up the snow and eating the dried grass underneath.

I went over with my man Peterson to interview the new arrivals. From what I could glean it seemed that they had some idea of trying to locate here and also taking up some land.

I had known this man Shorty Bigelow long before at Chilkat, and many others knew of him.

Well, this party stated that they were there to explore this route to the lakes, and report on its feasibility for trails, roads, and traffic to his principles back East, and that they would start up the valley on the ice as soon as it moderated a little. He expressed himself as being sure of finding the right route through and over the summit to the lakes, especially since he had Long Shorty with him as well as Schwatka.

In the course of two days they got started, and eight days later the whole party returned – frostbitten, cursing the whole surrounding country, and plumb disgusted with everything. I learned from them that they had gone way up a wrong draw in the mountains, had to return, got lost for a day or two, and so

174

forth. Mr. Seeley argued with me for hours trying to illustrate the futility of my spending my time in such a place as Skagway, saying that there never would be travel through this route, let alone any trail or wagon road built; and even if there were, there wouldn't be enough miners' supplies shipped over to make it pay.

All this time old Schwatka wore his everlasting broad grin and motioned and gesticulated all about the awful trip they had had, and upheld Mr. Seeley. Long Shorty and the rest added their arguments that the Skagway route could never amount to anything for traffic to the interior.

In fact this party made a complete failure of even finding their way to the summit, to say nothing of getting through to the lakes, and tried very hard to discourage me from spending any more time and energy on my location at Skagway. They remained at Skagway Bay for eight days or so, and then the Rustler called in and took them all to Juneau. I have not heard of or seen either Mr. Seeley or his nephew since then, but have often seen the old Indians Schwatka and Henry, because scarcely anyone who has been in up in this country for any length of time could help hearing of them.

Long Shorty Bigelow, as will be seen hereafter, later became very much interested in my location and rights at Skagway. He tried very hard to assist the contestants to our claim (to) win out against me in the land office at Sitka, when I proved up on the location. Later he was convicted of a heinous crime committed in the Yukon country, and sentenced to about fourteen years' imprisonment at McNeil's Island, Washington. But after serving seven years or more he was pardoned.

My father was now employed steamboating in British Columbia on the Kootenay lakes and rivers to earn a little money.

On the 22nd of February, my man Peterson and I pulled out from Skagway and boarded a small steamer on her way down the channel from Dyea, and arrived at Douglas a couple of days later. I found my wife and little Benny and Edith – or Gertrude, as we sometimes called her – all well. But the weather had been something awful in my absence, which one could easily see from the appearance of the beaches and small floating wharves at Douglas and Treadwell's. They were covered with heavy ice a foot thick, for February is generally the worst month up here, or at least the first half of it.

I worked around Douglas at the sawmill and mines for the next two months, then left for Berner's Bay again to get employment there for a while and try to finish and rig the schooner. I left Douglas about the middle of April, taking my family up with me in our blue-painted skiff, to which I referred before as having been built at the sawmill at Douglas.

I arrived at Berner's Bay with my wife, Benny and Edith after a three days' trip. To our great regret, we lost our fox terrier dog, Buck; he had fallen overboard from the steamer *Lucy* while on a trip to Chilkat during a heavy northeaster when abreast of Seward City. The loss of this great friend and companion was keenly felt by my wife and me, and also the children.

Arriving at Berner's Bay I found my schooner intact, just as I had moored it on the beach at high tide. My wife and I gave her another coat of paint all over inside and puttied up all the nail heads.

I wrote a letter to my sister, Mrs. A.M. Taylor, at San Francisco, and sent her a description and sizes of the mainsail and foresail for the schooner, asking her to have them made and forwarded to me. This she did at once. Later I received oars, anchors, wire, rope, and so forth, from Juneau, which my father forwarded from Victoria along in May. I started work in the sawmill again. About this time my father arrived in Berner's Bay from the south and helped me to make the masts for the schooner and rig her up. Then, in June, my father proceeded with the schooner to Skagway and remained there for a couple of months. During that time he employed a couple of Indians to clear a little land, and slash brush and burn it. This brought us about to the middle of September.

My father then called in to Berner's Bay for me and my family, and we proceeded to Haines Mission. My wife and Benny and Edith remained there with my wife's mother. My father and I went on up to Dyea, and after a few days' layover we took on eight passengers bound to Juneau from the Yukon, at eight dollars a piece. We called in to Haines Mission on our way down Lynn Canal, picked up my wife and the two children, and sailed again for Juneau.

On the way we experienced some strong northerly winds and heavy seas, and were obliged to go into anchorage one night at Yankee Basin or Cove, which lies on the port side going south a few miles below Point Bridget or Berner's Bay.

We arrived safely at Juneau with our passengers. Later I rented a cabin there, and a week after that Mr. Fred Knowell engaged me to take three tons of giant powder up to his wharf at Seward City for his mines. So my father and I loaded this powder – which was packed in small square boxes – into my little schooner, and next day, as Captain Malcolm Campbell was going up Lynn Canal with the *Rustler*, we got him to tow us up to Seward City. We had one native boy with us.

On arrival at the wharf at Seward City we had to use great care (though it happened to be calm weather) in unloading this dangerous cargo of Giant Powder, for if a box were allowed to fall, it would in all probability blow up the whole load of it; and even if it did not, one box is enough to blow up a whole ship anyhow. We formed a row leading from the schooner to the wharf, and passed or threw boxes from one to the other.

For this trip I charged the Knowell Company seventy-five dollars, and it was fully worth it.

We then proceeded up to Dyea, and brought another batch of Yukoners down to Juneau. This brought us to the month of November. We beached my little schooner *Gertrude* at high tide just a couple of miles above Juneau and lived aboard her in the cabin, where we were comfortable. But I, especially, had to stoop over, for there was not quite depth enough for me to stand erect in the cabin.

My father went below to Victoria for the winter, and to see if in some way he could get someone interested to advance a little necessary money to help us make some more improvements on our location at Skagway Bay.

33. WE AT LAST GET ASSISTANCE TO MAKE SOME FURTHER IMPROVEMENTS AT SKAGWAY (1896)

The winter of 1896 here at Juneau eventually dragged by, and in April, I left in my schooner with my family for Skagway, where we arrived in the middle of April after a fairly good trip.

Shortly after my arrival I received a letter from my father in Victoria to the effect that he had taken a contract to convey the British mail to and from Forty Mile Creek and Fort Cudahy, at six hundred dollars per round trip, and for me to meet him at Skagway Bay.

Along about the beginning of June my father arrived at Skagway Bay on a little steamer called the *Sealion*. I met him, and we talked matters over. He explained that he had met an E.E. Billinghurst in Victoria, and through him became acquainted with a gentleman from England who was a promoter; Billinghurst was his agent.

My father explained to them all the great advantages of Skagway Bay, and the pass through there into the Yukon and so forth, and the great navigable streams putting into the Yukon, and his own firm belief for future big finds of placer mines in that country. In fact my father went into the whole matter at great length.

Mr. Wilkinson, the promoter, then took the matter under advisement. But before my father left Victoria, Mr. Wilkinson arranged through his agent, E.E. Billinghurst, to advance my father eighteen hundred dollars in supplies, two horses, a couple of cows, six thousand feet or so of rough lumber as well as other materials, including the guarantee of payment of wages to five men to work at our location at Skagway for this season, 1896.

It was arranged between myself and my father that I should make the second or intermediate trip with the mail. My father was under an eighteen hundred dollar government bond to faithfully and diligently fulfill the contract for three round trips from Victoria and return there.

My father then proceeded up to Dyea and went in over that route with his mail and, as will be seen later, continued on down the Yukon to St. Michael's, then out back to Victoria via San Francisco to Victoria.

In the meantime I remained at Skagway with my family. My wife and I worked together fixing up the log house, chinking it better, putting in a good window, a back and a front door, a rough floor, and making pieces of rough bunks and furniture out of poles.

On arrival at Dyea one day, along about June 5th, to see if there was any mail for me, I found a letter for me from E.E. Billinghurst dated from Victoria, B.C., advising me that two horses, harnesses, wagon and feed and a small amount of supplies had been shipped to me from Seattle to Juneau, and asking me to come there to have them transported to Skagway.

I immediately went to Juneau, using an eighteen foot sealing boat to make the trip, leaving my wife and children alone at Skagway.

I arrived at Juneau in two and a half days, having rowed portion of the way and sailed part of the way. On my arrival I found more advises there by letter for me, including some credit to draw on Messrs. Koehler and James for provisions and some funds.

The two horses sent up from Seattle, however, I was obliged to trade off to Mr. George Miller, in exchange for two horses that had been raised in Juneau. The two that Billinghurst had sent up were good-looking horses and cost considerable money, but no one could get near them. They kicked at anyone who came close to them, and struck out with their forefeet, and the blacksmith to whom I spoke about reshoeing them said he would not undertake the job without throwing them down and lashing them down for safety. How George Miller made out with them afterward I did not learn.

While at Juneau, I hired one George Buchanan, formerly of Enumclaw, Washington; also an Indian by the name of John Jack. There was also a young boy of about seventeen who came up from Victoria to stay at Skagway part of the season, whose name was Dick Hindle. The boy's father had been employed on Parliament buildings which were then in the course of construction at James Bay, Victoria, B.C., and sent the boy up to Skagway to us for his health, for his heart was weak and he was also subject to fits of some kind.

Well, I made arrangements with Captain Malcolm Campbell to take our horses, a small batch of blacksmith's tools, some lumber, shingles, groceries, and other supplies up to Skagway, also to take myself, George Buchanan, John Jack, the Indian, and the young Dick Hindle, and about June 15th we arrived in Skagway, all safe again, and discharged our stuff there.

We swam the horses ashore, and on reaching the shore they went flying up and down the beach, for they felt very well at having the whole uplands of the bay of Skagway all to themselves.

I shall state here that these two ponies, Molly and Daisy, became my favorites, and proved to be the two best little workers that ever landed at Skagway. Molly was taken to Cape Nome in 1901, and Daisy was still working in harness at Skagway in 1907; she was ten years old or more when I got her from George Miller at Juneau, and was, as I understand, the mother of Molly.

After straightening things out, hauling lumber up from the beach, and placing George Buchanan in charge of some work such as the building of a small log table and a lean-to blacksmith shop, and a frame house about sixteen by twenty-five feet, including some clearing, fencing, and other preliminary work, I started to get ready to leave for Juneau for the Canadian mail for Forty Mile Creek and Cudahy.

34. IN HER MAJESTY'S MAIL SERVICE – JUNEAU TO FORTY MILE CREEK AND RETURN (1896)

Early on the morning of July 5th, I provisioned our little sealing boat, including a sheet-iron stove, an eight by ten-foot tent, blankets, and so forth, and taking my wife, our two children Edith and Benny, and young Dick Hindle, we rowed out of Skagway Bay about 7 a.m. At about 11 a.m. we arrived at Haines Mission, at which place my family was to remain with my wife's mother and sister, while I went to Juneau for the mails and made the entire round trip inside.

At Haines, however, I found that my wife's folks were stationed at Chilkat, across the trail. So leaving Dick Hindle to look after my boat at Haines, I packed Benny across the peninsula over the old Murray Wagon Road, which had supplanted the first native trail; and my wife packed Edith, lashed in a heavy shawl, on her back. When we arrived at Chilkat she and the children joined her folks, then they sent a couple of natives to bring up the luggage and bedding.

I pulled out from Haines that same evening. The weather was very warm, and the sun beat down on us hard. Young Hindle was learning to row fairly well, and we made very good time. We rowed practically every inch of the hundred miles or so to Juneau, stopping only twice for half an hour to make coffee and get a bite to eat.

We arrived at Juneau twenty-nine hours after leaving Skagway Bay, and pitched our tent a couple of miles north of Juneau near the beach, not far from the cemetery. We camped there till the Pacific Coast Steamship Company's steamer *Idahoe* arrived at 5 a.m. on July 8th. At 8 a.m. on the same day I received from Richard Nelson, the then acting postmaster at Juneau, a fifty-pound locked and sealed leather mailbag, for which I made out a receipt and sent it to Mr. Nelson.

Half an hour later I shoved off from the beach where I had been camped with young Hindle, and started up Gastineau Channel and over the bar and on up past the head of Douglas Island.

We were fortunate in getting a good, strong, fair sailing breeze. I took the tiller, stationed young Hindle in the bows, and we went bowling along at great speed. I had gotten at Juneau a small young puppy dog, and a little black-and-white kitten which we kept in a box. These were the first cat and dog brought to Skagway. The little pup was about six weeks old, and we called it Mosquito (of which more will be told later)

After twelve hours I landed at Haines Mission Beach at about 8 p.m. Since there was a very heavy southerly wind still blowing and a big sea on, I decided to camp for the night here, then run over the portage trail and bid my wife and children good-bye before I left for Skagway, from where I would go into the Yukon via the Dyea route.

Next morning, July 8th, I left Haines Mission at 10 a.m. It was still blowing very heavy from the southward. We arrived at Skagway Bay at about noon and sailed way up the creek, the tide being quite high. On the way up, a few miles south of Skagway, young Hindle jumped up from where he had been reclining in the bows and started to whistle and act queerly; he rushed to the halyards of the sail, whipped out a pocket knife and cut the halyards before I could lay hold of him, and the boom and sail dropped and hung in the water, and very nearly overturned our boat. After that he had a fit, and it was with the utmost care that I got both of us out of this scrape without being drowned.

I spent two days at Skagway getting things ready and making pack straps and talking matters over with George Buchanan, then left with the mail for Dyea. Buchanan and Hindle accompanied me in the sealing boat, and helped me to pack my stuff up to Fields' store. Then I bade them good bye, and they returned to Skagway with the boat. This was on July 12th, at 2 p.m.

In the meantime, at Victoria an agreement, or contract, had been drawn up between my father and E.E. Billinghurst. My name also was placed in it as party of the first part, my father as party of the second part, and Billinghurst as party of the third part. Billinghurst acted as trustee for certain principals not disclosed. Affected by the contract were one hundred and sixty acres of land bordering on Skagway Bay, for which I, or we, should give the party of the third part a lien on same for their advancing us the sum of eighteen hundred dollars in supplies, materials, houses, and so on. This agreement I did not see up to the time of my departure for the Yukon.

I will state here that I started in with this mail trip and made the round trip without a cent of ready cash with me (nor did I have any to take with me).

I proceeded to pack my small light outfit up to old Joe Fields' log store building situated about a mile above the Healy and Wilson post, where I made arrangements with Fields to lend me two buckskin ponies he had brought back to Dyea from Skagway some time before. I wanted them to pack the mail sack and my outfit up to Sheep Camp; also to pack the outfit of an Interior Indian, whom Fields helped me to get to accompany me in on the trip without pay, and who wanted to get inside with a small outfit he had.

I was delayed at Dyea with the mails, and had a lot of trouble and some annoyance caused by Bob Wright, a notorious character, as will be seen shortly.

Fields and I rounded up both ponies and hobbled them; also we put a long rope around their necks so we could catch them next morning. But the hobbles were removed during the night by Bob Wright, who also stole the long ropes from their necks. Fields and I saw him carrying the ropes over to his cabin across the slough, where he had much other stolen goods stowed away.

July 13th: Rounded up the horses again and tied them up outside of Fields' store so we should be sure of them next day when they were needed. Arranged with Fields to procure the services of an Indian, Nan-Suk, his wife and his boy from Sheep Camp, where they were camped, to go with me to help over with my outfit from Sheep Camp to Lake Lindeman. I had a tent, blankets, and so forth, which made a bulky pack, and the Interior or Stick Indian had a sewing machine and his own stuff that he was taking in to his wife at Sixty Mile Creek above the Klondike.

My provisions amounted to very little: one half sack of flour, ten pounds of bacon, twenty-five pounds of sugar, fifteen pounds of beans, two small cans of yeast powder, two rolls of butter, two pounds of coffee, five pounds of dried mixed fruit, and five pounds of rice.

My cooking utensils were a frying pan, a coffee pot, two tin cups, and a bean kettle. The bean kettle I have kept ever since, and I still have it.

Got the two ponies packed and started from Dyea at 4 p.m. today. Reached the mouth of the canyon some eight miles above Dyea at 7 p.m. The deepest ford, thus far, took us to the hips. We unpacked our ponies, got supper, and camped here for the night. There was not a single Indian here at Dyea except the Interior one I took along; but we expect to see a few at Sheep Camp.

Had a heavy rain fall last night.

July 15th: Got up at 4 a.m., packed the ponies, had breakfast, and left here – the mouth of the canyon – at 5:20 a.m. Arrived at 8 a.m. Made arrangements with the Indian, Nan-Suk, and his wife and boy, who we found camped here as Fields expected, to pack two hundred thirty-eight pounds over to Lake Lindeman at two cents per pound, amounting to twenty-three dollars and eighty cents, for which I was to give Nan-Suk an order on Joe Fields for that amount.

I turned the two ponies loose and started them back toward Dyea where, as I learned later, they arrived all right at the Fields' store, where they belonged.

Left Sheep Camp at 9 a.m., and at 5 p.m. arrived at the log cabin with an earthen roof called the Miners' Rest, which my father built in the summer of 1895, about a mile or so from the upper end of Lake Lindeman. We had overtaken and passed the Richardson-Obelander party carrying United States mail on the way over near Sheep Camp, where they were camping for about two weeks.

I continued down the trail to where it strikes the Lake near its head. I expected to find some miners or a camp of some kind, but no one was there. I found one good-sized canoe and one old smaller cottonwood canoe lying bottom up a few yards from the edge of the lake. So I returned to the log cabin again to await my Indian packers, who had not arrived as soon as I did, for I only packed the sack of mail and a lunch kettle.

Traveled fifteen miles today, mostly all up hill. Waited here at the cabin for about twenty minutes, when the Richardson-Oberlander party came along with the U.S. mails. I then decided to go back to the lake again, and camped there for the night by 10 p.m. It is quite raw, cold, and windy here tonight.

Traveling over this summit and pass now is different at this time of the year from what it was nine years ago, early in the spring of April 1887. Then there was deep snow, snow everywhere; now bare rocks, earth and foliage everywhere except, of course, on and near the summit of the pass. My Indian, Nan-Suk, and his family arrived with their packs shortly after I got to the lake, but my other Interior Indian has not yet turned up. I settled with Nan-Suk and his family by giving him an order for twenty-three dollars and eighty cents on Joe Fields for the packing.

July 16th: Still here, unable to get across the lake. Some Indians came along, who asked six dollars, or two dollars per hundred pounds, to take my outfit to the foot of the lake. Weather still quite cold and stormy for this time of the year.

My other Indian came along this evening at 6:30, with his own pack.

July 17th: Still blowing very hard from the south, and cannot get any Indian to take us to the portage at the foot of the lake. What few Indians were here left again for Sheep Camp and Dyea this morning. Mr. Richardson and party are here now too with the U.S. mail, awaiting a chance to get across the lake. He offered an Indian twenty-five dollars to make three trips across with a canoe, and offered to put in his own help and that of his three men to get his stuff across, but the Indian would not do it. Richardson has about three tons of stuff and the Indians asked two dollars per hundred pounds.

We intend to take or borrow one of the canoes we found here as soon as the gale moderates. The Indians took three of their cottonwood canoes away yesterday and had them way up one of the creeks at the extreme head of this lake.

No moderation in the wind as yet this evening. Low clouds scudding from the southward, and it is so cold that we had to set up a stove in our tent. No likelihood of getting across the lake, unless we take a canoe.

Mr. Richardson offered the Indians thirty dollars to take three canoe loads across for him.

July 18th: Still lying here, stormbound. Heavy, cold southerly wind with drizzling rain. I certainly did not expect weather as chilly as this at this season of the year.

July 19th: I and my Indian started from here (the head of Lindeman Lake) this morning at seven o'clock in a small cottonwood canoe loaded down heavily and leaking freely, necessitating one of us to bail water continually. Wind moderated to some extent. Arrived at Payer Portage at the foot of the lake at 7:30 a.m. Gave the canoe in charge of an Indian named Stick Charlie to tow back to where we took it from at the head of Lake Lindeman, giving Charlie an order on J.T. Fields for four dollars, of which I explained to him, he was to take two dollars for his services and with the balance of two dollars pay the owner for our use of the canoe.

Portaged my outfit and mail to the head of Bennett Lake, and there met Billy Rudolph and Ned Ellingen camped and running a small sawmill, cutting boat lumber from logs six to eight and ten inches through, and occasionally building a boat. Rudolph had already built a boat for me with paddle, oars, and mast complete. This had been prearranged for me by my father on his first trip in.

I rigged up a sail, had lunch with Rudolph and Ellingen, took a letter from them addressed to Ellingen's brother at Forty Mile Creek, and left here at 12:30 p.m.

Now I really felt good. Our boat was a good one and fairly tight, and we went scooting down Lake Bennett, sailing before a strong southerly breeze which kept increasing right along until we had to go ashore just abreast of the island, which is near the right shore about midway between the upper and lower end of the lake. There I cut down our sail to a smaller size.

Started out again and made fast time. Arrived at Caribou Crossing at 6:30 p.m. Passed the mouth of Windy Arm. Light wind and choppy sea. Here we sighted the Hyde's party tow boats about four miles ahead of us. They left Rudolph and Ellingen's camp at the head of Bennett Lake four hours in advance of us.

Passed Hyde's party, camped and all turned in on the beach, about midnight. We kept on pulling till 2 a.m., then went ashore and lay down to rest and sleep for two hours.

July 20th: Monday. Got under way again at 4 a.m. Arrived at Tagish Lake houses and wrote the date and my name on one of them. Left again. Passed through the sluggish connecting stream to Marsh Lake. No wind yet today. One of us pulling at the oars, and paddling and steering alternately an hour each. When about nine miles from the foot of the lake a very light southerly wind came up, for which we were thankful because the sun was beating down on us fiercely. Passed the island near the foot of the lake, also an Indian fishing camp, thence into the outlet leading in to the Twenty-Six Mile River. Current sluggish here. Kept rowing hard right along and arrived at the head of the canyon at 6:30 p.m. Found the water very high. Therefore I did not deem it prudent to run the canyon.

Turned in to snatch a couple of hours' sleep if possible, but the mosquitoes were as thick as cheese. Our run from the head of Lake Lindeman to the head of the canyon, including portage and stop-over at the head of Bennett, was accomplished in thirty-three and one-half hours.

July 21st: Tuesday. Had a hard job portaging my outfit and boat, especially the latter. Laid skids down, and I on one end, and my Indian on the other, pulled, hauled and lifted till we got her up the first hill. Then it was somewhat easier. On reaching the foot of the canyon I wrote a note and fastened it to a conspicuous tree addressed to my father in the hope that he would see it on his way out, in case I missed meeting him.

Had a bite to eat, loaded up the boat, and started again. Passed through about two miles of very strong water, and landed a little above the White Horse which I could see looked pretty wild. Portaged the mail, blankets, and provisions, lashed the oars and other stuff tightly under the thwarts, and dropped the boat down through the rapids all the way on left-hand side using a long rope and bridle on the bow.

Loaded up again and started. Passed the Takhini River on our left, fifteen miles below White Horse. Entered Lake Laberge by a narrow channel or a slough on the left, and here and farther in the mosquitoes are thick and furiously hungry. Stopped on the left hand side of the lake near some old fish houses about two miles from the mouth of the slough or entrance to the lake to snatch a little sleep, for I was nearly worn out. After cooking supper, with three or four smudge fires all around us, we ate and turned in around 10:30 p.m. but got hardly any rest, to say nothing of sleep. The mosquitoes were thick on top of the netting and blankets and got at us in spite of all we could do, till I could not lie here any longer.

July 22nd: Wednesday. Left here again at 4 a.m. without breakfast. Mosquitoes too thick to allow us to cook anything. Just after starting, a light southerly breeze sprang up, so I raised our sail. Sun shining warm, and mosquitoes still keeping us company way out here on the lake, a mile from shore, though they are not so thick.

Entered Lewes (Thirty Mile section of the Yukon) River after a long hard pull across the lake, for the wind did not amount to much and soon died out again. Many large flies, which resembled horseflies, also bothered us a great deal while rowing over the lake. Have not met or passed a single boat or canoe since passing the Hyde party.

About six miles or so from the entrance of the Lewes River from Laberge, the river makes a regular horseshoe bend where there are many high-cut clay or sand banks. A good current of four and a half or five miles flows here. This remarkable bend in the river is almost a complete circle, and the distance across from water to water at the nearest points cannot be more than a few hundred feet. The Indians call it Too-tel-Wa-ta. A few miles below this place, without any warning, a heavy upstream wind struck and whirled my boat around and very nearly capsized it. I quickly sheared her over to the nearest bank and tied up there for nearly an hour, during which time some rain fell accompanied by a few flashes of lightning.

Started again. Passed the mouth of the Hootalinqua (teslin) River at 9:30 p.m. Saw the island where I had built my boat in the spring of 1887. Landed at 11 p.m. on the left-hand side about ten miles below the Hootalinqua, where there are three houses, and had a few hours' rest.

July 24th: Thursday. Got under way at 6 a.m., shoved off, and ate our breakfast in the boat out in mid-stream to be clear of the pesky mosquitoes. Passed through another horseshoe bend. This (Lewes) river is very crooked off and on nearly all the way from the upper end to Big Salmon River. Passed Cassiar Bar, which was all under water with quite a large drift-pile at its head. Noted the grave and board cross where Jim Williams was buried at the top of the beach toward the upper end.

Passed another bar where considerable mining had been done. There is another bar above Cassiar, where a good deal of prospecting and mining work had been done some time ago. Passed the mouth of Big Salmon River on our right, and about thirty-seven miles farther on we passed the mouth of the Little Salmon. Here my Indian asked me to land at a little nook close to a small brook. I did so, and he looked about for something in the way of an Indian sign or message. As he later explained, he had expected to find a message from one of his friends. He did find it. In reply he cut a slit in a small willow, then took a small spruce twig about two feet long, stripped off all the green from it except a little tuft on the small end, and inserted this twig or little branch in the slit in the willow with the green tuft end pointing downstream. This, he explained, would tell his friend when he called into this nook that he, my Indian, had passed downstream this summer.

Passed a boat along here with five men bound for Forty Mile Creek. They started, I learned, five days in advance of us from the head of Lake Lindeman. This boat got swamped on Lake Bennett, and they had been laid up there for twenty-four hours. I noted the low gap or pass on the left, twelve miles or so below Little Salmon, which leads by an Indian trail across to Lake Laberge in three days' travel.

Islands and sloughs have become numerous now. Passed George Carmack's house where there are also two other houses built by Indians, about fifteen miles above the Five Finger Rapids. Went ashore about five miles farther down, bent some strong willows till the small ends touched the ground, then spread our tent over them and tried to get some much needed sleep. But the mosquitoes quickly got us; they are still wickedly hungry. The salmon have not as yet made their appearance along here, but they are expected to reach Forty Mile Creek in about a week from now.

Our willow-supported tent or wigwam – tight as we tried to fasten the canvas to the ground and net in the inside – had no effect in keeping the mosquitoes away. They appeared to help each other through the netting and tortured me and my Indian until we both had to get up and prepare to make another start.

July 25th: Friday. Started at 6 a.m. This is the most crooked river I have ever seen. The longest stretch that one can see from point to point along the river, it seems to me, would not exceed one and one half to two miles.

Just below George Carmack's old house the river makes almost a complete circle, all but about a hundred feet, so it appears. Passed by Carmack's lignite coal prospect on the right hand side, situated on a steep side hill, five and one half miles from Five Fingers. Quite a strong current makes along here with broken-like water. This was about twelve miles above the mouth of the Pelly River.

I understand the Alaska Commercial Company's steamer *Arctic* is due to arrive at Forty Mile Creek in three days. Learned this from a couple of Indians who were twelve days out from Forty Mile Creek.

Passed the mouth of the Pelly River at 8 p.m. And one mile above its mouth on the opposite or left-hand side, saw Healy's house and the mouth of the slough where he and Harper and McQuesten winter their steamers. One small steamer is now lying there which, I understand, is the *New Racket*, the same boat to which I have referred previously in this writing, and on which I went downriver to St. Michael's on my first trip in 1887, nine years ago.

Islands are quite numerous along here. About a half a mile below the Pelly, one of Harper's posts is located on the left-hand side; also some mission houses and Indian shanties. Stopped here for half an hour, then went about twelve miles again and went ashore to try to get a little sleep. But, as usual we had to turn out again without a wink because of mosquitoes and rain. Our blankets and pillows are all wet. Noted the high, sheer, rocky bluffs along on our right beginning just below the Pelly.

July 26th: Saturday. Started at 2 a.m. Heavy rain off and on during morning. Then at about noon it started to blow hard upstream and rain came down in torrents. We had to run the boat ashore and seek shelter under some large trees.

Jim, my Indian, threw himself down on the soaked ground under one of the large trees with a wet blanket partly under and partly over him, and went to sleep while huge drops of rain fell on him from the large spruce boughs, so completely worn out was he for want of sleep.

After some trouble I got a large fire going and hung up some of our clothes near it to try to dry them out faster, if possible, than the heavy rain could drench them, for I did not expect it to keep up long. I then got the tent and my blankets ashore, and put up the tent. My Indian then awoke, shivering with cold. It was necessary to heap wood and roots on the fire continually to keep it going.

Jim then helped to cut some more wood and we piled a large heap on the fire. Then we arranged a bed in the tent, and after bailing the water out of the boat, both of us lay down to sleep.

This was really the first sleep we have had since leaving the head of Lake Lindeman on July 19th, for the extraordinarily heavy rain and strong, upriver wind, while it lasted, had the good effect of banishing at least most of those miserable mosquitoes.

I woke up at 9 p.m. The wind had died out, and the rain was over. I aroused the Indian. We made a new fire, had something to eat, and started off again. This is about forty miles above the mouth of the White River.

35. TRIP TO FORTY MILE CREEK WITH THE CANADIAN MAIL (July-August, 1896)

July 27th: Sunday. Passed the mouth of the White River on the left at 5 a.m. Very cold all night and this morning, with a white fog rising up out of the water and strong, upriver wind. The White River is very shallow at its mouth, with numerous islands and bars. Passed the mouth of Stewart River at 7 a.m. on the right-hand side. It also has a number of islands at its mouth, and I noted a bluff about two hundred fifty feet long and forty feet high a little below its mouth on the left-hand side. The old houses and post store that used to be located on the right-hand side have been chopped up for firewood for the steamers.

Arrived at Sixty Mile Creek sawmill at 10:30 a.m. Remained here until 1:30 p.m., and had dinner with Joe LaDue. My Indian left me here, so I pulled out alone at 1:30. I worked hard at the oars without stopping, and reached Klondike at 8:30, a distance of fifty miles in seven hours, on the right-hand side. Stopped here and cooked supper, saw Stick (Skookum) Jim and family here, and camped for the night. Fort Reliance is also on the right side, three miles below here.

(Editor's note: This was just three weeks before Skookum Jim, his nephew Dawson Charlie, and his brother-in-law George Carmack discovered the Klondike gold on nearby Rabbit Creek.)

July 28th: Monday. Left here at 5:30 a.m. Last night was the coldest night I experienced on the trip. A very heavy dew fell. The salmon have not as yet made their appearance here. The natives are anxiously waiting for them, for it is very late. I have learned that the first riverboat could not leave St. Michael's until June 26th, owing to the presence of so much ice in Norton Sound, and it is supposed that the salmon are so late on account of the ice is in such large quantities at and near the mouth of the Yukon.

Passed another boat this morning bound for Forty Mile at Klondike. This morning I succeeded in selling my downriver boat and purchased a good upriver boat twenty-seven feet long.

The weather is very warm today, with hot sun and not a cloud to be seen. Mosquitoes vanished yesterday evening, but they will appear again in swarms during the day. Passed three boats on their way out. Arrived at Forty Mile at noon; eight days exactly. Delivered mail at Fort Cudahy and Forty Mile and got receipts at both places.

July 28th: Tuesday. The *Arctic* arrived at 11 a.m. with a cargo of supplies for this place, and will return to St. Michael's tonight. Reports from Circle City very good, some men making ten dollars to the pan.

The North A.T. Company's sawmill is running steadily and shipping lumber to Circle City. Supplies very scarce here until the Arctic arrived today. I put up notices on the post offices that the outgoing British mails will close on July 30th, and commenced making preparations to go out upstream. A rich new creek has been struck near Circle City, called Harrison, which is turning out very rich. About seventy-five men left here on the Alice a few days ago; some for Circle City, and some for outside. The Arctic left here for St. Michael's at midnight tonight. Good news from American Creek, fifty miles below here. It promises to turn out good.

July 29th: Wednesday. Still here giving the miners a chance to answer their mail.

July 30th: Thursday. Left here with the Cudahy and Forty Mile mail today at noon for upriver and out to Juneau in company with Mr. Anderson. Camped twelve miles above from Forty Mile run till 10 p.m. Heavy rain falling and continued all night.

July 31st: Friday. Got under way at 6:40 a.m. Still raining all forenoon. Had supper at Twelve Mile Creek and saw a large moose come out on the bar. Passed Fifteen Mile Creek three miles below here on the same side.

August 1st: Saturday. Got under way at 6:30 a.m. Passed Richardson, the U.S. Mail carrier, right below Klondike about one mile, and got an order from him for his next September

August 2nd: Sunday. Got under way at 6 a.m. Keeping to right-hand side all the way from Forty Mile and going through all sloughs whenever any current shows at the foot. Had a very hard day of it. Hardly any towing ground at all, and a great deal of rock bluff to get around. Camped on a bar about five miles below Indian River, or twenty-three miles below Sixty Mile Creek. Mosquitoes very thick. No sleep at all. Commenced raining during the night, and no tent.

August 3rd: Monday. Got started at 6 a.m. Poled up the mouth of Sixty Mile Creek and poled up on that side until nearly a mile above the post, then made the crossing to the sawmill. Arrived there at 11:30 p.m., just four and one half days from Forty Mile Creek. Making good time.

Joe LaDue here at the post is out of supplies and expecting the steamer.

August 4th: Tuesday. Fixed one of our pile poles, and left here at 11:30 a.m. after a fair night's rest. Kept the left-hand side of the river now, and had some very long bluff rocks. Camped about ten miles below Stewart River at 10 p.m. Mosquitoes bad all night.

August 5th: Wednesday. Started at 6 a.m. Our boat handling hard and leaking badly, but could not find the leak. We took a long slough about five miles below the Stewart River, then crossed over to the right-hand side at the bluff rocks, and kept that side until within about four miles from the mouth of the White River, when we crossed over to the left again, near some islands and bars, and kept the left-hand side. Camped at 11 p.m., about one mile above the mouth of the White River, and had to make our bed on a drift pile as darkness overtook us.

August 6th: Thursday. Started at 5 a.m. Had strong water but good stretches of two beaches. Took a slough about four miles above White River, but had to return and go around – no outlet. Camped at 7 p.m., ten miles above White River. Caught two young wild geese. Met Hyde's raft with horses. They run the canyon, White Horse, and Five Fingers.

August 7th: Friday. Got up this morning at 5:30 a.m. all wet, with our blankets and pillows soaked through, and pools of water around and under us. Rained all night. Had our sail up all day with good upstream wind. Strong water, but lots of good tow beaches. Made about twenty-five miles today and camped sixty miles from Pelly River in a mosquito hatchery.

August 8th: Saturday. Heavy rain all night and thundering. It commenced just after we went to bed in our wet blankets, and kept up all night. We were actually lying in water and all blankets were wet through, for we had no tent to put up. So we got up without any sleep and started off again. Had a very strong upriver wind all day and made big time, sometimes walking right up against the current at the rate of three and one half miles an hour.

We towed where the swiftest part of the stream struck up, keeping sail on the boat, also poled with sail on her for a change. Camped about forty miles below Pelly River at sundown at 8 p.m. Built two large fires, then wrung the water out of our blankets and tried to dry them partially, but could not get them dry. So we had to sit up all night around the fire, and keep putting on wood because it turned pretty cold. No mosquitoes.

August 9th: Sunday. Got up at 3 a.m. Could not sleep in our wet blankets. Started at 5 a.m. Passed the mouth of the Selwin River on our right, thirty-five miles below Pelly, at 7 a.m. Met Brad Cole on his way from the Pelly to Forty Mile. Rounded two very bad drift piles. This part of the Yukon is completely filled with islands. At sundown passed the mouth of the creek fifteen miles from Pelly on our right, and camped at 9 p.m. twelve miles below Pelly River.

August 10th: Monday. Started at 7 a.m. Very foggy. Ate dinner near the lower end of the lava bluffs. Passed a large creek about five miles below Pelly on the right-hand side. Crossed the river again just below the islands about four miles below Pelly to the right, and rounded a very bad elbow or bluff just two miles below. Arrived at the Pelly River post, Harper's, at 8:30 p.m. and camped here tonight. Fixed my pike pole, and bought a tent six by eight feet for five dollars. Learned here that Buck and his party, also Chilkat Paddy just left here at 2 p.m. They left Forty Mile Creek three and one half days ahead of us. Traded three cups of tea for one whole salmon.

August 11th: Tuesday. Left the Pelly post at 10 a.m.; boat leaking badly. River from here up very swift and poor towing beaches. Camped at 8:30 p.m. about ten miles above Pelly River. The river is still very wide here, and completely cut up with islands and sand bars.

The river is still very wide here, and completely cut up with islands and sand bars.

August 12th: Wednesday. Got started at 7 a.m. and had a very hard morning of it. Swiftest water we have had on the trip and tow beaches very scarce. The only way we could make headway was to keep the boat's bow close up to the grass roots and willows. A large bend in the river can be seen opposite on our left, and the river must be four miles wide from bank to bank including islands.

Crossed the river this afternoon expecting to find better water just below a log house at the head of a slough. We started up one slough, where the water was very swift next to the mainland, and the boat bucked on us twice. So we turned back to go around the island and had a very hard time getting around its head where there was a drift pile and heavy water. We had to cross the head of the slough with oars. The Lewis River is rising a little today. Weather fine, and mosquitoes plentiful this evening just at sundown. Camped at 9:30 p.m. about twenty-five miles above Pelly River. Anderson has been pretty sick yesterday and today.

August 13th: Thursday. Got started this morning at five o'clock. Sun very warm all day, but most of the forenoon a strong wind blew downstream. Had a little easy water on an average today. Towed around some very long coarse gravel banks, which make traveling most difficult and tiresome; feet keep slipping, and the gravel gives way and slides down to the edge of the river.

I got pretty sick this afternoon from overexertion and being continually wet about the feet, knees, legs, and arms, so we camped at 4 p.m. and I went to bed immediately to get some much needed rest. This is about forty miles above Pelly, or twenty miles from Five Fingers.

August 14th: Friday. Got under way at 5 a.m. Had middling fair current and came round some very long, high gravel banks where the current was generally pretty heavy and towing very bad. Ran about one mile above Rink Rapids, and camped at 8:30 p.m. We cooked beans and fruit, and pitched tent because the weather looked threatening. Did not get to bed until 1 a.m. Mosquitoes hungry. Noted two green islands about one half and one quarter mile respectively, below Rink Rapids; and two brown rock bluffs on the right-hand side about five hundred yards apart.

August 15th: Saturday. Got started at 4 a.m. Saw Jack Dalton and party building a raft about two miles below Five Fingers on the right side where trail comes out. Lined our boat through the Five Fingers in a half an hour, and then, about seven miles above Five Fingers, we had to hurry into camp at sundown on account of thunder and lightning and a heavy rainstorm.

August 16th: Sunday. Started at 7:30 a.m. Arrived at George Carmack's old post at 8:30 p.m. and camped there for the night. Also found Jim Cannon and Hopkins, of the Dalton party there. It is about twenty miles over their trail to two miles below the Five Fingers. They left there this morning at 10 a.m. and got here at 6:30 p.m.

August 17th: Monday. Started at 5:30 a.m. and ran till 9:30 p.m. Rounded a long, hard drift pile just before camping. We are in sight of, and about three miles away from, three prominent white marble bluffs on a straight line, but the river is very crooked here at this point, especially at about twelve miles from the Little Salmon River.

August 18th: Tuesday. Got under way at 5:30 a.m. Poled around some very sticky clay banks, the pole often going in three feet and almost stopping the boat's headway, when we pull it out. Passed the mouth of the Little Salmon at 4 p.m., and camped at 7:30 p.m., five miles above from this. It is advisable to cross the river more often.

August 19th: Wednesday. Started at 6 a.m. Strong head wind part of the day. Islands becoming very scarce now. Camped at 8 p.m. about sixteen miles below the Big Salmon River.

36. DIARY OR LOG KEPT ON MAIL TRIP FROM FORTY MILE CREEK TO DYEA (August-September, 1896)

August 20th: Thursday. Started at 5 a.m. During the forenoon we passed two deep bends and very wide places in the river dotted with islands, sand bars, and slag banks. Also, in the afternoon we passed a heavy whirlpool about five miles below Big Salmon, which we passed at 5 p.m. Camped four miles above it at 9 p.m., after supper.

August 21st: Friday. Started this morning at 4:30. Had average easy water today. River very crooked and tow beaches scarce, and wind blew very hard downstream all last night. Had numerous good eddies. We kept the left-hand side all the time, and have had the left-hand side all the way from twenty-five miles above Pelly, except for one crossing about five miles below.

Carmack's house, on the left side coming up, appears to be the best on this upper river. Our feet, arms, and legs have been wet every day as usual, ever since we left Forty Mile. Met Ellengen and the internal revenue collector this evening, about twelve miles below the mouth of the Hootalinqua on their way to Circle City. Camped at 7:30 p.m. to bake some yeast bread. Noted four oblong sand or clay spots or bluffs standing in a line on the right-hand side going down, about one mile above the Big Salmon River.

August 22nd: Saturday. Started at 5 a.m. Arrived at the mouth of the Hootalinqua River at 1 p.m. Poled up the left-hand bank five hundred yards and then crossed over to the other shore to go up Lewes. Saw a boat tied to the bank with miners' outfit of tools and rockers thrown away, about fifty dollars' worth. Poled up the Lewes till about one half mile above the rapids, then crossed to the left again and took the usual tow beach. Camped at 9:30 p.m. about ten miles above the Hootalinqua.

August 23rd: Sunday. Started at 5 a.m. Crossed the river three times this forenoon, in four hours, running at places in the river to avoid strong water banks, to get good water on the opposite side. Came up to Buck's party and Chilkat Paddy. Camped at 9 p.m. about fifteen miles above the Hootalinqua, or halfway to Lake Laberge. It was raining pretty hard, so we went in to camp too, baked some bread, and took the first layoff and rest since leaving Forty Mile.

August 24th: Monday. Started at 6 a.m., crossed the river five times today; took a slough on the right-hand side one half mile below a bald marble bluff high up on the mountain and situated about six miles below the head of the river on the left side. The clay banks and landslides have put us back about four hours or more on this river since we left the mouth of the Hootalinqua. Had stretches of very easy water today, and at times some very swift places. Arrived at the head of the river at 6 p.m. and found a strong south wind blowing on Lake Laberge. So we went in to camp, cooked supper, and took a few hours' rest.

August 25th: Tuesday. Lying here at the head of Lewes River. Heavy gale of wind from the south on Lake Laberge, and raining. Choquette and party, also Indian Paddy and his party, are lying here, also windblown.

August 26th: Wednesday. Wind and rain continued all last night but calmed down about 1:30 a.m. Left here at 4:30 a.m. Pulled seven hours through heavy rain and light head wind and went ashore at noon to get some dinner. Wind went down at 3 p.m., so we started again and arrived at the mouth of Six Mile River at 7:30 p.m. It was very dark before we got supper. We kept to the left-hand side of the lake going up and entered the river about in the middle, or a little to the right at its head.

August 27th: Thursday. Got up at 3:30 a.m., and started at 5 a.m. Ice in the boat last night, and noticed quantities of new snow on the mountain tops. Poled up the mouth of the river for about two and one half or three miles and took a slough coming in on the right-hand side, which cuts off a long, deep bend in the main river. Had nice easy water all day, especially to within three miles of the Tahkiena (Takhini) River, and passed the mouth of the Takhini at 12 a.m. Noted a very high straight clay bank opposite the mouth of the Takhini on the Lewes. The Takhini, the Takhini at 12 a.m. Noted a very high straight clay bank opposite the mouth of the Takhini on the Lewes. The Takhini, like the Big and Little Salmon Rivers, has confined banks with no islands or sand bars at its mouth.

Crossed the river twice today to avoid some clay banks. These landslides and mud banks have been the greatest detriment to poling out, particularly from the Hootalinqua up; in many cases the pole pulling us nearly out of the boat, and we often had to let the pole go and back up the boat to get it out.

I was wet through today and miserably cold. It rained hard all day, and stormed from the south. Passed a large round-shaped basin nearly one mile each way across, resembling a lake surrounded at intervals with clay banks and a low willow island with some spruce. This island lies at the upper end, near the upper opening of the river and about eight miles below the White Horse. Camped at 5:30 about six miles below the White Horse. The valley here is very wide, and contains lowlands and islands. Deep poling all the way.

August 28th: Friday. Started this morning at 6 a.m. Poled up on this left side until within one quarter mile below the foot of the White Horse, then crossed over to the right-hand side and towed up to the landing at the point where the trail comes in. Had good towing over low scrub willow bank commencing about one and one half or two miles below the White Horse on the left.

Arrived at the White Horse at 9:30 a.m. Lined my boat through, but the rope parted three times and nearly lost the boat once, swamping her completely, with me in it, taking a shear out in the strong water. The river here is booming high. Had two five eighth-inch ropes, one hundred feet long, on the bow with four men on them, and they could not hold her when she took the out shear and swamped at the time one of these ropes parted. I jumped into her stern, and she took a shear into the bank. We then hauled her out, tipped the water out, and went ahead again. Buck and party and Paddy's party would not chance lining their boats through, so they portaged their boats and everything.

Got through with the three boats and left ahead of the White Horse at 1 p.m. Towed and poled up through Squaw Rapids on the right-hand side (a very bad piece of water, too) commencing about three quarters of a mile above the White Horse, having two rock points on the left-hand side less than a quarter of a mile below the foot of the canyon, and towed up to the landing. We arrived there at 4:30 p.m., cooked supper, ate, took two packs over the portage, then rigged our tent and went to bed.

August 29th: Saturday. Was up at 3:30 this morning, breakfasted, took three more packs apiece over the portage, then started out with the three boats at 8 a.m. and got them all over by 11:15 a.m. The gnats were thick as soon as the sun rose and almost blinded us; our faces, eyes, and hands were badly swollen. We put a little caulking in our boat at head of the canyon, and portaged, but it did not help her much. Left head of the canyon at 1 p.m. after dinner. Poled up on the left-hand side. Water a little strong for about two miles, then had pretty mild current. There were a few clay banks, and deep poling water as usual. Strong downstream wind all afternoon, also heavy rain. Got wet through, and had to camp at 4 p.m. Was obliged to stop and land the boat every twenty minutes or so to bail out water on account of the straining she got at the White Horse. We only have six pounds of flour left, no sugar, and all the provisions short in proportion.

Reports state that Circle City and Birch Creek are almost drenched out by rain this season, and at Forty Mile Creek there is no water at all. American Creek, fifty miles below Forty Mile on Mission Creek, also Wolf Creek, are new strikes and very good. American Creek empties into Mission Creek, one and one half miles from the mouth of the latter.

(Editor's Note: Moore was unaware of the Klondike strike at this time, having left Forty Mile just days before George Carmack arrived there to register his claim, and those of Skookum Jim and Dawson Charlie.)

August 30th: Sunday. Got under way at 7 a.m. Kept to the left-hand side all the way on this river. There is no advantage in crossing this river above the canyon. Had hard rain again part of the day. About eight miles from the head of this river there are two clay banks, one on the right and one on the left, which stand at about right angles, and just above these there is a wide place in the river with many islands and sloughs. Streams very sluggish, and average good poling, but deep. Arrived at the foot of Marsh Lake and camped at 5:30 on the right side for a half hour to eat and fix our mast thwart, then started again at 6 p.m. and pulled up Marsh Lake on the left-hand side.

August 31st: Monday. Arrived at Tagish at 6:30 a.m. Buck

morning. Later in the day it was fine and clear and not a ripple on the lake, but gnats thick. Went ashore for supper at 5:30 p.m., about one third of a mile from the head of Tagish Lake, and started out again at 8 p.m. Noted three small rock islands about one mile above the Tagish. Houses on the left side coming up.

Made a very bad mistake by keeping along the left side of Tagish Lake, and followed up Taku Arm, but noted an opening in the hills on the right-hand side that looked very narrow. Not thinking that it was the right and proper channel to take we kept on up Taku Arm, for it looked so large and appeared to be the main lake. We camped at 7 p.m. on the right-hand side of the Arm, had supper, left again at 8 p.m. and pulled in the dark for four more hours; a distance of twelve miles.

September 1st: Tuesday. Went ashore and camped at what we thought and felt sure was about one and one half miles above Windy Arm. Froze very hard for two hours, and we were awakened by heavy rain. Had breakfast, and started up the arm again at 7 a.m., feeling sure we had passed Windy Arm, which resembled it very much.

Pulled for nearly three hours longer, and after getting about thirty miles up from the mouth of this arm, the truth dawned on us that we had taken Taku Arm instead of the right channel; and we could see up the arm, forty miles farther, blue hills in the distance, and in some places the arm was five and six miles wide.

We lost no time in turning around and had a long, hard, and tedious pull back till we got nearly to the mouth of the arm, where we camped in the dark for supper at 8 p.m. This mistake cost us lost time and sixty miles of hard pulling.

September 2nd: Wednesday. Started this morning at 6 a.m. Raining hard. Sailed down Taku Arm to the right opening and arrived opposite the Windy Arm at noon. Had dinner there, and noted three small rock islands right at its mouth; also one large timbered island. Saw a large boat going down and hailed it several times, but it would not stop to give us any grub.

Sailed on up to Caribou Crossing. Here the wind petered out, and we had to take to the oars again. Rain came down heavily. Pulled up Lake Bennett about five miles to the left-hand side, but the wind increased and, together with the sea, it was heavy pulling and little progress. So we camped for the night at 5 p.m.

Diary Of Mail Trip Out To Dyea

It seemed strange to me that a strong wind should follow us down from Takun Arm this morning, and that we should have a fair wind up to Caribou Crossing, then get a strong southerly wind on Lake Bennett, which no doubt had been blowing all day here. Noted a large gap in the mountains to my right on this lake, abreast of here, which must be Wheaton River. We are out of flour altogether, and have only about two dozen hardtack left, five pounds of bacon, one pound of sugar, and one handful of tea, and one teacup full of beans to get from here (near the foot of Lake Bennett) to Dyea, and a strong head wind blowing.

We have to put up our tent every night now, for it is generally raining every morning. Our great mistake of keeping to the left-hand side of Tagish Lake and going up Taku Arm thirty miles has given us no end of trouble and extra hard work.

September 3rd: Thursday. Started from our camp this morning at 6 o'clock. Passed the mouth of the Wheaton River on our right; also an opening in the hills bellow it, about eight miles from the foot of Bennett Lake. Pulled hard all day against a strong southerly wind and quite a strong sea. Also it is raining hard, and we got wet through again as usual. Boat leaking badly; forty gallons in one half an hour. Made the head of Bennett at the trail at 6 p.m., but found no one here except a tent and camp with grub. So we cooked what we had in the dark and rain, and intend to portage our boat and pack our stuff.

The left-hand side of Bennett is best coming up.

September 4th: Friday. Was up at 3:30 this morning and commenced getting our packs across the portage to the foot of Lindeman. Blowing very hard from the south, and raining heavily. Hauled out my boat, also Buck's boat, at Rudolph's sawmill at the head of Bennett, and took a small stray boat which we found at the foot of Lindeman.

Then the four of us, Mr. Choquette and his son, Mr. Anderson, and I went to a tent at the head of Bennett, where there was quite a quantity of supplies but nobody around. We took five pounds of bacon, ten small tin cups of sugar, and one sack of graham flour, for we actually were in need of food. It was understood between us that we should meet the party at Dyea and pay for the food.

We made a double trip up Lindeman, about two miles, but had to camp at 1 p.m. again – on account of the heavy wind and

We made a double trip up Lindeman, about two miles, but had to camp at 1 p.m. again – on account of the heavy wind and sea – on the right-hand side just north of the first big bluff point. Our tent has not been dry for the last two weeks.

September 5th: Friday. Started from camp here, one and one half miles from the foot of Lindeman Lake, at 6 a.m. Blowing very hard from the south, and raining. Low, heavy clouds scudding along. Made one trip to the head of Lindeman and the landing, then went back for the second load and returned. Packed up to Moore's House, remodeled our packs, and had to throw away all my clothes, a good tent and other stuff, in order to lighten my pack. I just took the mailbag and a little grub.

Found lots of things thrown away. Good tents, provisions, and other stuff. Lake Lindeman rose about one foot last night. Left our house at 3 p.m. and went about three miles to where the timber got very scrubby, then camped at 5:30 p.m. Weather very bad, and no sign of a change.

September 6th: Sunday. Left timberline, or three miles above Moore's House, at 6:45 a.m. in a heavy southerly storm. Raining hard, and fog driving and banking up all round the pass. Buck threw away his tent and other stuff; could not pack it. And his dog gave out on the way and lay down under a sheltered rock to die. Fresh snow on some of the surrounding mountains, and very cold. We were anxious to get across, for we were without an Indian guide, and should fresh snow fall, we could not make it through at all.

Left the string of lakes on our right and passed Crater Lake, the last also on our right, and ascended the five hundred-foot rise right at the head of it. Had some difficulty in finding and keeping the trail sometimes, especially where it ran across bare rocks. Arrived at Sheep Camp at 5 p.m., wet through to the skin and hungry. Built a large fire and got our supper, partially dried ourselves, then spread out to try to get some sleep. My pack was about seventy-five pounds. Stopped raining just a little while before reaching here.

September 7th: Monday. Left here (Sheep Camp) at 6:30 a.m., arrived at Dyea at 5 p.m., and heard the news that father had gone in to Forty Mile again about ten days ago and we missed him on the way at Taku Arm. Stopped at Fields' over night, and found ten men camped there waiting for a steamer to take them to Juneau.

September 8th: Tuesday. Got up this morning at 6 o'clock and began to get ready for the trip to Juneau. Engaged Nan-Suk with his canoe to take me, Buck's son, and Mr. Anderson down to Skagway Bay. Left Dyea in the canoe at 11:30 a.m., but had to get out again with our packs and pack over the trail from Nan-Suk's house to the upper side of Skagway Bay, and Nan-Suk took the canoe and told George Buchanan, who came over with the sealing boat, to take us across the river. We arrived at the house at 1 p.m., and found everything all right. Wind blowing heavy from the south.

September 9th: Wednesday. Could not get away today. Heavy southerly wind all last night and today, with rain at times, and heavy sea running up the channel. The tide rose and backed way up behind the log house at 3:30 p.m. George Buchanan shot a goose today.

September 10th: Thursday. Wind calmed down during the night, and we – George Buchanan, myself and young Choquette – left Skagway in the sealing boat, with the Canadian mail, at 5:30 a.m. Had a heavy north wind shortly after starting, which sent us right through to the bar. We arrived there at 6 p.m., then camped for the night.

September 11th: Friday. Started over the bar at 3 a.m. on the tide. Dark as pitch. Got over the bar and hurried all we could to catch the Topeka in order to forward our mail on her this trip, for we heard her whistling to leave Douglas Island far below. But we arrived just an hour too late – in time to see her steam out. Delivered the mail this morning to Mr. Nelson, the postmaster, and got a receipt for it.

Round trip: fifty-one days. Eight days' layoff.

AFTERWORD

Note on Mr. J. Bernard Moore, the author of these memoirs of early pioneering days in Alaska:

J. Bernard Moore's dream of a future Skagway was fully realized in the years following the period with which his diary and recollections deal, and his early struggles were rewarded by a well-deserved- prosperity in the succeeding years.

In 1906 Bernard Moore left Alaska for the United States, to make his home in Tacoma, Washington. He brought with him the simple honesty and straightforwardness which were characteristic of most of the men in the Yukon country of his day, and lost most of his well-earned money to shrewd and unscrupulous businessmen with whom he happened to come in contact in the United States.

Moore died in San Francisco in 1919, regretting that he had left the country of his adventurous youth and energetic middle age.

To order more copies of this or other Lynn Canal Publishing titles,
please contact us at:
Lynn Canal Publishing, P.O. Box 498, Skagway, AK 99840
907-983-2354, phone • 907-983-2356, fax
E-mail: skagnews@ptialaska.net